A NOVEL OF THE KRAKEN MC

MARLIN'S FAITH

The Virtues BOOK II

AJ Downey

Second Circle Press

Published 2016 by Second Circle Press
Book design by Lia Rees at Free Your Words (www.freeyourwords.com)
Cover art and Virtues logo by Cover Your Dreams
(www.coveryourdreams.net)

Text copyright © 2016 AJ Downey

This is a work of fiction. Names, characters, businesses, places, events and incidents are either the products of the author's imagination or used in a fictitious manner. Any resemblance to actual persons, living or dead, or actual events is purely coincidental.

All Rights Reserved

ISBN: 978-1530627929

Author's Note

Being a spin-off, the events of this trilogy take place *after* the events of Damaged & Dangerous, The Sacred Hearts MC Book VI. If you have not read the SHMC series, references and events that are talked about in this book may not make sense to you. I highly suggest reading the SHMC series first, followed by Cutter's Hope, the first book in this trilogy.

DEDICATION

A special thanks to Carian Cole and Bibi Rizer for giving me permission to pull our worlds together, thus giving our readers who are fans of all of our series some fun Easter eggs to discover in this trilogy. I think it's fantastic as a group of indie authors that we can do this. Much love and keep on keepin' on, the both of you. I'm dying to see what you come up with next.

THE VIRTUES BOOKS IN ORDER

1. Cutter's Hope

2. *Marlin's Faith*

3. Charity for Nothing

Contents

Chapter 1	*1*
Chapter 2	*8*
Chapter 3	*10*
Chapter 4	*14*
Chapter 5	*16*
Chapter 6	*24*
Chapter 7	*31*
Chapter 8	*38*
Chapter 9	*46*
Chapter 10	*62*
Chapter 11	*68*
Chapter 12	*74*
Chapter 13	*78*
Chapter 14	*82*
Chapter 15	*86*
Chapter 16	*90*
Chapter 17	*97*
Chapter 18	*103*
Chapter 19	*110*
Chapter 20	*116*
Chapter 21	*122*
Chapter 22	*125*

Chapter 23	*136*
Chapter 24	*143*
Chapter 25	*148*
Chapter 26	*153*
Chapter 27	*160*
Chapter 28	*168*
Chapter 29	*172*
Chapter 30	*176*
Chapter 31	*181*
Chapter 32	*186*
Chapter 33	*190*
Chapter 34	*195*
Chapter 35	*201*
Chapter 36	*206*
Chapter 37	*214*
Chapter 38	*220*
Chapter 39	*226*
Chapter 40	*231*
Chapter 41	*237*
Chapter 42	*241*
Chapter 43	*249*
Chapter 44	*254*
Epilogue	*258*
Charity for Nothing: Cover	
About the Author	

CHAPTER 1

Marlin

I stared out of the floor to ceiling windows of the safe house's master bedroom and asked, "That you bobbing out there, Captain?" The running lights were just that, indistinct lights, rising and falling gently with the swell of the sea. No telling if it were the Captain or not, but with Hope as feisty and insistent on remaining with her sister, I had to guess it was.

"Yep," Cutter grated into my ear. I smiled to myself.

"Oh, cool; night then." I lowered the phone and ended the call with a heavy sigh.

I looked back over my shoulder; she was asleep… for now. Her pale skin was washed out and made nearly translucent by the moonlight. Her long blonde hair, so brittle, crackled around her face like spider silk. Deep, dark, circles were etched under her eyes, a combination of the drug, fatigue, stress, and the cherry on top? Malnourishment. Her body was so frail, her bones standing out in high relief, her cheek bones standing out so sharply, they could cut.

Still, she was beautiful. One of the prettiest girls I'd ever seen. She made Hope look ugly by comparison and Hope was a fucking knock out. *Twice over,* when you stopped to think about it.

Faith's brows were drawn down, her lovely face pinched with pain and sorrow, even in sleep, and I was afraid it was only going to get worse. We'd had quite the candid conversation downstairs after Cutter and her sister had left. I'd taken her into the living room and sat her down and talked to her about what she could expect if she did this the way she wanted to.

"How do I do this?" she'd asked me, licking her lush lips and biting them together.

"A day at a time, Darlin'."

"What's going to happen to me?"

That had been hard to tell her, the truth of it, that she was gonna be sick for *days* with how bad her body wanted what she was on. There was no real way to gauge how long she'd be sick; not with no tellin' how long she'd been on the shit they'd been pumping into her veins. She was looking at a good couple of weeks of the physical stuff. A couple of weeks of pure hell, livin' with something aping the worst case of the flu she'd ever had, times a hundred or more.

"I can't remember the last time I had the flu," she'd said, drawing her knees to her chest, resting her chin on them. She'd pleaded with me, with her eyes, before her voice had caught up to her.

"Please, just tell me what to expect. I can't stop it and not knowing…"

"I get you," I'd told her softly. She was gonna be brave. Sometimes it's almost better not knowing, but she'd wanted to know, so I'd told her the truth. The pain, the aches, and fatigue. That's how it would start. She'd be irritated, agitated beyond measure for no reason at all. Then, the tears would start. Like she'd sprung a leak. Pouring down her face, til she was sick of 'em, but it wasn't crying; not really, near as I could tell. Her eyes would just be watering, tearing up something terrible. Then, the sweating and the not being able to sleep when all she would want would be *to* sleep to get away from the symptoms. Except she wouldn't and that was just the beginning.

Next would come the *real* sick. The cramping that would be so bad she would beg to be killed. Then the throwing up and the runs. She'd be sick to her stomach, sweating and shivering as the poison gave up its hold and her body fought to hang onto it. By the time I finished talking the tears had run silently down her face and she'd looked more afraid not less.

"I won't go anywhere, I promise. You won't have to do it alone."
"Did you?" she'd asked then.
"Did I what?"
"Go through it alone?"
"No, Darlin'. I never went through it at all…"
"Then how do you know about this? About what's going to happen?"

"I've helped someone through it before," I'd told her honestly.

"Who?" she asked.

"My little brother, Danny was his name."

"Oh… what happened to him?"

"He died."

I'd failed him. Couldn't keep him off it. He'd gone back to it after I'd cleaned him up and took too damn big a dose and killed himself. Faith had looked so solemn then. She'd raised those startling aquamarine eyes to meet mine and we'd sat in silence for a long time. That's when the Captain had shown up with my shit.

I'd watched her carefully as they'd had their little exchange of words and he'd left to go back to his woman, Faith's sister… which damn but those two didn't look nothin' alike.

"Am I going to die? I mean is there a chance..?" she asked softly.

"No, Darlin'. You aren't going to die," I'd said, and it fuckin' killed me that she looked almost *disappointed* by that. It was a fleeting look, twisting into a grim resolve, but it was hard to banish that flicker of misery from the deep dark part of my brain. That part where the ghosts of bad memories liked to live.

Faith moaned, more like groaned, into the silvery dark of the room and I snapped out of it, turning from the window and going to her. I knelt beside the bed and using two fingertips, took her pulse the way Nothing had shown me when it was Danny, my little brother, three years gone. It was speeding against my fingers and sort of a bitch to take.

She had on this leather cuff, some kind of bracelet that laced up on the underside. The leather black and broad with an old fashioned key plate set into it. A newer, shinier, thin metal filigree behind it to make the key plate pop. She'd thrown a goddamn fit in her highest, most traumatized state when me and her sister had tried to toss it, and everything else she'd been wearing. The shit was so filthy it needed to be burned; the wristband was in good enough shape though, so we didn't figure there was any harm in her having it. Was a bitch and a half convincing her to let me take it off just to get her bathed and *that shit?* That had busted my heart six ways to Sunday...

That first night had been fucking awful while she'd been in the throes of that poison. I'd had to put the skills that Danny had shown me to use, and fuck if that hadn't made me feel both guilty and sick. Nothing had helped me out there, too. Being the ex-medic, he knew how to find and tap a vein. I didn't have the first fucking clue what I was doing other than to cook the shit up. I'd seen my brother do it enough to at least get that part done.

I wrestled myself back to the here and now in time to see Faith's eyes snap open as she inhaled sharply. There was this brief, shining moment where our eyes connected and something passed between us. Couldn't tell you what, but it was something. Trust maybe? Though I didn't know why she would trust me or any of the other boys, *any man* for that matter, not after…

"I'm going to be sick…" she gasped, voice tinged with fear and I knew what was next. I shoved the little bedside trashcan into her too thin arms, she doubled over and heaved. Shit. It was bad. It was like throwing up in and of itself scared the bejesus out of her. She jumped and shook and cried as her poor stomach rebelled. The sour smell that came from the can didn't help me none either. I gritted my teeth and held the can steady for her with one hand, smoothing her hair back with the other, but it was already too late. She'd nailed that too. It'd gone into the trashcan as she'd heaved.

"Easy, Girl," I murmured as she broke down in sobs.

"I'm sorry!" she warbled brokenly and I shook my head.

"It ain't your fault. Steady though, gotta get you cleaned up. This ain't gonna be the last time either. Just you hang on, put your arms around me… that's it."

I lifted her easily; she was just so fuckin' frail, and carried her into the master bathroom. I contemplated shower or bath and settled on shower. The tub would take too damn long to fill. I set her on the counter and she gripped its edge, shaking like a little leaf caught in hurricane force winds.

"I'm going to get the water started, remember what we talked about?" I asked her.

"Some, not all," she answered truthfully, "But if it's the naked talk you're talking about…" she trailed off and wouldn't look at me.

I sighed, "Yeah, that would be the one."

She nodded miserably, and my heart went out to her. This was a fuckin' shame on so many levels. After Cutter had left, we'd had some more candid conversation. I'd told her the time would come where she'd be weak as a newborn kitten. Sick on herself, that I'd have to do this for her and here we were already.

I'd also promised I would keep my fuckin' clothes on and wouldn't do anything that made her uncomfortable.

I got the water going and turned back to her, but she already had the tee up and off over her head. I gritted my teeth and she drew those solemn aquamarine eyes up to meet mine. They were just as startling in their brilliance every damn time I saw them. She didn't look at me direct much but this time, I got the full effect. More so because her pupils weren't swallowing the color whole. I kept my eyes locked to hers and didn't dare wander.

"No sense in being shy," she said miserably, "You've seen it all before anyways."

Her tone held so many things. Anger, bitterness, derision… all of them she'd come by honestly, and none of them bothered me any. She was hurting; she was going to be all over the map. It was how this thing was gonna play out and I couldn't pay no never mind to it. Getting butthurt over it wasn't gonna help the situation, or her, so I simply nodded and let it roll off me. I don't think it was directed at me anyways.

"You steady?" I asked her when she'd slipped off the counter and stood for a moment on her own; still trembling, but a damn sight better than before.

"I think so," she uttered softly and was back to staring fixedly at something, anything, that wasn't me.

I helped her the rest of the way out of the sweats we'd bought her and stripped my tee off over my head. I had a wife beater on under it, and she was pretty much out of clothes for the time being. One bit of torture at a time. Clothes could be gotten tomorrow after I put what she had through the wash.

I set the tee aside on the counter, made sure there were enough towels and stepped into the large, glassed in shower with her, shirt, boots, pants, and all. She made a noise that sounded almost like protest and I tipped her chin. Her eyes flashed to mine and I did my best to silently communicate my best intentions. She gasped softly and I turned her under the shower spray.

"You think you're gonna be able to sleep after this?"

"Truthfully, I don't know…"

"Fair enough. Might as well do this again then. Didn't get the best opportunity to actually comb your hair for nits. Think you can hold still and let me try?"

"Nits? What are those?"

"You've got head lice, Darlin'," I reminded her gently.

"Oh god!" she muttered horrified.

"Don't remember much of last night do you?"

"No… I'm sorry," she closed her eyes and put her face in her palms and began to cry, "I can't remember, I don't…"

"Shhh, s'okay. You don't need to. You were scared, and out of it, and you really don't need to. We doused your hair pretty good, everything should be dead but no harm in having a go at it again right?"

"No, god no! Please," she dropped her hands to her sides and her eyes to the shower floor. She shuddered and twitched gently and I sighed silently.

"Okay, here we go. Stay out of the water, but head back, Darlin'."

She tipped her head back but stayed out of the shower spray and I followed the pesticide shampoo's directions and applied it to her hair. Her hands found their way to my sides and rested just above my hips, holding on for dear life. I imagine she was afraid of falling and I couldn't blame her. I worked the pesticide shampoo onto her head, making sure to get her entire scalp all the way to the ends of her long blonde hair, and checked my dive watch.

"Ten minutes, Baby Girl, can you hang on that long?" she nodded, her eyes closed and I brought her forehead to my chest.

"Just rest, hang onto me. I won't let you fall."

"Why are you being so nice to me?" her muffled voice asked.

"It's about time someone was, isn't it?"

She shivered, but it was warm enough in here, so without looking to confirm I could only guess she was crying. As far as detoxing junkies went, she was being incredibly brave right now. She wasn't begging for a fix, she wasn't whining about how much it hurt; she just simply rested against me, let me hold her up, and cried. It was probably the most heartbreaking, and at the same time, most inspiring thing I'd seen.

I checked my watch and absently massaged the goo into her hair, grimacing as I felt some of the damned bugs in her hair run over my fingers and hands, trying to get away from the shit that was killing them. Guess we hadn't gotten them all after all. It made me wish there had been more of the bastards that done this to kill back in that house. Fuck.

"Okay, Beautiful." I tipped her head back and rinsed her hair gently but thoroughly. Letting the water detangle it, cautious not to let it catch or pull.

"Th-thank you," she stuttered dully and I took my attention from her hair to her face. She stared off into space, shivering in withdrawal and I think I swore to myself then and there, that no more harm would befall her. Not while I was around. She'd had her lifetime of pain bundled into just a couple of years and every one of my protective instincts screamed that enough was enough.

Faith needed a friend, and while I'd only ever pulled the white knight routine once, for my brother, she made me want to protect her with everything I was worth. I just wasn't quite sure how to protect someone when the only monsters that were left to fight were the memories inside her head. I couldn't even begin to fathom what'd happened to this girl.

Could. Not. Even…

CHAPTER 2
Faith

I sat as still as I could; it was hard with how much I twitched and jumped. Muscle spasms happening seemingly out of nowhere and often. I hurt. A deep and abiding ache in every bone, every joint. It was the worst I had ever felt in my life. So awful. The only thing to make it bearable was the tenuous link to the man who sat behind me, gently pulling a comb through my hair. I shuddered and it had nothing to do with the lifting fog of whatever drug my captors had me on and everything to do with the deep revulsion I felt knowing what it was he patiently combed from my hair.

He was deeply methodical, sectioning out my hair, clipping it up out of his way so he could make sure he got everything out of it. He'd been doing this for over an hour and we weren't even halfway through.

"How you holding up?" he asked softly.

"Okay," I murmured back, which surprisingly, was true. Despite feeling so nauseous, despite the cramping and the twitching and the aching and the generally wanting to die, overlaying that was a peace I hadn't known for a very long time… I felt safe and cared for. The gentle, rhythmic pull of the comb through my damp hair was soothing, and a gentle, pleasurable, tingle suffused my scalp, washing over my neck and shoulders. The simple pleasure of having something done for me, of being cared for.

I hugged my knees and huddled in his oversized tee shirt and closed my eyes, concentrating on the feel of his hands moving my hair, the light scrape of the comb through my locks. The glow from the bedside lamp suffusing the room with golden warmth.

"Is the air conditioning on?" I asked.

"Yeah, why?"

"It's hot."

I wiped a bit of sweat from my upper lip and he sighed, the sound of it carrying the weight of the world. I gasped at a particularly sharp spasm in my leg.

"It's only just starting," he said quietly.

"It gets worse?" I swallowed, and with how dry my throat was is very nearly gave an audible click.

"Yeah, Faith. It gets much worse, but it'll be okay, I promise. I'll be right here. I'm not going anywhere." He drew the comb steadily through my hair, as if he were determined to see the long process through before the even longer one got started. I was afraid. I wanted to believe him, I really did… I gripped the leather cuff around my wrist with the opposite hand and sighed as another shiver wracked through me.

The boy who'd given it to me had been sweet. The boy who had given it to me had shone a light in my eyes that not everyone was out to get me. The boy who'd given it to me had reaffirmed my faith that there were still a few good people left out there. The man behind me, who carefully tended to me, reaffirmed what the boy had shown me with his simple gift, and I wanted so badly to believe…

But it wasn't long until the pure fire of an ultimate living hell overtook me and burned every sweet and kind sentiment away. Regardless, I clung to that simple gift, and the solemn vow of the gentle man of the here and now…

It'll be okay, I promise. I'll be right here. I'm not going anywhere.

CHAPTER 3
Marlin

I could almost feel her slip away, the lucid moments just before the withdrawals really set in were always so fleeting, but she'd hung on. As if the gentle tug of the comb through her hair were an anchor or a lifeline. She shivered hard and harder and I knew it hurt. I knew it was bad, and I also knew it was just beginning. I'd promised her I would be here for the whole thing and I'd make good on that promise. Faith had every reason to never trust another man again, to never trust *anyone* again. I wanted to prove there were still a few of us left that could be relied upon.

I finished her hair just as she doubled over and the sobbing began. Soon it would be screaming and that screaming would morph into crying uncontrollably as her body rebelled. Bucking wildly with muscle spasms. She would throw up and worse. Possibly wet herself. It would be the absolute worst thing she would ever go through in her life and then some… and there wasn't a damn thing I could do for her.

Faith doubled over and let out with this high pitched keening wail and that was it. It'd started. She was past the point of no return and it was going to be *days* of this. The worst part of it was, that for whatever reason, with withdrawals came insomnia. She wouldn't even be able to *sleep* through any of this. Let alone the worst of it. I folded the towel around the ruin of stray hair, bug parts, and *eggs* and threw the whole damn thing away in the trash bag I had at the ready in the bathroom.

I came back out to Faith curled on her side, crying. Her eyes squeezed shut, her teeth gritted tight against the pain. I got back up onto the bed and, fuck, I gave in to my own moment of weakness. I couldn't not touch her. I knew after what she'd been through that touching her too much might not be the best thing, but I was fucking human. Being fucking human meant that when someone as fragile looking as her was in pain, you gathered up the broken pieces and tried to make them whole again. Which is what I did. I gathered her up against me and made soothing noises as the despair and agony took hold.

So what if she puked on me? So what if she pissed herself or worse? I wasn't going to stain. I could suck it up and wash it off. I held her while she bawled and struggled to get away from what was hurting her, but it was her own body wreaking havoc and throwing a tantrum like a two year old denied a piece of candy. Her body wanted the drug so fucking bad and she didn't. She'd never wanted it.

"Shh, I got you, Faith. You scream, you cry, you do whatever you need to do, Baby Girl."

It was that fact that made this whole thing worse, as she bucked against my hold and thrashed. When it'd been Danny, I was so pissed at him for getting involved in the shit in the first place I'd been downright fucking cruel during his time kicking the habit. I was so mad, I'd told him he could suck it up. That he didn't have the option to be a pussy about it. My anger had been my shield against feeling any kind of sympathy or empathy and I didn't have that shield here. I needed to find another and I needed to find it fast, or this was liable to destroy a part of me I would never get back.

I wrapped my legs around Faith's and held her as still as I could so she wouldn't hurt herself. Danny had scratched himself bloody and raw and he didn't really have fingernails to speak of. Faith did, and her peaches and cream skin didn't need any more permanent reminders of her captivity.

The first few nights would be the worst. If she were anything like Danny, the turning point wouldn't be until around something like day fucking four. A few hours into this initial struggle the doctor from up north appeared in the door.

"How's she doing?"

"Not keeping anything down, sweating, she's getting weak. I know she ain't gonna die of the withdrawals…"

The doctor nodded and put on his glasses, coming forward,

"Dehydration is still dangerous, so is a high fever." He peeled back Faith's eyelids and shone a light into them and she started thrashing and screaming.

"I'm going to start an IV, some anti-nausea meds, too. They don't always work, but I wanna see if I can't get her hydrated; maybe get a sedative on board for good measure," he sighed, "Wish I could help rapid detox her, but they look at the kinds of drugs we prescribe and the shit I would need? They'd flag that so quick… Damn it to hell, can you hold her arm? Just like this."

The doctor got an IV started and fluids going, but Faith kept ripping out the tubes. She was wearing out. Exhausting herself, so the fourth one finally stuck. The sun was climbing in the sky and the doc and I looked up at the open and shut of the door downstairs. My MC brother, Nothing came up, and mercifully, Faith was out for the time being.

"Hey," he said.

"Hey." I grunted back.

"Take a minute, we've got this."

I nodded and carefully detangled myself from Faith. I needed a fucking cigarette, bad. Grabbing up the pack on the bedside table, I trekked downstairs. I went out the back slider and took a deep breath of the clean, sea air.

"How's she doin'?" Cutter asked, coming around the side of the house.

"Rough. She's hurting, jonesing hard for a fix that I ain't got shit to give her," I bowed my head and palmed the back of my neck. "It's worse, somehow, you know?" I asked him bleakly. Shit, this was only day one… I lit up and sucked in a lungful of my own vice. I didn't smoke 'em unless I was stressed. I blew out.

"Yeah, man. I know," my Pres supplied.

"Thanks," I nodded and sighed, took two more drags and put out my cig.

"You need to talk, you can reach out." Cutter called as I slid the back slider open.

I nodded and went back inside. I was jumpy being this far from Faith. Didn't want or need her waking up in her fucked up state and me not be there. Hell, I couldn't be sure if she was with it enough to know that I'd gone.

I went back into the room to a flurry of activity. Nothing was moving things around, tossing pillows and peeling back blankets. The doc was capping her IV.

"Shit, she sick?"

"Yeah," Nothing affirmed, "Get her cleaned up, we got this." I nodded and it was back to the bathroom. I drew a tub full of water this time. Shower just wasn't going to happen. She couldn't hold herself up. She felt so small and so delicate in my arms. She was way too thin and needed at the *very* least ten to fifteen pounds put on her just to make her look healthy again. I think it would take even more than that for her to actually *be* healthy though. I would ask the doc before he took off back up north to be sure.

She roused a bit when I put her in the bath and she reached for me, scrabbling at me to keep her out of the water.

"Faith, Faith! Easy, Darlin', I got you. Just take it easy," she focused on me for a moment and whatever it was, this thin and tenuous bond we had going on, it was there and she settled, whimpering, into the warm bathwater.

"You good, Brother?" Nothing called from out in the bedroom.

"Yeah! I got this." I held Faith against me, so she wouldn't slip under and I took care of her.

CHAPTER 4
Faith

I felt like I was dying. If there was ever any mystery surrounding what dying felt like, it was certainly dispelled... this had to be what death felt like. I was suddenly afraid that maybe I was already dead. That maybe I had already passed through the gates of Hell and I was burning. Maybe this would never end. Maybe this was what it was going to be for all of eternity. This fiery burning ache. This feeling like fire ants had gotten beneath my skin and were eating me alive, one nerve ending at a time.

I whimpered and hot tears leaked across my skin at the corners of my eyes and even *that* hurt. I opened my eyes and he was there. I blinked and tried to focus and when I did, he was still there. He was good. So very good to me. He took care of me, and was so careful with me; like the boy had been my last working night. My last night as one of their whores. I felt for the wrist band and cried out. It was gone.

"Oh hey, hey, it's okay!"

Leather and metal were pressed into my fingertips, beneath the wristband his hand felt warm and alive. I grasped it and blinked and tried to focus on him again. Summer skies smiled out from his blue eyes and his other hand wrapped around my one. He cradled my hand and the wristband between the both of his own, as he squatted down beside the bed.

"Am... am I dying?" I asked, and fresh hot tears slipped free.

"No. No, Darlin', it just feels that way..."

"Promise."

"Promise you what, Baby Girl?"

"Promise me I'm not dying, I don't want to die." I sobbed. It was true. I didn't want to die. I wanted to see my sisters again. I wanted to live and do so many things, something; *anything*, with the rest of my life. I wanted so badly to know this man who selflessly took care of me and made me feel safe again.

"Shh, you're not dying. You're not gonna die. You're okay, Baby Girl. This is normal for day three."

I closed my eyes… *what had happened to days one and two?*

CHAPTER 5
Marlin

"What's your name?" she asked softly and I reached back and pushed her hair off her face so I could see her better.

"My name?" I asked, surprised, "Didn't I ever tell you?" I immediately internally chastised myself for the casual touching. It was tough to remember not to do it when all I wanted to do was comfort her.

"If you did, I don't remember..." She looked up at me, huddled small and in on herself. She'd tucked herself into the corner of the large, triangular bath, next to the wall closest to the outside edge. I was sitting on the outside, back against the side of the step and short tiled wall leading up into the large bath that was big enough for three. I twisted so I could see her. My fatigued body didn't like the position so I adjusted so I was sitting alongside the tub, leaning against it. I propped my chin in my hand and kept my eyes on her face.

"Boys call me Marlin," I said finally when she kept staring, waiting for an answer. She frowned slightly.

"Like the fish?" she asked and I smiled. She was finally lucid again. Looked like Faith had pulled through and was one with the rest of the world, for the most part.

"Yeah, exactly like the fish. It's what I do. I run a sport fishing operation with my other brother, caught one of the biggest Marlin's on record about six years back. When I patched into the club, it stuck, been Marlin ever since."

"Club?" she asked hollowly.

"Yeah, the motorcycle club. Your sister, Hope, she's with our president, Cutter. We all came to get you."

"I know, Hope was there..." she scrubbed her face with her hands, "And another man, I remember him yelling and then there was you. You picked me up and then I was back in the van they took me in, and everything was awful and confusing…"

Her terror back in the van when we'd got her out of there made some sense now. Being all fucked up on the opiates, she'd probably had a flashback. Past and present melding into one awful big tangle of line that was so snarled there wasn't nothing for it but to cut it and start fresh. I sighed inwardly. Nothing could be done except explaining things some so they made sense for her now. Couldn't take the fear or the pain away, the unpleasant memories, but maybe giving her the tools to properly process the truth of things now, would help the raw fear of a week ago and more scab over and heal quicker.

"Think that was the drugs messin' with your mind, Baby Girl. Can I tell you what happened? Maybe it'll help some?" She stared me in the eye and finally nodded slowly, so I told her. About how her sister had gotten the call and how we'd gone looking. I skipped some of the gory details, leaving it at we'd found out about the house. Not how or why or what'd been done to get that information… She stared into the mound of bubbles around her, providing her the illusion of modesty as I spoke. She didn't interrupt but I could just *see* her wheels turning. She was soaking up the story like a sponge.

"Captain called me from out front, I came in and your sister had a hold of you. I'm the only one of our crew that's had to deal with addiction, even second hand like I did with Danny, so I picked you up and took you out of there."

"The van…"

"Set you off like a firework," I nodded in agreement. "But that's okay. You had a good reason for it, and that's gonna happen. You been through a lot, Faith. We're going to get you some help. One step at a time."

"I still don't understand, you don't know me… why are you helping me?"

It was a valid question, but none of the answers I had were real satisfying… because I liked her sister, because my Captain had asked me to, because I was a nice guy, but mostly and most truthfully it was likely to fix past mistakes that could never *be* fixed. Because I'd fuckin' failed and my brother was dead... Then the reality set in, the hard truth: because every time she looked at me with those beautiful eyes, the color of the waters around here that I loved so damn much, I was like a drowning man that didn't *want* to come up for air. None of these explanations sounded real good. None of them sounded anything less than what they were, sort of creepy. So I simply pursed my lips and patted the top of the edge of the tub. Resisting the urge I had to give her knee a reassuring squeeze.

She didn't need me touching her. No matter how much I *wanted* to gather her up, hold her close and keep the horrors away from her, I couldn't do that. I had to fight every instinct I had *to* do just that. It was basic human instinct. You saw someone hurting, you put your arms around them. You held them and soothed them, except what do you do in a case like this? When every touch she'd endured over the last couple of years was for someone else's gratification?

Her clear, bright eyes roved my face and something flashed in their depths. She closed them and turned away from me, laying her head on top of her knees. It killed me that there wasn't anything I could do.

She'd been sleeping more, after the initial hell of detox had passed, she'd finally fallen into a deep, exhausted sleep. Over two days she'd been up in one form or another. The doc had left this morning with his crew to go back up north now that she was out of the woods. Not like I'd let him do much. Nothing either, for that matter. He'd been forced to put antibiotics through her IV a time or two when it was clear she couldn't keep any of the pills he'd brought with him down. The anti-nausea medicine, for whatever reason, didn't work for shit on her. The pediatric popsicles Doc had me give her to help keep her hydrated only stayed down some of the time. Of course, the red ones were her favorite, and of course, they stained like a motherfucker. Didn't it figure? As soon as she could keep some broth and crackers in her, maybe some pudding, she'd have to start the antibiotic pills again.

I sat with her while she soaked in her sorely needed bath, and counted the knobs of her spine and every rib, where they stood out prominently against her back. She was so *thin*... It'd killed me when the doc had said she was lucky, that the sexually transmitted infections she had were all fixable with a course of a couple of weeks' worth of pills. She had three, apparently... Gonorrhea, Chlamydia and some shit I ain't never heard of called Trichomoniasis.

She would need regular bloodwork for a while to keep checking for HIV or any of the Hepatitis', but he said the initial tests had come back clear, which was a real good sign. All I could keep thinking was there weren't no good here. None at all.

"You cool for a minute?" I asked her softly and she nodded without looking. I pulled myself up, pushing off the edge of the tub to get to my feet and felt like I was getting too old for sitting on the floor like that, which was a bitch seeing as I was only thirty-six. I went out into the main bedroom and stretched for a second before I changed the bedding. It needed it. She'd been sweating hard. That done I went back in to check on her and found her crying quietly. It broke my fucking heart that there wasn't a damn thing I could do except for what I'd been doing all this time. I sat back down on the floor and just hung around near her. Just there, for whatever she might need.

"I'm sorry," she uttered and raised her hands from the bath, scrubbing her tears away with her damp fingers. She held her breath and splashed water onto her face and I turned my head away, staring at the glassed in shower, trying hard not to study her reflection and to give her both support and privacy in equal measure. I mean, what else could I fucking do?

"Thank you, Marlin," she said and I jumped slightly.

"For what?"

"Everything."

"I ain't done nothin' really."

She finished her bath in silence and I let her, standing and waiting out in the room for her to dry off and get dressed. She was unsteady on her feet when she slipped out into the room and blinked up at me owlishly when I turned around and looked down at her from where I stood sentinel.

Wordlessly she held up that leather wrist band with the old fashioned key plate set into it and I smiled and nodded. She slipped it over her hand and held it in place, turning up the delicate underside of her wrist so that I could tug the laces tight and tie it off for her. Silently we stood while I carefully tied the thin leather cording off in a bow.

"Someday you gonna tell me what it means? Why it's so important?" I asked quietly.

"Maybe."

"You ain't gotta tell me anything you don't want to, Darlin', but I sure would like to get to know you."

She looked thoughtful at that and with a halting step, took one out into the room, but stopped.

"What's the matter?"

"I don't want to sound rude, but I'm sick of it in here… can we go someplace else in the house?" I smiled.

"Yeah, you're not a prisoner, Baby Girl. You're a guest, you can go wherever you want. You good to make it downstairs? Sit in the kitchen while I make you something to eat, see if you can keep something down?"

"I think so," she nodded but wouldn't look at me. She hugged herself around the middle and looked so wrung out, but at the same time, she was on the mend. Her color better, the dark circles under her eyes still prominent, but her bright eyes, from beneath her pale lashes, were more alert than I'd seen them since I'd met her. Forget lucid, she was back from the hell the drugs had dragged her down into… which meant she was going to have to start clawing her way out of the pit of memory sooner rather than later.

I was wondering how tough this talk was going to be. None of us were fuckin' equipped for this kind of mental and emotional damage. Faith was gonna need help. Real help, from a professional equipped to deal with this level of trauma to a person's psyche. I put out a hand and motioned for her to lead the way and she padded gracefully on her bare feet across the light, lush carpet.

Hope had dropped off a few clothes the day before, quiet, pleading with her eyes for me to tell her that Faith had changed her mind and wanted her older sister, but Faith hadn't said a word about her. At least not until now.

"Do you think Hope will want to see me?" she asked and I cocked my head to the side and pulled out a chair at the dining room table. Faith drifted down into it and I looked her over. She wore soft looking heather gray leggings beneath an oversized white boat neck tee. At least I think that's what they called the kind that hung artfully off her thin shoulder. She'd swept all that long blonde hair over her shoulder. Both of us thankfully lice free, so it would seem. My jacket and cut were in a plastic garbage sack and tied off in the garage where they had to sit for a few more days yet. Just to make sure.

"Honey, I think I'm gonna have a tough time keeping her away much longer. You want I should call her here now?"

She gazed out the back slider, out over the sun bleached beach, eyes distant as she took in the faraway lapping waves of the sea.

"Tomorrow okay?" she asked.

I sighed inwardly. She'd been programmed to go along with everyone else's wants and desires so long it was going to be an uphill battle to get her to a place where she was comfortable expressing what *she* wanted. This was going to take patience. Something I both had and didn't have depending on the situation.

"I'll call her and let her know."

I got something simple to eat started and called Hope and let her know that Faith was ready to see her. Then I spent the next ten minutes talking our President's girl out of coming right then and there and holding off until tomorrow. The call ended with her tellin' me we weren't friends for at least the next five minutes before she huffed out a breath and thanked me for taking care of her girl. There was a reason we liked Hope. That would be one of them. It was like she was a female version of the Captain, only a little less sure of herself in some ways and feistier in others.

"There we go," I set down a steaming mug of a simple broth in front of her and some saltine crackers on a plate. If she could keep this down, I was under doctor's orders to give her a supplement shake after a while.

"Thank you," she murmured and blew on the steaming liquid.

I sat across from her, and kicked back in my chair. She wouldn't look at me, but I kind of expected that.

"Tell me something you like to do, or liked to do, before all this." I said gently. I wanted to try and get a conversation started but half expected she wouldn't tell me. She stared for long moments at the leather on her wrist before she spoke, haltingly.

"I… I liked to party. I would go out to bars and clubs and drink and dance, just hang out with my friends. You know?"

I chuckled, "I do."

"My sisters and I would go shopping. I liked to do my makeup…" she frowned, "Do you think that's part of why she sold me?"

My mouth went dry, she didn't have to talk about any of this to me, but who was I to deny her? I didn't know what to say, I didn't have a truthful answer, or extreme certainty, the only truth I had was the one I gave her.

"There's no telling what people like that think, what they look for. You're a beautiful girl, Faith. Makeup, no makeup, puking on me…" I grinned to take any bite out of it but it quickly faded. She was staring into her cup of broth, her eyes drifted shut and twin crystalline tears dropped from her lashes and into her lap. "Even crying." I breathed and she sniffed. I wasn't helping anything so I shut my fucking trap and got up, tearing a paper towel off the roll and bringing it to her. She took it and dabbed at her eyes.

We sat in silence for the rest of the meal and for a long time after she was finished. Her stomach finally gave an unhappy, clearly audible roil and she visibly paled.

"That way," I pointed at the open and darkened bathroom door and she nodded, got up and swiftly walked that way. She hit the light and closed the door and I waited for the retching, but it never came. I sighed. *Oh. Right. That.* I thought to myself and went about cleaning up around the kitchen. I made myself a sandwich and ate; she still hadn't come out by the time I was through. I tapped on the closed door.

"You okay, Darlin'?" I asked through the wood.

"I'm fine…"

But she wasn't. I knew she wasn't, but like so many things thus far when it came to Faith, there wasn't anything I could do except wait this out like all the rest. It was day seven of detoxing for her, but I somehow doubted she remembered the first four or five and that was okay. I could be the strong one and endure those memories for her. I sighed and sat and waited for her to come back out of the bathroom. When she did, she was sweating and pale, a light sheen of moisture on her upper lip, her arms wrapped protectively around her middle.

"Think you're done throwing up. You want help back up to go lie down?" I asked.

She bit her lips together hesitantly and nodded finally. I helped her back up to bed and she lay down on her side. The poor girl was miserable and uncomfortable, and again, there wasn't anything I could do.

Damn.

CHAPTER 6
Faith

My sister and I clung to each other on the big, overstuffed couch in the living room for the longest time. I could think again, which was both a blessing and a curse. Marlin tried valiantly to give us space, but he was just there, always there, hovering at the edge of the room. Hope kept glancing at him, and back to me and I shrugged, finally pulling back enough to let the corner of the couch support me. Although our hands were still clasped in one another's in our laps between us. I couldn't bear to let my sister go. The cast on her right arm was rough beneath my thumb where I rubbed it back and forth over it, over the back of her hand. The thought she couldn't feel it didn't even really occur to me, and when it did, it didn't make me stop.

"You okay, Bubbles?" Hope roved my face with her deep dark eyes that I had always envied growing up. Deep, dark, smooth liquid brown, and remarkable with how *un*remarkable they were. Everybody always had something to say about my eyes. Sometimes I wished I were just… I don't know… more *ordinary*. Maybe if I'd been born plain, maybe I wouldn't have been chosen, maybe I wouldn't have had to…

"Faith, come on, Darlin', look at me…" I blinked several times and focused and as ever he was there, a constant, stable. A wall to lean on when I couldn't stand on my own, and ever the perfect gentleman while providing that service to me.

Of course, why wouldn't he be? Who wants a nasty used up druggie whore on their arm?

"I… I'm sorry…"

"Shhh, it's okay, really. You back now? You solid?" he asked. I searched his handsome face, the bright blue of his eyes and nodded faintly.

Hope sighed and squeezed my fingers with her good hand, "Faith, will you let me find somebody to help you, Sis?" she asked quietly and I dragged my attention back to my sister. I bit my lips together.

"What, like therapy?" I asked. I knew that's what she meant, and I couldn't fool myself, even if I wanted to, let alone anyone else. I needed help. I didn't even know how to crawl up and over this *mountain* of issues on my own; I couldn't even begin to figure out how to deal with this. Any of this. I closed my eyes and let the despair of my situation wash over me.

"Yeah, Bubbles. There's a woman about an hour away. She specializes in this kind of thing… if I made an appointment would you talk to her?"

I sniffed back tears, Marlin's presence beside me lending me strength to face this, my sister's hands in mine…

"I can't afford to pay –" I cut myself off abruptly, "I mean, you, I…" I would need to find a job; I didn't even know how much money I had left, if any. Was I even still legally alive? Don't they declare missing people dead after a time? Anxiety and panic trilled up and down my spine, crushing the center of my chest in its fist and rattled me back and forth. I felt like I was drowning, like the house was closing in and swallowing me up, but as ever, Marlin's voice chased back the dark, which was warring to crush me between its gnarled hands.

"Easy, Baby Girl, deep breaths, just breathe…" it was the mantra that had pulled me from the deepest, darkest, despair of my sickness. The sickness those evil bastards had shoved into my veins, and fogged my brain with. I squeezed my sister's hand and resisted the urge I always had when he spoke to me this way. The urge to crawl into his lap. To huddle against his chest and hide from the world like a frightened child. After all, he didn't want to touch me. I was an unclean thing. Every time he did, he would startle and jerk his hands back as if he'd been burned, or like I was diseased and he would catch it. Which who knew? Maybe I was.

Maybe the test results the doctor had called with were all lies and I had something horrible and incurable and I would die from it…

Sometimes I wanted that. To die. Then I would see the fierce look in Marlin's eyes, I would think of Hope's disappointment and Charity's heartbreak and those thoughts would be chased back into the dark for the time being.

God, these thoughts… I knew I needed help. I knew I needed to talk to someone about these things. Someone who I wouldn't hurt with the telling, someone not my sisters… Marlin ducked and captured my gaze with his, determination radiating out from his summer sky eyes.

"Will you take me?" I asked, before I could stop myself.

"Absolutely, Darlin'," and I could hear the solemn vow in his tone.

"I'll make the appointment, Bubbles, don't worry about anything for now. Okay?" Hope searched my face and where I'd been blind, I swore I could see now.

"You really worried about me didn't you?" Guilt spiraled out of the sky and crushed me beneath its weight.

"Never stopped looking," she said, eyes welling.

"Why!? I always thought I was a pain in your ass!" I didn't understand, all the fighting and disagreeing and her riding my ass…

"Of course you're a pain in my ass!" She pulled me into her arms, "You're my little sister, you're meant to be a pain in my ass. Doesn't mean I'll ever stop loving you, Faith. Doesn't mean I would ever stop trying to find you. You're my blood, you and Char are my reasons for being. I love you guys. I will always love you guys."

I reached for my sister and we hugged and cried some more. Marlin stayed nearby, and eventually, quietly, disappeared into the kitchen right around the corner to fix a meal. My body still wasn't fully cooperating. I felt run down, fatigued, hollow and empty. The bathroom was still where I found myself spending the majority of my time, with the bedroom and bed a close second.

We ate, quietly, and I disappeared into the bathroom swiftly, though it was becoming less awful and less frequent. Although the less awful part *could* be because I was growing used to it. That was a depressing thought.

Twilight deepened into night and a knock fell on the big house's front door. Marlin went to get it, and the man from the house in

New Orleans, the one who'd been yelling, followed Marlin back to where Hope and I were sitting together. I frowned. I remembered more of him now. I remembered… I closed my eyes and tried to grasp it.

"You okay, Firefly?" his voice was rich and familiar and I placed it, what he called me.

"We've talked before, here in this room, right?" I asked softly.

"Yeah, we did." He nodded and everything rushed back to me, like a rogue wave coming further up the beach than expected. I couldn't place his name, or who he was, I just remembered that he was somehow important. Important to Marlin.

"Faith?" Hope asked; voice tinged with alarm.

"It's hard to remember things. I remember him at the house, back in New Orleans. I remember him yelling, right before Marlin came, and I remember we talked here… but I can't remember your name. I'm sorry."

The man smiled kindly and put his hands over the back of the couch, letting them fall in a familiar touch to my sister's shoulders, kneading them gently. Her posture which had been stiff, eased under the gentle prying of his fingers and it looked like it felt really good. Soothing.

"Name's Cutter, I'm the President, or as we call it, Captain, of The Kraken motorcycle club. This is my house, Honey, and you're welcome to stay here as long as you need to." He fell silent and his warm brown eyes roved me over, taking me in. I shifted a bit uncomfortably under the scrutiny, it was almost an echo of the way the men who, well… *paid for me,* looked at me when they were choosing between girls.

"Feel like you're gettin' better? In a physical sense, I mean." I jumped, his voice wasn't loud, just unexpected in the creeping silence.

I nodded and tried a tremulous smile, "Yes, thank you for letting me stay here." I twisted in my seat, "And thank you for taking care of me." I directed the last at Marlin who was leaning a shoulder against the wall, arms crossed over his muscular chest. He wore faded jeans today, and scuffed motorcycle boots, which he had crossed at the ankle on the gleaming hardwood floors. He nodded, carefully, a tension around his summer sky blue eyes. I swallowed hard, a bit nervously.

"Well, I just came by to pick Hope up, we're headed back to the Mysteria Avenge; you need anything from the Scarlett Ann?" I twisted back, but Cutter was looking over my head at Marlin.

"No thanks, Cap. I'm good."

"You want me to come over tomorrow?" Hope asked, her brow was furrowed and she shook my hands gently back and forth in her own. I nodded and my sister smiled. She used her free hand to push my hair back from my face and behind my ear, like she'd done when I was a child. The memory of such a long ago and innocent time made my eyes water.

"You want me to stay tonight?" she asked, and I took a deep breath and held it, I did. I really did, but I didn't want to be a burden to anyone. I didn't want to be a weight on my sister's shoulders, so I shook my head.

She leaned across our laps and kissed my forehead. I closed my eyes and sighed and she got up, and let Cutter guide her around the end of the couch.

"You need anything, anything at all, you call me. Okay? Marlin has the number."

"Yes, Mom." I cracked weakly and rolled my eyes slightly. My sister stilled and roved my face with an unreadable look.

"I love you, Bubbles," she said finally.

"I love you, too, Buttercup." I sniffed and gave her the best smile I could and her expression swirled with something akin to pity. It was okay though, I mean, I *was* pretty pitiful at this point.

"You're gonna be okay, Firefly." Cutter's tone was judicious and he nodded once. Marlin saw them out, letting out a hard, long sigh the moment the door was shut tight behind them. Guilt twisted the center of my chest into a knot, so hard I placed my hand over my breast. Marlin's broad back was to me, his head hanging low, bowed with exhaustion. He paused for a long moment before his hand slipped from the door handle with a slight rattle. He turned in my direction and searched my face from across the room.

"Aren't you going to lock it?" I asked nervously.

"Anybody tried to come up in here, they'd have a real bad night, Darlin'. You're safe with me, but if it makes you feel better…" he reached back and flipped the deadbolt into the locked position for my benefit. It felt strange to be on this side of a locked door after so long.

"Thank you," I uttered.

"No problem."

A vast silence filled the room between us, as if time were suspended and all that was and had been, hung between us. I bit down on my lower lip and felt a rush of shame heat my cheeks. This man had silently and stoically endured the worst parts of me and it was as if I were finally awake and all of the embarrassment and humiliation had piled up and waited patiently for it to be so, before they made their presence known.

"Hey, stop. Don't do that," his tone was hasty but gentle, "There's no shame here. No shame for any of it. It wasn't you, Baby Girl. It was *done to you*… there's a big difference there, Sweetheart. Huge. Okay? I knew what I was getting into. I committed. Don't forget, I've seen it all before, I've done it all before…" he stopped talking, searching my face as I searched his, sighing he gave a shrug, "Truthfully, watching you come down off that shit was one of the bravest, most inspiring things I've ever seen."

I blinked, bewildered, my voice hollow as it emanated from my mouth, "I don't understand."

I'd dropped my eyes to my hands, folded in my lap; to the boy's wristband and the silver metal plate and old fashioned keyhole set into it. The boy had been incredibly sweet. Incredibly kind. Like Marlin, certainly, but…

The scrape and swish of denim was incredibly loud. The thunk of his boot heels on the hardwood dull, as he moved from the front door and came around to sit on the couch. He put distance between us and my heart cracked further under the weight of my stigma. *Druggie whore…*

"You were hurtin' bad up there," he said gently, by way of explanation. "Thing I remember most about when my brother went through it was him beggin' me to kill him. He was hurtin' so fucking bad –"

He stopped abruptly and stared sightlessly at the huge, dark, flat screen TV against the wall opposite us for a long time. "Ain't never told anyone about this," he confessed, returning his gaze to my face which I felt was set in solemn lines.

"You don't have to…"

"Psht! Yes I do. You need to understand. What you went through, up there," he pointed to the stairs, "Was fuckin' awful, Girl." He dropped his strong arm to the back of the couch and let it lie there casually as he continued, "It was fuckin awful, and you handled it. You handled it better than a grown ass man. Danny begged me to kill him. He begged me six ways to Sunday to put him out of his misery. All he could talk about was how much he wanted to die but you…" he sighed out harshly and looked at the ceiling and shook his head.

"All you could talk about was how much you wanted to live, and that's sayin' somethin'."

I went back to staring at my clasped hands in my lap for a long time and closed my eyes, sighing out; my shoulders dropping. I didn't feel brave or strong. I didn't feel like I'd done anything particularly impressive.

"I just want to pull you into my manly bosom and just hold you for a while, damn."

I startled and blinked, looking up at Marlin sharply. A halfhearted smile played on his full lips, framed by his golden goatee and it called up a tremulous answering smile of my own. His smile grew with mine and I was struck by how extremely grateful I was that he was here, and again that feeling of safety overtook me even as his words registered and I found myself laughing softly.

"Manly bosom?" I asked and his eyes sparkled with barely suppressed laughter of his own.

He flexed and it was an impressive display, "Come on now, I work hard for this."

I laughed outright then, and it felt incredibly good. Marlin smiled, seemingly satisfied and winked at me.

For a glimmer of an instant… I felt almost normal.

CHAPTER 7

Marlin

I watched her sleep. It was so late at night it was early, and she was passed out. Dead to the world. The lines and grooves that sorrow had etched upon her face smoothed out when she was like this. She's fucking beautiful when she sleeps, when she feels safe, and she dreams... I wonder for a fragment of a moment if she dreams of me.

I reach out a tentative fingertip and trace some of her long, fair hair out of her eyes, letting my fingertip linger guiltily against her smooth skin. She's soft, and despite having been so violated, still so pure.

It amazes me, her resiliency. Her willingness to trust me after so many men, hell, and women too, had given her plenty of reasons to never trust another soul ever again. Her brow furrowed, and she moaned a little. I silently sighed and backed away to see if she'll find an even keel again or if this was going to morph into one of the big ones. Rarely does a night go by where she doesn't have some kind of nightmare or terror. Of course, she's only been about three weeks out of hell, so it's kind of to be expected.

She writhes and another moan creeps from her, cascading into a whining whimper that's become familiar. It's a bad one this time. They're almost all bad in the end, but this one is particularly rough. She doesn't always talk about them, but when she does… the shit is fucking awful, man. Her legs jerk, her knees making a rush for her chest and she cries out and I have a sinking feeling I know what this one is about. I switch on the bedside lamp flooding the room with golden artificial light in an attempt to chase back the shadows. It usually does the trick, chasing back the invisible ones inside her head too. The light goes on and those aquamarine eyes pop open and slay me all over again.

Not this time though. This time requires a little extra effort on my part.

"Faith!" I call out and I put my hands on my knees. I want to touch her. To gently shake her awake, but I know what a bad idea that is. You're not supposed to touch victims. It's a rule somewhere or something. Especially folks that have been victimized like her. She twists and sobs in her sleep and it breaks my fuckin' heart every fuckin' time.

"Faith! C'mon Baby Girl, you gotta wake up for me. C'mon Sweet Thing. Wake up!" I keep talking and finally it happens. She sucks in a breath like I tossed a bucket of ice water on her and those eyes of hers lock on mine. She half crab walks back on hands her feet sliding along the slick cotton sheets trying to find purchase and my heart sinks in my chest.

"You're alright. You're safe. You're okay now, Baby." I let my hands slide off my denim clad knees and straighten into a standing position as the tears well in her eyes, turning them jewel bright and beautiful. So wide, her face slack with realization of where she is, that it's the here and now.

"I'm sorry!" She blurts.

"Hey, no. None of that, now. You hear?" I shake my head and swallow hard as she hugs her knees. Sliding the soles of her feet against the bottom sheet.

"Bad one?" I asked, already knowing the answer. They were *all* bad. She didn't have good dreams, and when she did, they never stayed that way.

She nodded and I sat carefully on the edge of the bed, a fair distance from her. Giving her space. She looked at me, a little wild eyed, reminding me of these feral cats out at the marina… hungry little things. Half-starved bags of bones that'd look at me, hoping for fish scraps. I always gave them if I had them, but I wasn't sure what Faith was hungry for and I didn't feel right in askin'.

"Want to talk about it?" I asked softly.

"I have," she said, averting her gaze, "Talking about it hasn't helped, at least not yet."

"Always willing to listen, you know that Baby Girl."

"I know," she says and smooths her long beach waved locks behind her ears. Most girls spend hours and hours in front of a mirror putting all kinds of crap in their hair to get it to do those soft waves. Not Faith, though. Far as I could tell, her soft wavy curl was all natural.

I didn't miss how much her hands shook as she smoothed back her long hair. Or how she pulled the ends until her ears bent. She let go and wound her arms around her shins and hugged herself into this little ball.

"I tried to run," she said by simple explanation and bile rose, hot and fierce to tease the back of my throat. I nodded solemnly. She scrunched up her toes, curling them under and I tried very hard not to stare at her feet. They'd burned the soles with cigars and cigarettes to teach her a lesson on that one. She'd told me when I'd asked what the shiny pink pock marks were. Then she'd told me she'd never tried to run again after some more gory details.

I figured that if Faith had had to live it, then the least I could fuckin' do was be a fuckin' man and listen to it. She needed a box to keep her horrors in. A safe place to hold her nightmares so she didn't have to hold them inside all the time. Until we could get her to that shrink her sister had the hook up for, I could be that fuckin' box and I would be stone about it as she passed it off.

"I shouldn't tell you these things…" she murmured.

"Why not?" I demanded and she flinched at the hard edge in my tone. I silently cursed myself and took a deep and silent breath, letting it out slowly.

"I don't want to be this weak and wounded thing," she murmured, averting her eyes, staring fixedly at some invisible point in the bank of bedroom windows. Or maybe it was at our reflection. Who knows? She laid her cheek atop her knee and those amazing eyes drifted shut.

"Wounded? Yes. Without a doubt you are that… but weak? Aw, hell no. Not at all." Those eyes opened up and fixed on me, moving slightly back and forth to track the movement of my shaking head.

"I miss it," she confessed quietly, "I dream about it, the not thinking, the numbness it brought. If I could go back to it I would."

"Ah," I nodded my head in understanding. "Danny used to say the toughest part about getting clean were the dreams. Said whenever he dreamt of anything for a long time, the best dreams were the dreams of him getting high. It's normal, I guess." I shrugged lamely. I didn't know what else to do.

"Do you think I should go to a meeting or something?" she asked.

I chuckled, "Do you think it would help?"

"I don't know," she said honestly, "I guess I won't until I try it…"

"I'll find one for you if you want."

"Okay."

Silence slid between us but it was a calm one, a comfortable one. We sat quietly for a time before I cleared my throat.

"Ready to try and sleep again?"

"Yes, I think so." That brave little smile she sometimes got tugged at the corner of her mouth and I felt an answering smile of my own.

"Let's get you untangled." I stood and grabbed the sheet and she squirmed her way out of it. I made her into the bed, and was rewarded with a giggle. An actual small laugh. It was sweet and clear, like a cool drink of fresh out among all the stinging salt and punishing sun of the open water.

"Sit with me?" she asked.

I dropped onto the edge of the bed and she took my hand, I startled and looked down where she'd fitted her small palm against my own, her delicate fingers curving around the deeply suntanned, broad back of my own hand, scarred and rough as it was from use in my trade.

When I looked back up at her face, it held apprehension. I gave her small hand a tiny squeeze of reassurance and she visibly relaxed.

"I wanted to say a proper thank you, but I'm not sure that simply saying 'thank you' is enough for everything you've done."

"Don't think nothin' of it, Baby Girl," I said, "You just work on you. Don't worry none about me."

We lapsed into a comfortable silence and I leaned back against the headboard, hyperaware of how warm and gentle her hand was in mine. It felt good, that small contact, but I couldn't help but feel uneasy about it at the same time. I mean, she'd been through *a lot*, and I know it was just holding my hand, but she was in a bad place and needed to heal and I felt like this big dumb ox next to her... shit, I don't know.

"When it was quiet, like this, they sometimes let us listen to the radio."

I went very, very still. I swear it was like her light, clear voice stopped my heart right in its tracks. I felt my breath catch in my chest and I dared not breathe, waiting for her to continue. It wasn't the first time she'd spoken about her time with those fucktards, but it was the first time she'd spoken with anything other than total anguish in her voice.

"There was this band that would come on. I liked their music; it was like their songs spoke to me. Encouraged me in my darkest hours to hold onto the light. Ever hear of Ashes & Embers?" she asked me.

I nodded carefully, "They're that band from up in New England, aren't they?" I asked quietly.

"I don't know. I just know that's who sings the song."

"What song? Do you remember the title?"

She was quiet for a long moment and when she spoke it was almost too quiet to hear, "Hope Never Dies."

I chuckled, "She is kind of a superhero isn't she?" I joked and I was rewarded with a smile.

"Or a super villain, depending on the day and her mood."

It was my turn to smile. The Captain sure had his hands full with Hope. She damn sure opened a can of whoop-ass on the bunch of us boys back when Tiny had run his mouth... which fuck, that seemed like ages ago with everything that'd happened between then and now, 'cept it really was only like last month or something. Three weeks before on the outside.

"What was that?" Faith asked and I came up for air out of my deep sea of thought.

"A lot's been going on the last few weeks. It all blurs together sometimes. You know?" Faith gave my hand a gentle squeeze and nodded against the pillow.

"I know. I'm sorry..."

"Oh, hey, no. Nothing to be sorry about. You don't get to own none of this. We all know this was something that was done to you. Not something you picked to have happen, not something you got into without a fuck ton of help from all the wrong people. I know that, your sister knows that, the Captain and all the rest of the crew knows it too. You don't get to go blaming yourself for none of it, Baby Girl."

I watched storm clouds of emotion traverse her too-sharp features. Each one blooming and twisting, her thoughts whirling behind those bright, aquamarine eyes of hers before she finally murmured, "I want to believe you."

"Well that's up to you, Honey. I don't expect you to. Hell, I never expect you to trust another soul let alone another man again, but I'm telling you, you *can* trust *me*. Okay?"

She settled into deep thought after that. Her eyes far away and distant while she presumably searched around inside herself. For what, I don't know. For now, I was just content to watch her think. To watch those aquamarine eyes drift shut and to listen to her light breathing deepen and even out. Her sleep was slightly more peaceful, but by no means perfect, but I can say one thing... her hand in mine, it was oddly more perfect than I wanted to admit to myself.

When I was sure she was down for the count and wouldn't come back up out of her slumber anytime soon, I extracted my hand from her light grip with a heavy sigh and moved myself over to what was becoming my customary post in the chair by the bed. I slouched down and closed my eyes, my lips hooking up into a slight smile at a particularly brilliant stroke of an idea that hit me like a bolt out of the blue.

Yeah.

I would get right on that tomorrow, I just needed to check and see if I had the money for it. I should. Business was good, sucking a little wind with my absence, but I could get by. I could do it while Hope took Faith clothes shopping.

Decision made I dropped off into a light sleep myself, but it wasn't particularly restful. I didn't get restful sleep anymore. Jerking awake at any movement or sound Faith made. From the moment I'd laid eyes on her, I'd sworn to myself I wouldn't let her go down the way Danny had. Faith was my atonement for how I'd treated my brother and so far she'd soothed the fiery torment of my guilt.

I couldn't bring my brother back. I couldn't save him from the grave. But I could save *her*. It wasn't perfect. Hell, maybe it wasn't even right… but it mattered and I needed to do something that really mattered at least once in my damned life because at the end of the day, successful business, pride of the family, none of it meant shit fuck all in the grand scheme of things. Not when you were willing to let a family member go. Willing to let them die, just because they pissed you off or disappointed you.

Hope belonged to the Captain, and my club was my second family. By extension, Faith was family too. Cutter'd put me in charge when it came to her care, I wasn't about to let my Captain, my brothers, Hope or Faith down. It was just what it had to be. I was okay with that. My life needed a change up from the same old routine anyhow.

CHAPTER 8
Faith

"Faith?" I jumped and turned mutely back to my sister. I swallowed hard and she frowned. "You okay?"

I pressed my lips together and nodded rapidly. I wasn't. I felt like they were all staring at me. Like everyone in the store *knew*. I felt dirty, ashamed and like the weight of the universe was pressing me inexorably into the floor.

"No, you're not." Hope said judiciously and hung the dress she'd pulled off the rack back up.

"I… I think it's just a little bit much for my first time out." I murmured and she nodded.

"There was this famous general back in the day, like world war one and two, right? He used to say that he didn't measure a man's success by how high he climbed or how good he was at anything. He used to say 'The measure of a man's success should be taken by how high he bounces when he hits bottom.' You always did bounce the best out of the three of us. This is no exception."

I rolled my lips together and thought about what my sister was saying, finally nodding. A measure calmer than I had been before, even though my heart still raced in my chest and every breath I took made me feel like I was going to explode.

"Concentrate on the clothes, Bubbles. Let's find you some stuff to wear that you'll be comfortable in. It's hot around here, some shorts? A couple of swimsuits maybe?" Hope kept talking and I followed her dutifully around the little clothing boutique, looking at clothes without really seeing them.

My blood rushed in my ears, my heart thundered in my chest and it felt like the world was losing focus. I was falling but I was standing still. I felt crazed and like a total lunatic and when gentle hands fell on my shoulders I jumped clean out of my skin, shrieking, clapping my hands over my mouth to stifle the terrified sound. I quickly glanced around the shop and with a sinking feeling realized that if they hadn't really been staring before, I was definitely the center of attention now.

All conversation had ceased and every single set of eyes in the shop was turned on me. Pinning me in place. My eyes grew hot and wet and Hope's boyfriend's voice wrapped around me from behind.

"Aw shit; sorry, Firefly. I didn't mean to sneak up on you. Thought you knew I was here." I shook my head back and forth and he gave my shoulders a gentle squeeze, thumbs digging just a bit to ease the tension between them.

"Sorry, I was…" I sniffed, "I guess I got lost in thought a little. I wasn't paying attention."

"It's okay, Bubbles. You're good, but maybe we should stop for now." Hope lowered the clothing items she'd been prattling about and I shook my head furiously, tense beneath her boyfriend's hands. I knew he meant well, but honestly, the casual touch was a bit much for me, or maybe it was the hulking male presence behind me or…

"Hey, Cap. I know you mean well, Man, and I'm sure she does, too, but let her go, Man. She's not digging it."

Relief flooded out from the center of my being at Marlin's low and controlled voice. The Captain's hands left my shoulders and Hope sighed. I blinked my eyes open, having not realized I'd squeezed them shut and looked at my sister. She looked equal parts aggravated and heartbroken and I felt my stomach drop into my toes.

"Not your fault, Darlin'. Don't none of us think it is." Cutter, said to me. I nodded, throat tight and we all stood in awkward silence for several moments.

"I, I like this." I slid a dress off the rack, a maxi dress that was strapless but fell to the floor. It would cover more of me and with a light cardigan it would work well. My sister smiled and as if she'd read my mind held up a three quarter sleeve loose and flowy white cover-up that would go well with the aqua and white chevron printed dress.

"That's nice," Cutter commented nodding and I raised my eyes to Marlin's. He gave me a slightly off kilter smile that both warmed me and encouraged me. Still, his eyes spoke volumes. They whispered to me that he knew that I was being brave and that he believed in me. I took the strength he offered and stood a little straighter.

"Um, a swimsuit. That would be good. I think I'd like to go swimming if that's okay." I looked from one to the next, and Marlin and Cutter both smiled.

"You can do whatever you want, Sweetheart. You don't need our permission for anything." I swallowed hard and tears sprang to my eyes and Hope was suddenly there. She hugged me tight and I crumbled a bit and cried, clinging to my sister as the enormity of what transpired caught me off guard.

While I knew I was free, that my sister had saved me, I still didn't feel it yet. Marlin and I had spoken on it just this morning actually, before we'd left the house that had quickly become the center of my world and my sanctuary.

"I'm sorry! I'm sorry!" I cried into Hope's shoulder as we stood in the middle of the sea side clothing shop, in the middle of the little town's bustling boulevard.

Warmth and what had become the familiar smell of Marlin enveloped my back as he stepped near. I closed my eyes and breathed deep the combination of leather, cigarettes, and whatever he used for his shampoo, the faint smell of peaches and alcohol rounding things out. I thought it strange. The combination of cigarettes and alcohol should leave me feeling ill after so many had come to me reeking of it, but the alcohol smell on Marlin, I don't know. It was so faint and under everything else it was mellow. Bespeaking of time spent around bonfires or sipping cold beer while working in the sun.

Marlin's smell was what I imagined hard work, patience and decency to be like and his words, when murmured, did nothing to dispel that notion, but rather reinforced it tenfold.

"Baby Girl, don't forget that you're human. It's okay to have a meltdown. Just don't unpack and live there. Cry it out and get refocused on where you're headed. You can do that for me right?"

I nodded against my sister and sniffed, words weren't something I was ready to voice, my mind scrambling around in circles, caught in a never ending loop of panic and fear.

"Shhhh, you're okay, Baby. We get it. Your sister gets it, right Hope?" he whispered.

"Right," she affirmed.

"The Captain gets it."

"I surely do," Cutter agreed kindly.

"I get it," Marlin's voice pitched low, just for me, and he said, "Fuck everyone else in here, Baby. You've been through hell and none of these motherfuckers know what that looks like. You survived. It's all good. You aren't embarrassing us. There ain't nothing humiliating about this. For you, for me, for the Captain or your sister. You just take your time. Anyone has anything they want to say about it then they can come talk to me."

He straightened, the comfort of his close presence receding like the water from the shore down the beach outside the bedroom window where I'd been staying. I pushed back from my sister, sniffed and wiped at my eyes. Hope gave me a smile and I gave a tentative one back.

"She's going to need jeans at the very least if she's getting on the back of one of the bikes, which if Marlin's taking her out to that doc tomorrow, is a pretty likely scenario." Cutter pointed out. I stared a little wide eyed at my sister who smiled even bigger.

"Good point. I think you'll like riding, Bubbles. Let's go find you some suitable bike wear."

We went from the boutique to another little shopping center and finally ended up at the local motorcycle shop. I felt better with my sister walking in front of me and Cutter and Marlin at my sides and just behind me. Insulated and protected. Still, by the end of the shopping excursion I was exhausted, sliding gratefully into the back seat of Nothing's tired station wagon. Marlin got behind the wheel. Cutter rode up front while Hope sat in back with me.

"Home, James," Cutter said and Marlin called him a dirty name. I half expected Cutter to be angry but he just laughed and settled back further into his seat.

I stared out the window and felt bitterness for a time, looking at all the shiny, happy, and carefree people flitting by the window as we passed. I took the time to wallow in my own self-pity. Staring sightlessly yet seeing it all as it went by. Women smiling, men laughing, children playing in the sand on the beach… none of them having a single clue as to what went on in dark corners. In swanky and shady hotel rooms alike. In 'private' parties for the rich and famous. Of the tears and the hopeless nights that reeked of desperation and sex.

"Hey, you're okay. Look at me." I blinked and realized my face was wet. Marlin was crouched outside my car door, hands on his knees, sky blue eyes focused on mine. His dark blond hair crackled around his face like a mane, and the set of his mouth and the taught lines of his shoulders spoke of both power and determination. Looking at him, looming so close, in my personal space, I felt nothing other than utterly safe.

The tension in my own shoulders eased and he nodded as if something were confirmed for him, "Maybe a bit too much for today, huh Baby Girl?" he asked quietly and I sniffed and nodded.

"Okay, come on," he stepped back from me and let me get out on my own. Hope stood a little behind and off to one side, Cutter's hands on her shoulder's kneading the muscles there.

"You okay, Bubbles?" she asked and I could see in her dark eyes that she knew as well as anyone that it wasn't. She just didn't know what else to ask… what else to say. Neither did I… so I just went with the old standby.

"I'm okay," I lied, "Just tired, I think." Which was true, now that I thought about it. I felt, completely drained from the small outing. Like I could sleep for a week now, and that was all I wanted to do. I just wanted to go upstairs and sleep. Crawl into bed and lie in an exhausted heap and never come out again.

"Come on, we'll get this stuff put away and you can take a nap. Sound good?" Marlin's voice was patient and kind but all I could see was how much I was hurting my sister. How much Hope felt like shit, and honestly, my mood spiraled ever downward. I suddenly wanted to fall asleep and simply never wake up. I was miserable.

My sister led me to the house and up the stairs to the big bedroom at the top and down the hall, with its beautiful floor to ceiling windows and view of the ocean. I couldn't bear any of it. My emotions kaleidoscoped within me. Roiling and crashing into one another only to explode in a giant confused mess. It made me just want to curl up and cry. My heart raced, my throat squeezed tight, and I didn't know what was wrong with me. I sat on the end of the large bed and Hope stood silently for a moment, looking me over.

"Bubbles, what's wrong?" she asked softly and knelt at my feet. Marlin and Cutter, they set bags with our purchases on the creamy carpet just inside the bedroom door and backed out slowly to go get more. My sister had gone a little overboard and I'd let her; I think it was honestly more for her than for me. Hope had always been a total control freak and all of this was so far outside her control. Mine too.

"Faith..." she said a little helplessly. I shook my head a little violently and scrubbed my face with my hands.

"I don't know," I said helplessly, "It's like I am feeling everything and nothing at once and yet, at the same time, I'm so horribly numb on the inside. I just feel so tired but I haven't done anything. I shouldn't *be* tired."

Hope stood and turned, flopping into a seat beside me and wrapping her long, slim arms around me. I rested my head against her narrow shoulder and burst into tears, letting my hair hide my face from the room. Hope shushed me, making calm soothing noises like she used to do when Char and I were kids and had scraped a knee and somehow, somehow that helped.

"You should too be tired, everything you're telling me is perfectly normal for someone dealing with anxiety and PTSD. I've got it myself."

"I thought only soldiers could get that." I moaned piteously.

"That's a myth, Firefly. Anybody that's been through some heavy shit can come up with post-traumatic stress disorder. Shit, some people get it from bein' in a car accident." Cutter stood to one side of the doorway, arms crossed loosely over his chest and raised his shoulders in a shrug that was strangely one I would describe as being... elegant.

"Did you hear him, Baby Girl? Anybody who's been through something sudden or shocking can come up with it. What's happened to you – "

Marlin paused abruptly, a muscle in his jaw ticking in agitation under his golden scruff of a beard coming in around his goatee. He took a deep breath, "What you been through? It surely qualifies to give you a boatload of serious issues. Issues you may not even be aware you've got until something happens and you have a rough reaction. You're good. We've got you. You agreeing to go see that doctor lady is one of the biggest hurdles in getting you better." He stood in front of me, hands loose at his sides as if he were afraid to touch me and I closed my eyes. Of course he was. *I was dirty, cheap... a diseased whore. There was barely anything human left.*

"You're a brave girl, Firefly. And you ain't doin' none of this alone. You got your sisters, you got Marlin here, and you got me. By default you got any number of our guys behind you too. One step, one day, at a time. No need to get yourself overwhelmed." Cutter's voice interrupted the self-loathing inner monologue and I opened my eyes. I suddenly felt sick. Nauseated by the thought of what a burden I'd become to these people.

The weight of the world seemingly rested on my shoulders and I just wanted to lie down. I just wanted to be alone but at the same time, I didn't want them to leave me. I couldn't have it both ways though.

"I really," I paused and tried to make up my mind on what is was I wanted and finally settled on the least selfish, "I really just want to lie down, be alone for a little while."

"Okay," Hope said quietly but I could see my sister was a touch crestfallen. Damn it. I sighed inwardly. She got up and the three of them moved the bags in front of the closet in a neat row before slipping out of the bedroom and shutting the door firmly behind them. I stood up and toed off the flip flops I'd been wearing, going around to the side of the bed that was toward the windows. I lifted the covers and slipped between the sheets fully dressed, turning my back on the serene, too-pretty-to-be-real view of the white sand, of the vivid blue sky the color of Marlin's eyes where it met the aquamarine water the color of mine.

I just didn't want to exist anymore and pretty soon, I didn't, or the world didn't. I couldn't really tell, because I was fast asleep.

CHAPTER 9

Marlin

"Her first appointment is tomorrow," Hope said, and the Captain pulled her into his side. Her good arm wound around his waist and they looked like they belonged together. Strong, more solid together than they'd ever been apart. It was good to see. The Captain deserved someone like that. We all liked L'il Bit but she was Reaver's and that had always been plain to see.

"I'll get her there, just like I swore I would. I don't go back on my word."

"No one's sayin' you would, or that you ever have, Brother."

I nodded. The Captain was right, no one ever said that I would, it was just me that knew that I had... I had gone back on my word, on my vow, when it'd come to my brother Danny. I'd lost my patience with my brother after he'd gone back to that shit time and time again. I'd quit on him when once upon a time I'd swore I never would... and now he was dead.

My phone went off in the front pocket of my jeans and I dug it out, one glance at the screen and I was swearing softly. I slid the indicator bar and answered it.

"What's up?"

"Just wondering, Man. Were you ever planning on bringing your ass back to work?" I gritted my teeth and fought not to snarl back at my surviving brother.

"Yeah, I'm kind of in the middle of something with the club, Johnny."

He swore softly, or he'd pulled the phone away from his mouth before he'd done it. Either way, didn't care, but I was gonna in a second.

"Well I booked you a client, they're at the Scarlett Ann now, it's only a four hour gig but the bills need to get fuckin' paid, Bro."

I was gonna fuckin' kill him. I ground my teeth together and tilted my head from one side to the other until my neck creaked and finally gave with a loud crack. Once, then twice and in the span it took me to do it, I got a lid on my temper.

"You listen to me you little shit. I say who gets on my boat when. You get me? I live there, you don't."

"Whatever, Jim. I got a fuckin' family to feed, you don't. Get your fuckin' ass down here and let's get some fuckin change in our pockets. My kid wants to eat this week."

The fucking little cock bite hung up on me. Cutter and Hope both locked me with looks of bemusement and wide eyed empathy.

"I'd throat punch him," Hope said judiciously. I huffed a small laugh.

"He's more'n just my business partner, he's my brother."

"I'd still punch him," she said with a blasé, one shouldered shrug.

"Trust me, it doesn't work."

She gave a dramatic sigh, "It really doesn't."

Cutter's shoulders shook with silent laughter and he finally shook his head, "You were headed that way anyways, go on. She's out like a traffic light and probably will be for a minute. Your brother's half right, it's been a leaner season than most. Of course it don't really get started for a while yet. We got this, man. Go do your thing."

I clasped hands with my P. and we pulled each other in, slapping one another hardily on the back. I gave Hope a nod and she gave me a serious one back.

"See you soon," she uttered and I made for the door.

It didn't sit well with me leavin' like this, but Johnny'd painted me into a corner. I fuckin' hated that shit and you'd best believe we'd be havin' words about it. *After* we'd gotten rid of whoever was on my fuckin' boat without me. By Christ, Johnny had better be on the Scarlett Ann when I got there, with whoever he'd given the go ahead to board.

You'd like to think he was the older of the two of us, but I out stripped him by a year and more. Danny'd been younger than me by four, mama's little miracle baby. Spoiled rotten 'cause of it too. Danny'd gotten away with fuckin' murder out of the three of us growing up. My parents had started late with me an' Johnny as it was. Mama had had Danny in her mid-forties. We'd all been named for the bible. God fearing, my folks. I'd gotten stuck with James, Johnny was after John the Baptist and Danny? Well, Mama'd decided that with how high risk the pregnancy had been, our little brother had made it out of the lion's den and so he'd gotten Daniel.

I made strides out the front door of Cutter's house and threw a leg over my waiting bike. I checked her over thoroughly. When Hope's bike had gone into the crash truck I'd bitten the bullet and let the prospect fuckin' ride her. There wasn't a scratch on her. I must have inspected her at least a dozen times over the last couple of weeks but she was fine. I still kept expecting to find some kind of flaw in her but the kid had taken good care of her for me. I think he was going to work out.

I pulled my sunglasses down over my eyes and started her up, my lips curving into an appreciative smile. Rides, even short ones, had been few and far between with the situation what it was. I was in some serious need of some wind therapy to blow out some of the cobwebs and ick coating my soul from the epic pile of shit I'd been shoveling. Not that I regretted one minute of it. Championing this particular cause had never felt so right, but that didn't stop it from taking its toll.

Faith was a beautiful mess. I didn't fault her for that in the slightest, not after what'd been done to her. It was going to be a long haul to reel her back in from the devastation that'd been visited on her. I still didn't know if she would ever be quite right. Don't suppose anybody could be after something like that. Better, sure, but some things left indelible marks that nothing would ever take away completely.

The struggle to pull my mind off of Faith and onto getting to my boat and whoever was on it *off it*, was real. I gave the throttle and the handlebars a twist, gently guiding myself out onto the street. The ride to the marina was way too fuckin' short, and did nothing to quench my thirst for beating the brakes off my brother. I backed my bike into my garage and locked her in. I was intentionally taking my time to piss off Johnny-boy, but at the same time I was itching to get on my boat and get this fishing trip over with. I double checked my pockets and satisfied my cargo was intact, headed for the dock my boat was moored at.

The Scarlett Ann was a thing of beauty. Forty-two feet and state of the art, she was all business, except when she was my home, which was when she was docked here. I tried to keep the scowl off my face as I made strides up the dock and down to my slip. Couldn't help it when I heard the off key singing and the discordant notes I was pretty sure was coming out of my guitar.

I hoisted myself up and onto my deck to four curious faces looking in my direction. Two dudes and two chicks, all young, like in their twenties and my fucking brother was not among them. The dude sitting in one of my deck chairs guiltily lowered my guitar and the dude that had been standing, back to the railing wasn't laughing anymore, but damn sure wanted to be friendly like. He stuck out his hand all bright and eager and I had to keep repeating to myself, over and over, *he's a paying customer, don't deck him. He's a paying customer,* be nice.

"Hi! You must be Jimmy."

"Marlin," I grated and begrudgingly took the dude's hand. It took everything in me not to crush his fucking fingers in my grip. "Folks around here call me Marlin," I said and forced a smile onto my face. As soon as this ordeal was over I was gonna have words with my brother and I'd probably let my fists do the talking. This shit was a million fucking miles away from cool.

"Right, Marlin. I'm Kevin, this is Douglas and this is my fiancé Karen, and Doug's girlfriend Kristen."

I pinned Dougie-boy with a look, "Does that belong to you?" I asked, eyeing my guitar.

"Uh, no…" he answered.

"Then why are your fucking hands on it?"

He hastily set my guitar aside and I turned back to Kevin and asked, "Any idea where my brother John is?"

"He went to get some ice," the blonde chick introduced as Karen pitched in.

"Uh huh, well, when this ain't our fishing boat, it's my home. You didn't know that though, did you?" Four heads shook as one and I nodded. *Fuck my fucking brother sideways.*

"In any case, welcome aboard," I said in a grudging attempt to ease the tension in the air my temper had caused, "Soon as Johnny shows up, we'll get underway."

"Woah! Johnny's right here!" my brother called cheerfully from the dock. I turned and he heaved a bag of ice up to me. I caught it and glared murder at him. The little shit just smiled up at me and oh, the fuck yeah, I would be wiping that shit right off his fucking face when we were done here, if not sooner.

Johnny's smile faltered as we loaded the built-in coolers on deck with ice. I left my brother to it while I set about starting up and casting off. The four paying customers began to ease up and relax under my brother's routine, which was fine by me. It was why we were partners in the first place. He dealt with certain kinds of people better than I could. Usually, the yuppie kind. I got along better with the true sport fishermen, but the amateurs paid more. I could teach them, even had the patience to teach them right – what I didn't have the patience for, especially now, was the small talk aspect of things.

All I'd wanted to do was come to the boat and grab my fucking laptop. I didn't *need* to be out here with these fucking yahoos, and neither would my damn brother if he didn't spend his share down to the fucking wire every time he got a bit of cash in his pocket. Greedy little prick. He was a lot like Danny'd been that way.

I undid the ropes and started to cast off. Johnny moved over to help and we worked in unison, the silence between us thick and alive, sitting heavy like one of Hossler's fuckin' snakes in the grass. Motionless, but you knew it was about to strike, could tell by that stillness.

I could barely keep a lid on it, and the way my brother kept glancing at me, these furtive looks to gauge how pissed off I was? Well, that shit wasn't helping. All it did was serve to piss me off more. Johnny moved closer to me and I knew he was about to say something so I did what I had to do to keep it cool. I took a deep breath and held it, bit the inside of my cheek, and kept my hands busy coiling the line.

"Dude, I'm sorry it had to come to this but…"

"Stop right there, little brother. I don't want no cock and bull fuckin' sob story about your money troubles. I'm here, I'm doin' it, but while I do, you need to shut the fuck up and keep *your* guests happy. We'll talk about it when they're gone. I'll tell you this right now, though." I leaned in real close and brought myself eye to eye with my brother, "You *ever* let *anyone* on my boat and you ain't glued to their ass, or I'm not already here, I will fucking *end you* Johnny boy. This is my *home* you little cock weasel. I don't let my boys into your house randomly. Don't you *ever*. You get me?"

I'd talked to Danny like this a million times, but I could only count on one hand the number of times I'd been this pissed at Johnny. Usually he and I were on an even keel. Then Danny'd died. Right after he'd knocked up his cunt of a wife, and rushed the wedding. Then, as soon as she'd dropped one kid, he'd knocked her up with the next. Wasn't no way he was getting away from that judgmental, gold digging bitch. Lynn had her hook set in deep and Johnny'd swallowed it. There weren't no catch and release when that happened. Not that I'd trade my niece and nephew for anything. Cute as bug's ears. The both of them.

I just wish my brother would grow some fuckin' balls and handle his woman. It was her spending that landed him in a tailspin nine times out of ten. She had her way, she'd work my brother to the bone. Even if he left her, he couldn't, and wouldn't leave his kids. She'd bleed his ass dry through child support anyhow. Still, I was getting tired of it. More so now that I had Faith to look out for. Second chances didn't come around every day, and she was mine. I couldn't save Danny, from the dope, or from himself… but Faith was different. She needed saving from the same demons, sure, but not from herself. Not as far as I could see anyways.

I was pretty certain that she didn't want to go back to that poison, even if the opportunity presented itself. The deck was stacked in my favor this time. I aimed to take full advantage. Get her clean, get her clear, get her the help that she needed, and set her free. Get her to a point she didn't need me, or no one else, to rely on. It was a long fuckin' road ahead.

Some wise old fucker once said that a journey of a thousand miles started with one step, or some shit. We weren't but ten into this journey, and had a lot of steps left to take. While I knew I needed to work for a livin', I thought I would have a little more time before I had to get back to it. Guess not. The knot of anger between my shoulder blades eased some as I took the wheel and started the Scarlett Ann's engines.

Bein' pissed the fuck off wasn't gonna get me anywhere. While it was true that my brother had some shit to answer for, there wasn't no getting to it right now. I might as well relax and enjoy the wind, the waves, and the fan-fucking-tastic weather we had for this. Besides, the sooner I got us out to sea, and these dipshits set, the sooner I could sit down with my laptop and hook up Faith's present the way I wanted it. Maybe it would give her some peace. Something to focus on, making going outside, and around other people, a little easier to swallow.

Johnny kept the two guys and their girls happy while I piloted us out into the open waters. I was hoping this trip would end up skunked, that nothing would bite, but I was probably going to be disappointed. The conditions were great. When we got out to one of the better fishing spots, I killed the engine and went to help my little brother get the customers set.

Both dudes were fired up to fish, and so was one of the chicks, the brunette, Kristen. Karen, the blonde, was content to lounge in the shade with a tablet in her lap. Fine by me. One less rod to man when the time came. Although, it wasn't like Kristen would be able to pull anything these rods were made for in; not by herself. Hell, I wouldn't even put her in the gear. She'd be ripped right over the side. She didn't have enough body weight to her to counterbalance what one of these fish could do, despite her athletic build. I wouldn't put her much over a buck, she was just that petite. I caught Johnny's eye and he waved me off. He knew what I was thinkin', I didn't even have to say it. There were several things my brother and I had no problem agreeing on, and safety for our customers and patrons was at the top of the list.

If Kristen's rod snagged something, it looked like I'd be the one fightin' whatever she'd caught on her line. As much as I hated to admit it, it was my turn to deal with it. Still, I would have time to do what I wanted to get done if I left Johnny to do the hard labor getting them set up the rest of the way, which is what I did. I'd wipe the dirty look off his face later. It wasn't my idea, or need, to even fuckin' be out here anyways; goddammit.

I left the trio and their rods to my brother to deal with, and ducked below deck to retrieve my laptop. At least it was where I'd left it, unlike my fuckin' guitar. I came back up and dropped into a deck chair next to the blonde girl who didn't even look up from her e-reader tablet thingy. Good deal. I didn't want to chit chat anyways. I opened up the laptop and started it up, clicking out of the business software book keeping crap I'd left undone before taking off on our wild ride to the crescent city. I could do it later; in fact, I'd bring it back with me to Cutter's place. I could do it while Faith was sleeping or doing her staring out the window thing. Just because I wasn't out on the water, didn't mean there wasn't shit to be done for the business.

I pulled the little iPod I'd picked up in town out of my pocket and plugged it in to my laptop. I didn't know if I had everything I wanted to put on it. I mean, I knew I had a song or two… I clicked through my iTunes account and, "Ha!" I must have uttered it aloud because Karen roused herself from whatever she was reading and looked over.

"Ashes & Embers, didn't take you for the type to like them. You struck me as more of a classic rock kind of guy."

I glanced at her sideways, "I like all sorts of sh-," I stopped myself, "Stuff." I muttered belatedly and admittedly a little distractedly, "Besides, it isn't for me."

I actually had one of A&E's first albums, not the one with *Hope Never Dies* on it, though. Still, it was my intention to put their entire discography onto this thing for Faith, and I aimed to get the rest downloaded and onto it right now, that is, if I had enough cell signal to get my hotspot working. It was tough out here on the water. They hadn't invented cell towers for the ocean yet, and I hoped to God they never fucking did. I sighed in frustration when I realized we were just this side of too far out and that I didn't have enough juice to get it done.

"What provider do you have?" Karen asked. I told her and she swiped across her phone.

"Try mine, they have the best signal. Password for my hotspot is…" I gave it a shot, knowing it wasn't likely, but no dice. I sighed.

"Thanks, anyhow." I grated and snapped the laptop closed.

"Who's it for?" she asked smiling.

"Who's what for?"

"The iPod."

"How do you know it's not for me?" I asked.

She laughed lightly, "Just like I didn't figure you for an Ashes & Embers fan, I really don't figure a guy like you is much into the color pink. A&E, a pink iPod shuffle… well that screams one thing and one thing only, my friend. Who is she?"

"What do you *do* for a living?" I asked, chuckling to myself. The girl was sharp.

"I'm in school, actually. Finishing up my master's degree in psychology."

"Ah," I nodded in understanding and set to work folding up the cord to the little music player. "She seems like she would like the color pink," I mumbled, suddenly embarrassed with the idea of giving her the gift. Shit, I was overstepping. I had to be overstepping. This was a dumbassed idea, for sure.

"You don't know what colors she likes?" she asked, and shit, it looked like I'd piqued her curiosity.

"She's my President's, Ol' Lady's sister," I said, then figured I might as well go for broke, "Hope isn't especially fond of the color pink, and Faith, I don't know. I figured if Hope wasn't a fan then it would stand to reason Faith might be. Besides, it was between pink and silver and the silver looked… boring." I shrugged.

"You really like this girl, Faith," she stated flatly.

I looked over at her, "Oh, yeah? What makes you say that?"

She laughed lightly again, "No man puts that much thought into what color iPod a girl would like if he wasn't totally either in love with her, or wasn't falling hard. It's okay. I think it's great, personally. She's very lucky." She looked over at her man, the respectful one, Kevin.

"He would do that for me, agonize over the color when I would just be over the moon that he'd bought me such an expensive, and *thoughtful* gift. I'm sure she'll love it."

I cleared my throat, still uncomfortable that I'd sorta been caught bein' such a softy. Finally, I sighed and decided that now would probably be as good a chance as any. That she might know, bein' as it was her line of schooling and all.

"Yeah, I don't know how to do this," I said snapping the laptop shut and leaning heavily back in my seat.

"Do what?"

"Faith, she uh, she's been through a lot and recently too. Some real heavy shit. Some seriously awful shit I wouldn't wish on no woman." I looked over at Karen and she softened, switching off her e-reader and setting it aside on the small deck table, on top of my laptop where I'd set it; right next to the music player in its offending bright pink color.

"Talk to me," she invited.

"She's been messed up pretty hard," I cleared my throat, "I shouldn't really be talking about it but you might know somethin' about how to…" I groped in the dark for the right words, "I don't know, how I could handle myself better surrounding her situation."

"I would have to know something about it before I could speak on it."

"She's a mess, addicted to heroin, and only a few days out of the worst of the detox. We got her going to some kind of head shrinker to help her, her first appointment is tomorrow," I was dancing around the ugliest part about it and I knew it, but saying it out loud still made me fuckin' sick and the anger surge hot and ridiculous.

Finally, I sighed out harshly and rushed out, "She was sold into white slavery. Trafficked for the better part of the last couple of years as a hooker in New Orleans. They were shooting that shit into her veins, keeping her hooked to keep her docile. I know what to expect when it comes to the whole addiction rigmarole, but I ain't got a fuckin' clue when it comes to the rest."

I couldn't believe I was spillin' my guts to this chick, a total stranger, a *paying customer on my boat*. I was a little startled to realize just how far down the rabbit hole I'd gone when it came to Faith. Just how far fuckin' gone I'd been right from the beginning; from the moment I'd lifted her too-thin frame up into my arms, and carried her out of that house of fuckin' horrors back in New Orleans.

Karen sat up straighter and wrapped her fingers around one knee, very prim and proper. I had to give it to her, she didn't flinch; instead, you could visibly see the gears in her pretty little head turning, her blue eyes sparking with intelligence.

"Right, you said that you're getting Faith some help, right?" She searched my face to make sure I wasn't blowing smoke up her ass. I liked her for that.

"Yeah, her sister found some doctor that specializes in cases like Faith. Some woman who's like top in her field. I take Faith out to see her tomorrow."

"Okay, obviously there isn't really anything I could, or should be doing there, seeing as I am both still in school and unlicensed. I shouldn't even really be talking to you about *you*," she frowned but it wasn't at me, more like at the situation. "In all honesty, I think you need to find someone to talk to or lean on yourself. Doesn't have to be a professional, but being on the front line, or a first responder to something like this takes its toll." I nodded.

"I got my brothers." Cutter'd told me if I needed someone to reach out to, he'd be there. I knew I could depend on him, or any one of the guys if I really needed to. I guess I just wanted an opinion from the outside. Somethin' a little more removed from the situation and here she was, all trained and shit. Well, mostly trained. The Universe provides, all you had to do was be willing to accept what it had on offer.

Karen nodded after several moments of reluctant silence, we both turned as Kristen let out a peal of laughter at something my brother said. Johnny caught my eye and the murder in his said he'd overheard some of what Karen and I were talkin' about, and that he wasn't happy. Well, fuck him, I wasn't happy either. The only *real* concern I had right now was how to do right by Faith.

Karen gave me an appraising look and sucked in a breath, "Let's go back," she said, "I want to ask you a question."

"Shoot."

"Why the iPod? What was your thought process in buying it?"

I sniffed, "Faith told me she liked a particular song that'd play on the radio sometimes back when..." I skipped over it and kept going, "Anyways, we've had to take her out a couple times and it hasn't gone well. She has these freak outs, gets all traumatized and freezes up and sh–" I caught myself again.

"And the iPod?" Karen pressed.

"I figured she could use it, you know? Plug the music into her ears and give her something else to concentrate on. Drown some of the other people around out.

"A coping mechanism."

"Yeah."

Karen's mouth turned down and she nodded her head thoughtfully, "It's a good idea. Something dependable that isn't bad for you. I think it was a really good, really thoughtful, idea."

"Yeah?"

"Yeah, I'd say you're on the right track. It can, and will, be a good tool to help ease her back into things. What else are you worried about?"

We talked, for a good long while. Kristen got a bite, and Johnny helped her reel in a red grouper. Enough for a meal for two, so that wasn't bad and seemed to satisfy her enough that she'd caught something before the boys, that she didn't feel the need to keep fishin'. She got her picture with it and I got the hook out of its mouth. I was about to toss it in the cooler when she squealed in protest. We weren't exactly a catch and release outfit, but she and her boys were the ones payin' so fuck it.

"Your lucky day, Man," I told the fish and leaned way over the side and let him go.

As I watched his tail wave back and forth, and his reddish brown body disappear into the blue, I couldn't help but wonder if this would somehow become a metaphor for my deal with Faith. Would she get better, wander off, and that'd be it? I'd never thought about what was supposed to happen *after*, you know? What came *after* all the therapy and recovery, when she was as put back together as she would ever be?

The universe provides, alright. The rest of the trip, we didn't catch shit. Their four hours were up and I got us turned around and headed back to the marina. I talked more with Karen, who was a smart girl with a good head on her shoulders and by all accounts, a heart made out of solid gold. Her and her man both, judging by the charity case his jackass buddy Doug, was.

One of the things I liked about my business was the people I met. There was somebody new on these decks just about every trip out; this trip had been no exception. I felt better, more right about some of the choices I'd made regarding my involvement in Faith's recovery. Of course, there was some advice I knew was coming, didn't wanna hear, and was pretty much choking on, but I knew I needed to hear some of the hard truths. Maybe if I'd heard 'em, or been more receptive to 'em when Danny'd been alive, I would have been more understanding. Maybe I would've been more patient, and maybe, as a result, Danny'd be less dead.

Kevin, Doug, Kristen, and Karen left all smiles after I'd backed the Scarlett Ann into her slip. I set about alongside Johnny in silence, going about the general cleanup. He was loading the rods back into the rocket launcher, which was basically a rack of tubes designed to hold and protect the rods when they weren't in use when he finally spoke up, but it wasn't with a fuckin' apology.

"You've seriously been blowing off our business for the last two weeks over some junkie fucking *whore*?" he demanded and I froze. *Oh, hell no he didn't.* I straightened and turned around slowly to meet his accusing stare.

"Johnny," I drawled quietly, and watched the uncertainty slide behind his eyes, "You're my brother, and blood is thicker 'n anything else, but you haven't met Faith, you don't know the half of what's been goin' on. Quite frankly, it ain't none of your fuckin' business either. Now, you got about two seconds to make some sort of apology before I beat the motherfuckin' brakes off you. You get me?"

We stared each other down for several moments and when no apology came, I lunged forward, catching my brother around the middle. We crashed to the deck and I reared up, bringing my fist crashing down into his face.

He swore and swung back, boxing me in my fuckin' ear which hurt like a mother and left it ringing. Wouldn't be the fuckin' first time though.

"I said fuckin' apologize!"

"Fuck you, Man! You should be apologizin' to me! I got a fuckin' family to feed." We grappled, and it wasn't my best game, but there wasn't much space to work with here on the aft deck with the butt seats and fighting chair. Even less when you factored in the two deck chairs and the small table with the electronics sitting on it.

"Gahhhh!" Johnny had his hand on my chin, fingers digging into my face as he forced me up and away from him. I let fly with an awkward punch to his ribs and he grunted, doubling in on himself.

We rolled around on the deck for a good long while, and I did as promised, I whooped my younger brother's ass. Though granted, he got a few good licks in himself.

Eventually, we each were sitting, legs sprawled in front of us, backs to the side of the boat, Each of us in a respective corner like a pair of wrung out prize fighters, glaring murder at each other as our chests heaved in great gulping gasps for air.

"What, this bitch's pussy made of gold or some shit?" he demanded.

I snarled back, "It ain't like that, and I could ask you the same thing. Better yet, when you gonna get your fuckin' balls back outta Lynn's purse?"

That shut his trap for a minute. He glared balefully at me through one eye swelling and wiped at the blood under his nose.

Heh, yeah, I got him good. Of course, judging by the stinging under my left eye, he got me pretty good too. Cocky little bastard.

"I need the money or we're gonna lose the fuckin' house. She opened up a bunch of credit cards I didn't know nothing about and has been skimping on the fuckin' mortgage payments to pay 'em, hopin' I wouldn't notice. The bank fuckin' called me. I'm going into default–"

"Jesus-*fucking*-Christ Johnny! When you gonna learn? Better yet, when you gonna start spending your money on something that matters like a fuckin' divorce attorney that specializes in child custody?"

"Man, you know how the fuckin' system works! They always, *always*, give the kids to the mother, then she'll have my balls in a vice when it comes to child support and who the *fuck* is going to take care of my babies then? You know she's only good for a few hours at a time."

I shook my head, I'd heard it all before, and I was sick and fuckin' tired of his goddamned excuses. What I said next, I admit, was pretty fuckin' shitty, but my brother had put me in an exceptionally shitty mood by this point and he still hadn't apologized for mouthing off about Faith; who he didn't even know.

"Fuck, Johnny. You're more like Danny every fuckin' day, except instead of smack, you're addicted to that cunt's pussy."

My brother recoiled like he'd been slapped, and just stared at me.

"Low fuckin' blow, Jimmy."

"Yeah, well so was the crack about Faith."

We stared each other down for a long minute.

"Never seen you go to bat so hard about some broad before, what makes her so special?"

"What makes Lynn so special, you little cock bite?"

"I asked first, you big bastard."

I laughed, and Johnny laughed. No one can fuckin' drive your ass crazy like family.

"Seriously," he gasped when we got our shit together enough to speak, "What's the deal?"

"I don't know…" I said honestly, and I didn't. I couldn't explain it, yet there it was. We sat and talked a little more after that and I tried to explain. This wasn't the first time my brother and I scrapped. Every once in a while it was like we each reached critical mass and had to blow off some fuckin' steam or explode. We never hung onto it, or let it come between us for more 'n a minute, and this here was no exception.

We finished cleaning up the boat, then took turns in the water closet cleaning ourselves up before I packed up the laptop and other electronics and threw some shit in my bag.

"You stayin' at Cutter's with this girl?" he asked.

"Yeah, for now."

"Mind if I do a few solo runs to catch up to Lynn?"

I considered it, "You gonna look into a divorce attorney? Shit ain't getting better, Johnny. If anything it's worse."

"Yeah, I know."

He stood there silent and I finally heaved a sigh, "You got keys. Be fuckin' careful and call and let me know, when, where, how long you'll be… all that shit, okay? In case I need to come by and grab something or, you know, want to fuckin' come home."

"Deal."

"Gimme at least the next three days before you hit me up to do anything, and keep my cut from this trip."

"No, not going to do that. You were out there too."

"Fine, whatever, I just don't want to hear from your ass for at least three days about babysittin' fucking tourists. You got it? I'm takin' Faith to some shrink an hour inland and down tomorrow. Not sure how that's going to go."

"You're fuckin' crazy putting your ass through this shit again, you know that, right?"

"No, Man. I'm right where I'm supposed to be, doin' what I'm supposed to be doin'. Never been more sure of it."

"I'm worried about you, bro."

"Not your job, Johnny."

"Yeah, then who's is it?"

"Mine."

CHAPTER 10
Faith

I was too warm and my mouth had a funny metallic taste in it. I was comfortable though, and I didn't want to get up. Still, my bladder demanded I move, and eventually it won. It always did.

I sucked in a deep breath to chase back the cobwebs and opened my eyes. I nearly crossed them to see what it was crammed and blurry in my field of vision, all pink, white, and yellow.

I backed my head up on the pillow and frowned. A pink iPod with white headphones coiled neatly next to it, a creamy yellow mini post-it note clinging to the controls.

Play me, Faith was written in a spidery scrawl on the post-it in black ink. The writing unfamiliar to me. I sat up on the bed and looked around the darkened bedroom. No one was there, nothing stirred… I felt my forehead crush down in a frown.

I looked around the room again, just to be sure, before I plucked the headphones off the smooth cotton pillowcase. I spent far longer than was necessary uncoiling them and tucking them into my ears before I plugged them into the little player. I read and reread the note before plucking it from the front of the little clip and touching the little triangle button to make the thing play.

My breath caught, and stilled completely as the first leading strains of *Hope Never Dies* spilled from the earbuds. The person playing the guitar was masterful, the notes solemn and quiet, building and subsequently building me up, surrounding me, tucking around me like an old and familiar blanket, or really, bandaging some of the broken bits of me. Holding me together again, just enough to allow me to mend.

Marlin. It had to be. No one else knew what this song did to me, *for me*, in those darkened nights of desolation and ruin. I stared out of the floor to ceiling obsidian glass, at the faint glimmer of silver as the water lapped upon the shore and let the music soothe me some more. My nap had done me some good, calming some of the disquiet of earlier, and I was glad for it. I let my fingertips idly play with the band of leather and metal around my wrist and thought about what the boy said to me back in the rank dark of that awful storage unit.

There are still good people out there, Faith. You gotta believe me...

Finally, my body wouldn't be ignored and I *had* to get up and take care of business. I set the little music player and headphones aside on the end of the bed and dealt with the unpleasantries of being human.

The giant house was so quiet. I stood in the middle of the room, near the forgotten packages from our shopping trip and listened carefully, for any signs of movement, people talking, anything to let me know who was here. Nothing but the air-conditioned hush and hum of electronics came back to me. The distant sound of music lured me back to the end of the bed where the little iPod still played and I clipped it to the hem of my tee, slipping the headphones under my hair and back into my ears. I backed it up to the beginning of *Hope Never Dies* and figured out how to put it on repeat before I went in search of whoever else might be in the house with me.

I padded barefoot out the bedroom door and down the hall, lightly slipping down the stairs, all the while Ashes & Embers playing soothingly in my ears. The living room was just as dark and vacant as the rest of the house, the only light on in the kitchen. I went that way and spotted him on the other side of the sliding glass, sitting in one of the chairs at the massive back patio table. He had his broad back to me and absently raised a cigarette to his lips, head turned to the side. He sucked on it, the tip flaring orange in the night.

He turned his head sharply at the sound of the slider opening behind him, relaxing when he saw it was only me. I slid it shut and hugged myself. It was warm out here, I just felt... I don't know, exposed? When I stepped outside. I padded along the warm flagstone of the back patio and drew even with his chair. He looked up at me, and squinted a bit in the light cast from the windows behind us.

"You doin' okay, Baby Girl?" he asked me and I smiled, a little sadly, but then again it was the best I could muster these days.

"This was you, wasn't it?" I asked plucking at my tee just above where the little music player was clipped to my hem.

He twisted in his chair some more to get a look at it and smiled, before grimacing. His face was revealed to me more with the motion, the light falling along the left side. A raw and angry scrape, puffed with swelling and turning ripe with a bruise adorned his left cheekbone and I stepped forward quickly, rounding in front of him, to keep him from having to hold the awkward pose.

"What happened?" I asked and grazed the injury with a light touch. He flinched back from it and reached up, gently capturing my hand with his much larger one. It was warm and calloused where it wrapped around mine, the knuckles scraped, bruised and swelling much like his face. The sight of it made me shiver. He immediately let me go and I tucked it into the crook of my arm guiltily. Of course, he didn't want me touching him.

"Business meeting," he grumbled and I felt my eyebrows go up.

"I don't want to know," I said faintly and pulled up a chair of my own to sit across from him.

He smiled thinly, "Sorry, Baby Girl. Nothing bad. I own a business with my younger brother. We have a... unique business model, bein' blood and all."

"I see."

I didn't really, but I'd meant it when I'd said I didn't want to know. Marlin sighed and reached out into the dark, toward the edge of the table. He brought a dark bottle to his lips and swigged down some of the beer inside. I didn't know what to say, and he hadn't answered my question. I placed my hands on the edge of my seat and kept my arms straight. My knees I kept together as well, leaning forward and back, hoping he would speak so I didn't have to.

He watched me for a few moments before smiling to himself, a fondness almost overtaking him. He slouched in his chair and saved me from having to make conversation by answering my question.

"Yeah, it was me."

"Why?" I asked softly.

"Figured it might help, you know, with going out there, around other people. Something to concentrate on other than what you got going on inside your head." He tilted his head to the side and set his beer, which was mostly full and still weeping condensation down the outside of the amber glass, aside on the table.

"Feel like taking a ride with me?" he asked. "I could use some wind therapy."

"What, now?"

"Ain't no better time. Can't imagine you're ready to go back to sleep, seein' as you just woke up. No need to talk on the bike, you can listen to your music and bonus points, ain't no one liable to be out this time. What do you say?"

I thought about it, I mean really thought about it, "I've never ridden before."

He nodded and captured my gaze with his, "Ain't no time like the present to learn. Why don't you head on up and go find some of that gear we bought you today?"

"O-okay." I stammered and pushed myself to my feet.

Marlin nodded and I went past him, opening the sliding door, I looked back over my shoulder at him and he smiled at me over his, giving me a last encouraging nod before I slipped inside.

I went back up to the master bedroom in search of the many bags we'd brought in earlier in the day. The bedside clock read that it was just after eleven pm, and I was startled to realize I must have slept harder and longer than I'd thought.

I rooted through the bags to find the one that contained the leather items and changed swiftly into what had been provided to me. When I was finally dressed, I stood staring wide-eyed into the mirror above the bathroom sink.

The leather pants were a touch loose, waiting for me to put on a bit more weight. The white tee beneath the leather jacket, however, fit well enough. I looked down at my booted feet and chewed my bottom lip. The clothing made me look sure; almost to the point that I could believe myself to be a capable human being.

I swept my long blonde hair over my shoulder and twisted it into a braid, certain that I wouldn't want to deal with the wind tangled mess that was certain to follow if I left it loose. I tied off the end with a thick black tie and stared for several moments more.

I was scared. Nervous beyond belief, but comforted by the fact that it would be Marlin taking me for the ride. I trusted him like I could trust no other, so, with a deep breath, I clipped my new little music player to the edge of the inside pocket of my new leather jacket and went down to meet him.

He was at the bottom of the stairs and had changed from cargo shorts to jeans and leather chaps. He'd placed his leather vest over his leather jacket and the added bulk of the protective gear made him seem even bigger and more imposing than he did before. I swallowed hard, mouth suddenly dry.

"Ready to take a slice out of life, Baby Girl?"

I nodded mutely, and knew my eyes were wide. Marlin chuckled and opened the front door for me, ushering me outside. His bike sat in the circular drive at the bottom of the wide, gentle front steps. The porch light gleaming softly along all the chrome and glossy black paint.

"Faith," he murmured softly and I tipped my head in his direction to acknowledge I heard, but I couldn't tear my eyes from the imposing yet beautiful machine.

"Faith, Honey. I need you to look at me. I need to know you're hearin' what I need to tell you."

I managed to tear my eyes free and look at him this time. He smiled and spoke sure and firm, telling me what he needed me to do as a passenger. How to lean with and not against, how to relax and go with things and to try not to remain stiff. I nodded carefully and he put a helmet on my head, adjusting the straps to keep it secure.

"Don't you need one?" I asked softly and he chuckled.

"I got the required amount of health insurance and such, you don't. Don't worry, I won't be ridin' dirty." He finished his sentence by pulling out a set of clear safety lenses from his saddle bag. Straightening he slipped them, gently and oh so carefully, over my eyes. With a last roguish smile, he swung a leg over and settled on the back of the machine. I took a deep breath. It was now or never, right?

"Get on up here, and hang on to me," he said helping me up behind him. I settled against his back and bit my lower lip apprehensively. I didn't think it would ever feel right having a man between my legs again, but this? This wasn't awful. In fact, it was the exact opposite. I tried really hard not to think too hard about it while he put on a pair of safety glasses of his own. That accomplished, he fired up the motorcycle. I couldn't help it; I jumped at the sudden noise.

"Hold on to me," he ordered again, loudly over the rumble of the engine. I settled closer to him, placing my arms around his tight waist.

"Here we go!" he called and he let out the clutch and pulled us around the driveway smoothly and out onto the street.

He went slowly at first, then picked up speed. I closed my eyes and freed one hand just long enough to turn up the music in my head. When I returned my arms around Marlin's waist, he poured on the speed and I found myself clinging to him just a little bit tighter.

The wind streamed across us both and carried our troubles far off behind us for the time being. For now, it was simply me, Marlin, the machine throbbing beneath us and the miles dissipating beneath the wheels. I couldn't believe I had never done this before! The sensation was like no other. Freeing, in so many ways. We rode for, I don't know, an hour? Maybe more? Until he pulled down this road and that, and the salty, briny smell of the ocean gave way to the heavier, earthier smell of what I presumed were the everglades.

Eventually, he pulled along a lonely lane and rolled us gently to a stop, putting down the kickstand and leaning the heavy bike onto it.

I had no idea where we were, but it didn't matter, because deep down inside, I knew I was safe. I was always safe with Marlin.

CHAPTER 11
Marlin

I was stiff in more ways than one, and I needed to get up and walk it off. I needed a break from the beach every now and again, and so I came out here to some of these farm access roads near the 'Glades and some of the orange orchards for a change of pace.

I looked back over my shoulder at Faith's too-pale face in the moonlight and put a damper on the sigh that tried to escape me as I shut off the bike so she could hear me. She woodenly pulled back her arms from around my waist and the stiffness I mentioned before? Yeah, it damn near became unbearable.

"Sorry, Baby Girl, I just ain't what I used to be. I'm stiffening up from earlier and I need to walk. I should have said something before pullin' off in what looks like the middle of fuckin' nowhere."

"Isn't it?" she asked.

"Isn't what?"

She gestured around us, "The middle of nowhere."

"Naw, my buddy growin' up all through school, this is *his* farm." I smiled reassuringly and heaved myself to my feet, helping her down off my bike.

"You're safe with me, Faith. You ain't ever gotta wonder, or question that," I said and popped the helmet off her head.

"I should know that," she murmured and I could hear the frustration in her voice, "I *do* know that, it's just…"

I plucked the safety glasses off her face and tried not to think too hard about how soft her skin was where my fingertips grazed.

"You're good, I get it. I figure after as long," I didn't want to say it out loud, so I just skipped over it, "…anybody bein' around that would be the same. You just do you, Baby Girl. You just do you."

She nodded and hugged herself tight, even though it was as far from cold as you could get out here. I figured I should warn her I was gonna pull a blanket out for us to sit on, so I did.

"Got a blanket to lay down to sit on, I figured we could walk out a ways and lay it out on one of the tracks. Good night for some stargazing, and it'll give me a chance to loosen up some for the ride back to the Captain's. You good with that?"

She nodded carefully and was bein' so fuckin' brave. She didn't remember half the shit she went through during the worst of the withdrawals. I know she didn't, so while bein' around her was familiar for me, bein' around me must have still felt pretty new, and me bein' a dude besides? I'm surprised she wasn't begging me to take her back right this minute, which I would have if she'd asked.

She tucked herself as close to my side as she was comfortable with, as I set out walkin' down one of the side tracks along the neat row of orange trees. I'd done some growin' up around these groves myself. Wasn't until our mid-teens that my folks moved us out closer to the water, when Dad was closer to retirement. I found myself telling Faith all about it, as much to fill the silence as to startle any wildlife into getting the fuck outa dodge while we were there.

Faith listened, surprising enough. She'd put her headphones away and walked, shoulder mere inches from my arm. I laid out the blanket over the dirt and sat down, laying back. It was a big thing, and I was surprised Faith lay out next to me. A healthy distance between us, studiously not touching, which who could blame her?

"What about you?"

She startled a little bit and replied softly, "What about me?"

"How'd you grow up?"

"With Hope. After our mother died, it was all Hope and our grandmother," she sighed, "I was nothing but a pain in the ass," she said and I could hear the weight of sorrow, almost taste the regret on the air.

I stared at the star scatter above us as the silence back filled in, like when you dug a sandcastle on the beach, and you watched the sand trickle back down and the water filled the hole, steadily... it was a lot like that. She lay beside me in silent reflection, and when I glanced over, tears slicked from those luminous eyes of hers down her temples.

"Hey," I said softly, but she just closed her eyes and covered her mouth with her hand.

"Hey, hey, hey; none of that, come on now." I couldn't help it, my arm snaked out and surprisingly, she rolled, and tucked herself into my side, taking the comfort that was on offer. The weight of her head on my shoulder felt incredibly good, and the way the slight curve of her body fit against mine? Well, it felt like two puzzle pieces coming together.

I knew right then and there, that it might be impossible in the here and now, but that I would be keeping my options open for the future. It might be a long fuckin' haul, but someday, when Faith was as close to whole again as we could get her, I wanted to visit the possibility of an 'us.'

It wasn't just the attraction, it was more than that. I think, on a deep, fundamental level, she understood the kind of guilt I carried over Danny. She felt something akin to it, even though there was no reason for it. We'd all exhibited a wild streak in our younger days to some extent. There wasn't anything unusual about that. We'd all, at one time or another, done some stupid shit to hurt or disappoint the ones closest to us. It was a fact of life. It was part of the learning curve, but in that moment, it snapped together and became clear, one of Faith's issues.

"Wasn't your fault, Baby Girl; none of it was your fault," I soothed and knew it was inadequate. That as much as I could, and would say it, she couldn't and wouldn't believe me. Not with her trust shattered into a million pieces so fine, that they were blowing away like sand up a beach. All I could so was lay there and comfort her with what amounted to nothing more than a bunch of meaningless bullshit.

I hoped like hell, that if she couldn't believe in me, or her sister, that maybe the chick with a professional license would help with it somehow. I knew it was backwards, and didn't make a whole lot of sense, but sometimes it took an outside source like that to open a person's eyes to the possibilities right in front of them.

The next time I opened my eyes was when a rough boot kicked my own. Faith startled and let out a terrified yip, crab walking her way off the top of our blanket. I glared up at my buddy, Bobby, who owned his family farm.

"What the fuck you doin' on my land, Boy?" he demanded, gun in hand and pointed at us and Faith – fuck – she didn't know.

"Put that fuckin' thing away, Bobby!" I snarled and rolled, groaning onto my knees, putting myself between my buddy and the girl I was pretty sure I had it bad for.

"Easy, Baby Girl. Bobby's just foolin', he's a friend of mine from way back. This is his farm."

"Oh, shit, yeah, I'm sorry. Didn't know she was that sensitive, dude. Why didn't you call or leave a message you were gonna be here?"

"Didn't expect to be here, we must have fell asleep."

Faith was nodding her head rapidly, eyes wide but tear free, "We're sorry!" she blurted.

"Hell, it ain't no thing. Why don't y'all come up to the house for some breakfast?"

I opened my mouth to answer him but my phone started going off, shrill in my pocket and buzzing up a storm. I rolled onto my feet and crammed my mitt into the front pocket of my jeans, fishing the damn thing out.

Uh-oh. That was Hope's number. I held up a finger to Bobby and Faith, and answered it.

"Hello?"

"Where the fuck is my sister!?" Hope's voice blasted out of the earpiece. I held the phone away from my head and watched Faith's face pale.

"Relax, Sweetheart, we went for a midnight ride –"

"Did you forget she has that appointment? Really, Marlin? Are you for fucking real!? She has to be there in an hour!"

"Calm your tits, Princess!" I snarled into the phone.

"We're closer to her appointment than Ft. Royal is, at a buddy of mine's place. I can have her there inside a half an hour." *Thank fuck we wouldn't be late.* I thought to myself.

Hope started railing and I winked at Faith who was positively ashen, but starting to smile at the funny faces I was making at her sister's diatribe.

"Okay, Hope. We'll see you when we get back. Bye-bye now, Honey," I said, talking right over her squawking, before I ended the call altogether by hanging up on her.

Bobby started laughing and I turned to him, "Sorry about crashing in your field," I held out a hand and he grasped it, pulling me into a hug.

"Ain't the first time I've found you out here, it *is* the first time I've found you out here with a girl, though," he said, eyeing Faith speculatively.

"Yeah, about that, Faith, this is my buddy Bobby, Bobby meet Faith, I been helping her out with some things." I mumbled lamely and I saw Faith's face shutter, just close up like folks shutting down the town when the big bad goes walkin' down the main street. Fuck. I needed some fuckin' coffee.

"Look man, I would take you up on breakfast, but we got some place we gotta be, and probably just enough time to hit a drive through and eat in the parking lot."

"I hear you. It's been a while, Man. Y'all should come back for a proper visit soon."

"Yeah, what about you?" I asked, bending to retrieve my blanket off the ground, wadding it, leaf litter and all into a bundle I could shove it in my saddle bags. I thrust my chin in the direction where I'd parked the bike and Faith fell into step on my one side, Bobby on the other, his rifle resting nonchalantly on his shoulder.

"What about me?"

"When was the last time you came out my direction, Boy?"

"You got me there, I could use a day on the water with some beer and some fishin'."

"Sounds good, you know how to hit me up."

"That I do," he stuck out his hand and I shook it, and then he stuck out his hand to Faith, who shied back and quickly grasped his fingers before letting go, equally quick.

"Nice to meet you, Faith." Bobby tipped his red trucker hat at her and turned, walking back the way he'd come after shooting me a look that clearly read he'd be hittin' me up sooner rather than later. Fine by me, we had to go.

"Ready, Baby Girl?" I asked her. She nodded rapidly, and I shoved the blanket back in my saddle bag while she donned my helmet and safety glasses I'd left on the seat for her.

We rode through a coffee stand and drank it in the parking lot, she barely picked at her pastry I'd bought to go along with it, but she put enough of it down to satisfy me. It was just to hold her until we got back to Ft. Royal.

I drove her over to the office building that the good doctor had her set up in and sat back against the bike, pulling out a cigarette.

"Aren't you going in with me?" she asked softly.

"Nope."

She frowned slightly, "Why not?"

"This is all you, Baby Girl. I'm not here to make you do nothin'. You asked me to drive you to your appointment and I've done that. The rest is on you. No one but you can make the decision to go in there, to get better. We can help you here and there, but this part of the journey is all yours." She stared at me, her aquamarine eyes wide and fuckin' stunning in the bright sunshine.

"You won't even come into the waiting room?" she asked.

"Nope, this place, this time, it's all yours. I'll be right here waiting for you to come out." I watched her chew her bottom lip in apprehension and smiled. Of course, that must be it. I pulled my keys to the bike out of my pocket and up ended her hand, dropping them in. I curled her fingers around them and said, "I promise, and you can count on that, alright?"

She stared at the keys, at her hand resting in my palm, and I took it away. She looked up at me solemn, but a big chunk of the anxiety that'd been in her face the moment before was gone. She took a deep, deep breath and handed me the keys back.

"I believe you, Marlin," she said quietly and I smiled.

"Glad to hear it, Baby Girl." And with one last lingering look over her shoulder she went into the building.

CHAPTER 12
Faith

I'd been quiet when I'd come out of the office, and on the ride back to the house. I'd had a lot to think about. I still had a lot to think about. Dr. Shiendland had been quiet and attentive, had listened and asked questions, and I was surprised to find that it was easy to talk to her. We'd talked about the boy, about his gift of the leather wristband and why I couldn't stop thinking about him, but I found myself extremely reluctant to talk about Marlin, so I simply hadn't brought him up.

When we arrived back at the house, Hope and Cutter were waiting on the front steps, my sister was agitated, bouncing in place, Cutter's hand on her shoulders as if he were the only thing holding her in place, and that very well could be. When we pulled up, I half expected it to fly out of her mouth how sick and tired she was about me being so irresponsible, but instead, she flew forward and wrapped me in a hug so tight, I thought she'd break me.

"Are you okay?" she asked, and all I could manage to do was nod. Cutter winked at me from behind her and I felt a faint answering smile.

"Jesus Christ, Hope. You wanna let her off the bike?" Marlin asked in front of me.

"Don't even get me started with you!" Hope snapped and I swallowed hard, *there* was my sister. *Corporal Badass*, as Charity and I liked to call her behind her back. Thinking of Charity immediately brought guilt and shame rushing to the surface. I hadn't spoken to her yet. I hadn't been ready, but I was out of excuses and I couldn't hide from her forever.

"I'd like to call Charity now, if it's alright."

Hope leaned back abruptly and searched my face, hers full of apprehension. Whatever she saw on my own smoothed it out and I wondered, not for the first time, what kind of horrible my sister thought I was going to do, what she thought I was up to. I kept silent, didn't try to argue with her, or snap at her. What was the use? Hope was always going to look at me and see the worst parts of me. The only difference was, now, when I looked in the mirror; that was all I saw too.

I felt guilty, keeping Charity away, not speaking to the sister who always and forever only saw the good in me. Dr. Sheindland had asked me a question about that. Then followed up with an open ended, ambiguous one that left me reeling and feeling three inches tall.

Don't you think your sister needs to hear from you? That she isn't sitting in agonized wonder?

"Sure, yeah, okay, Bubbles."

I let my older sister lead me into the house, glancing back over my shoulder at Marlin, still astride his motorcycle. His expression was unreadable, as he looked me over and watched me go. I wondered what it was he was thinking as we moved from his sight, and if he still stared after me as much as I did after him, still looking over my shoulder long after we passed from his sight.

"You okay, Bubbles?" I startled and looked at my sister, and felt my eyes were a little wide. She stopped us and turned me to look at her.

"What's going on?" she asked.

"Nothing!"

"You suck at lying to me, Faith. Always have, and always will. You know I'm always two steps ahead of you, so spill."

I didn't speak; I didn't know what to say. Finally Hope narrowed her dark eyes and asked, "Did he do something to you?"

"No!"

"Then where were you all last night?"

"We went for a ride." I stared at my sister and her mouth thinned down into that hard assed line, "I'm serious, we went for a ride and we stopped and we were watching the stars and we fell asleep. I swear, that's all."

Her shoulders dropped and she sighed out, "Let me guess, you're feeling like you're fourteen…"

"And just like when you caught me making out with Ray Tanzer in the back seat of his Mustang." I muttered dejectedly.

"But you're not fourteen anymore."

"No, I'm not."

She sighed, "I'm sorry, Bubbles."

"Me, too." I said softly.

"What are you sorry for?" she asked, face scrunching in confusion.

"That I'm such a pain in your ass, and for doing the wrong thing like all the time, I really don't mean to, Hope! I just…"

"You like him, huh?" she asked and there wasn't anything hard or accusatory in her voice; just soft resignation.

I looked up from my feet where my gaze had affixed itself and felt a little nauseous at the look of pity on my sister's face.

"It doesn't matter," I said softly, "No one is going to be interested in an ex-junkie whore."

"Faith!" Hope barked sharply.

"Don't 'Faith' me, Hope! Look, I don't want to talk about it anymore, I just want to call Charity. She needs to know." I stared my sister in the face and she wilted a little.

"Needs to know, what?"

"That I love her, and I miss her, and that I'm not okay but I'm going to try, really hard, to get better. I just want to have the time to do that before she comes down here. I don't want her thinking that I don't love and care about her, I don't want you to think that either, I just have a lot to deal with and nobody can help me do it. I just have to do it on my own. Nobody can help me but me with a lot of this."

"Sounds like you and Doctor Sheindland had a good talk today."

"I have a lot to think about," I agreed. Hope nodded and pulled me into a tight hug.

"Here for whatever you need, Bubs."

"Thanks, Buttercup." I sniffed, eyes welling hot and hugged my sister back.

She reached into her back pocket and dialed her phone, handing it to me.

"Hope, how's Faith, does she want to talk to me yet?" my little sister answered by way of greeting.

"I never didn't want to talk to you, Charity." I said sniffing and sank into one of the chairs at the large dining room table, where Hope and I had ended up. Hope went into the kitchen and poured a glass of water from the tap and brought it over along with a paper towel.

Silence greeted me on the other end of the phone and finally a muffled sob came through, "Are you okay?" Charity asked and I breathed in deep through my nose and out through my mouth and did what the doctor had told me, I didn't minimize it. I didn't lie and say I was fine, I did what I was told and confronted what had happened to me, head on.

"No, I'm not. I'm really not, Baby Sis," and then I took it one step further, I took a little piece of myself back from those bastards and gave it to my sisters. I looked at Hope, and I looked over, past the stairs at Marlin and Cutter coming through the door. I met Marlin's sky blue eyes and told Charity, "But I'm going to be."

CHAPTER 13
Marlin

She'd withdrawn some, after she'd got off the phone with her sister. She'd been quiet all through lunch and even when Cutter had pulled Hope away. She'd gone upstairs, equally silent and when she'd come back down, she was showered and in fresh clothes. I turned from loading up the dishwasher when I heard her soft tread behind me and had to stop and give her a once over.

She had on some short, cut-off denim shorts, which probably cost an arm to buy 'em in their current condition rather than make 'em herself out of a pair of jeans ready to give up the ghost. A swimsuit top peeked out over the nude, threadbare boat necked cover up she had on over it all. It hung longer in the back than it did the front and she swam in it, like it was her boyfriend's sweater back in high school and she'd never given it up.

"You look good, Baby Girl." I said, softly encouraging.

"Thanks."

The silence stretched between us and finally she blurted out, "Can I go for a walk? On the beach… I think I'd like that." She stood there looking so uncertain, like I'd tell her no, and that she had to stay in the house or something. It was probably going to take a while for her to get she wasn't a prisoner. That one of us didn't have to be with her at all times. I sighed.

"You don't need my permission, Darlin'. You want some company? Is that why you're askin'?"

She turned her upper body, and gazed out towards the water, finally giving in to one side of the war in her head and nodding mutely. I closed up the dishwasher and started it up, grabbing up a dish towel and wiping off my hands.

"Lead the way, Sweetheart."

We trudged slowly through the powder fine sand in silence, towards the water at a pretty good clip. Once we reached it, she stopped and stared longingly out over it, like it held some kind of escape for her but she was trapped here on land. I knew that feeling, but I'd found, even with the boat and going out on it, there wasn't no escape out there. The monsters don't live under your bed; they live inside your head.

I kept silent on the matter; she didn't need it right now. She hadn't asked my fucking opinion. I stopped to roll up the cuffs of my jeans and work my way out of my boots, tying my laces together and slinging them over my shoulder with the socks stuffed in 'em. Faith was up ahead by just a bit, and turned back to look at me, as if to make sure I wasn't leaving. Her aquamarine eyes were vibrant against the backdrop of white sand and with the sun full on out like it was... damn. It was like she was some kind of angel or something. Beautifully broken, trapped here on earth. She stood silently and held back a hand, waiting for me to catch up.

I smiled and caught up to her, but was careful not to touch, no matter how bad I wanted to. *Fuck all if I wanted to, so fuckin' bad.* Still, the girl was like fine art, and so fragile. It was my place to look, but not touch. Not yet, anyhow. Maybe someday, but definitely not today.

So you can imagine my surprise when she stopped abruptly and whirled and I crashed full on into her, my arms snapping up automatically to cradle her, to keep from doing any harm. She looked up at me, her breath catching and I was frozen, rooted to the spot and damn near slain by those bright, mystical eyes of hers, staring so deeply into my own.

"You okay, Baby Girl?" I asked and she blinked, once, slowly the wheels in her head turning at a furious pace. I went very still as she raised herself up onto her toes and leaned into me.

Her lips were silken fire where they brushed my own and I couldn't help it. My eyes slipped shut, and I held myself, so very, very still, as she leaned further into me, lips pressing minutely against mine.

Supple and soft, her body fitted against my own and I let my hands slide forward, around her back, smoothing down around her waist, tugging her lightly into me, closer, a more intimate embrace. I knew I shouldn't, I knew she wasn't ready, I knew *I* wasn't ready; but I couldn't help myself.

I breathed her in, and the mix of her scent, along with the salty tang of ocean water was a heady mix. Her tongue flickered out and touched my bottom lip and I groaned. I wanted her so badly I ached, but I couldn't do it. I couldn't let this happen, not right now, not so soon. I lifted my hands and softly cradled her face between them. I pecked her lips in a chaste kiss that tasted too much like goodbye for my liking and she lowered herself, sinking flat footed to the sand.

I opened my eyes and found hers, welling softly; a stricken look on her face. I smiled sadly and sighed out.

"I'm sorry; I shouldn't have let that happen." I murmured and she bowed her head, studiously not looking at me, suddenly finding the sand to be the most interesting thing in the world.

"It's okay, I…"

"No, it's not, Baby Girl. Sometimes it's easy to forget what's happened to you, I can't do that to you." I murmured. She flinched as if she'd been doused with cold water and turned; aquamarine eyes distant over the water that matched so beautifully.

She didn't speak again. We quietly walked side by side and she wouldn't look at me again, and I felt something like a falling sensation in the center of my chest.

"What was that for, anyways?" I asked a time later. She stared at me through her fractured innocence for a long, hard moment, before turning, her pace becoming brisk as she made her way back to the house we were nearing.

"Fuck," I muttered under my breath, "Way to screw the fucking pooch, Jimmy." I bowed my head and pulled on the back of my neck to loosen up some of the tension there and wondered how I would fix it before finally deciding there wasn't anything I could fix. Time. Time was the only cure for what ailed her. Time and a whole lot of patience.

I kept her in my sights until she disappeared into the back slider, and pulled out a cigarette once she'd gone. I smoked, and finished the walk back, dropping my boots on the retaining wall ledge and planting my ass right next to them to finish my cig. I glanced up and saw her in the bedroom window looking down at me, but the second she saw me look up, she disappeared again.

Something wasn't sitting right with me, but I couldn't put my finger on what it was. I didn't have time to think about it either, 'cause my phone was going off in my pocket. I fished it out.

"Aw, Christ," I muttered before accepting the call.

"Yeah, Johnny, what's up?"

"I was giving you the heads up; I'm taking the Scarlett Ann out tomorrow. I could use the help on this trip, I know you said three days or so, so if you can't I can get a temporary hire, I just thought I'd offer it to you first."

I glanced up to the empty window glass and decided I needed some familiar ground for a minute, and that Faith could probably use a break from me.

"What time?" I asked.

CHAPTER 14
Faith

I walked away. I felt so many things, but ultimately all I could do was walk away. My physical voice stolen from me by the one inside my head. *Of course he wouldn't want you. Junkie whore! Who in their right mind would want you after that? He's just being nice to you out of guilt.*

I was crushed under a mountain of self-derision and admittedly, a few broken hopes and maybe a shattered dream or two. I slipped up the stairs wraith-like and dejected heading straight to the bedroom I'd been staying in to sit on the bed.

What were you thinking!? I screamed silently at myself, locking it down, hiding it away, stuffing my hand in my mouth and doubling over as the tears rushed hot and fierce. *How could you have been so stupid?*

Helpless anger raged through me, and slipped through my fingers like rain. How could they have done this to me? How was I ever going to get past this? I breathed in deeply through my nose and held my breath before letting it out slowly, repeating the process over and over until I felt calmer and almost on the verge of sleep before rising to my feet.

I was so *embarrassed*, but there wasn't anyone I could talk to. Hope would just berate me for sure, make it my fault. Just like she had with everything else; school, boys, the trouble I'd gotten in all through school... *but all of that* was *your fault.*

It was true. As much as I had always hated to admit it, it was all true, it was always true; it was *all my fault.*

I touched the leather and metal band around my wrist and swallowed hard, remembering the little ray of light in my otherwise darkened world.

"You deserve so much better than this, Star, and I am so sorry. I didn't know, I didn't know. Please, forgive me?"

It'd never happened, not once before, not a single time... Not once. The sincerity in his eyes, the anguish in his voice, it made everything so real, shocked me out of my high long enough to hold onto the stolen moment with both hands. He'd taken off his leather wrist cuff and had pressed it into my physical fingers.

I believed him when he'd told me he'd get me out; then the cops came. It had to be him; he couldn't have known that they wouldn't believe *me*. He'd tried and that was what mattered, because I knew what it felt like to try and fail over and over again.

I went to the window and spotted Marlin sitting on the edge of the short wall lining the back patio. He was smoking, head bowed, hair falling loose in front of his face from the short tail he'd tried to tame it into. He looked pensive, and I couldn't help but sigh, my face flaming in further embarrassment.

He was gorgeous, and strong, and all of the things that I was not. I looked at my reflection in the glass and felt my heart drop. I was too thin; my bones standing out against my skin, stark and prominent and the haunted expression never seemed to leave my face. I refocused on Marlin and he looked up, squinting into the bright sunlight. I stepped back quickly, unwilling to meet his gaze.

Instead, I set about picking through the bags of forgotten clothes, putting them away. At one point I looked back to the bedside table and the little pink music player sitting there, charging. I guess it didn't really mean anything after all. Something to keep me quiet, make things easier, the fact it made things easier for *me* was just a bonus, right?

I sank to sit cross legged on the floor and sniffed, scrubbing my face with my hands. I felt like there was a firestorm of bitter and unfair emotions swirling inside my heart and head. It was hard to breathe, like so much broken glass, shards of memory and the catastrophe that was my life flying in a cyclone, shredding me from the inside out until I lay huddled on the floor, weeping silently but uncontrollably.

God, was this going to be me for the rest of my life?

"Faith? Faith, Honey?" The door swung open and Hope sighed, lowering herself in a crouch beside me. I sobbed harder and my sister sighed. She didn't say anything, instead she lay down behind me and pulled me back into her arms, her cast dug into my stomach but I didn't care. Instead, I cave into the despair and cried the broken and sour parts of me out onto the bedroom floor until I felt purged. Hollow and empty, I let my big sister cuddle me like our mom used to do to us when we were little, until the sun sank low behind the horizon.

"This about Marlin?" she asked some time later as we sat on the bed and ate ice cream. Cutter had brought it upstairs, handed it over to my sister wordlessly and with a wink and a little salute had closed the door behind us. The cold, creamy, confection felt good against my raw throat and it was mint chocolate chip, my favorite.

"It was stupid, *I* was stupid." I bit my lips together.

"No, it wasn't," Hope sighed and set her bowl aside. "He makes you feel safe, doesn't he?" she asked. I nodded wordlessly.

"Okay, Bubbles. We don't have to talk about it," she said with a sigh.

"I'm so embarrassed," I moaned.

"It's not the end of the world, I know it feels that way, but it's really not, I promise."

I snorted, "Why couldn't you have been like this when I was fourteen?" I asked.

"Like what?"

"Understanding."

Hope's expression changed and she looked out the window and sighed.

"Because I was stupid, and being unfair. I was still a kid myself when I started taking care of you guys, and let's face it, I suck as a parent."

I laughed a little and Hope laughed too.

"I didn't want you to be my parent, *mom* was the parent and she died... I needed my sister." I couldn't stop my eyes from welling and Hope sighed out defeated. She took my ice cream out of my hands and set it aside with hers and pulled me into a hug.

"I know, Bubs. I'm so sorry. I was hurting too and I didn't know what to do, so I did what I thought was right. It turned out to be all wrong, didn't it?"

I held tighter to my sister Hope, who had always seemed like a woman on a mission, a woman with a plan and now; now it was like she hadn't had one at all.

"I'm sorry," I warbled, suddenly soul crushingly guilty for having been such a pain in her fucking ass all this time.

"You were just being a kid, Faith. There's nothing to be sorry about, if anybody it should be me who's sorry for setting you up for failure. I pushed so hard, made it so you didn't want to talk to me."

It was true, "But that doesn't mean I had to stop talking, that was my fault…" we dissolved into a puddle of mutual goo in the middle of the big bed.

"What are we going to do?" I asked.

"The only thing we can, Bubs. We're going to keep going. Pick up the pieces, fit 'em together and move on. It's the only thing we can do, right?"

I nodded mutely. I wanted so desperately to prove myself to Hope, once and for all. That I could do this, that I could survive and still make something, anything, out of my life… I had to. Not just for my older sister, but for Charity, my younger sister, too.

I must have been babbling because Hope, smoothed a hand over my hair, "Forget me; forget Char, too. Do it for *you*, Baby. Do it for *you*."

I didn't have the heart to tell her that I wasn't worth it… I wasn't worth any of it, and right then, not for the first time, I just wanted to die. I just wanted to give up and die. *God, why didn't you just let me die?*

CHAPTER 15

Marlin

"Glad you called," Cutter grunted and dropped down onto his couch. I didn't bother moving my head from the back of the loveseat, just rolled my eyes in his direction.

"Yeah, well, I figure I'm the *last* motherfucker she wants to see right now." I sighed out and pressed the heels of my hands into my eye sockets.

"Probably, but you did the right thing, Brother."

I huffed a busted ass laugh full of disgust, mostly for myself. It didn't feel good, being in this position, but when I'd heard her muffled sobbing on the other side of the door, I realized my rejection had hit her hard, where it'd counted and I knew for sure I was the last person to handle that kind of shit. I'd called the Captain, and by default, the big guns – his woman.

"I wouldn't worry about it, Man." I listened to the scrape of denim and leather as he leaned forward. I pulled my hands away from my eyes and looked at him. He searched my face and sighed out harshly and bowed his head, bouncing it in a sloppy nod as if I'd confirmed something for him.

"She hit you right in the feels, didn't she?" he asked.

I didn't bother to deny it, but I didn't go out of my way to confirm it either. I felt my lips thin down into something like grim resignation. Finally, I broke and said, "I'd be a fuckin' liar if I said it weren't true."

"It always gets you when you least expect it. So, what're you planning on doing about it?"

"I think I already proved I ain't doing nothin'."

"Not now, you ain't, and a good thing too, but what about later down the line?"

"I'm gonna watch her, protect her, and when she's ready, she'll come back around. She'll get it figured out. I just hope that doctor is gonna help her."

"Yeah, about that doctor, I think she was a good bet. She wants to see Faith twice a week to start. You still gonna take her out there?"

"Fuck yeah, you just see what happens if anybody tried to stop me. I swore I'd give her a ride and I meant it."

Cutter eyed me speculatively and finally nodded, and I knew my Captain would have my back on this, and probably would smooth the way with her sister. I had a feeling when Hope got down here that I was gonna end up public enemy number one, but I knew I'd done the right thing by Faith. Even if it'd sucked doing it.

Cutter sighed, "I expect some of the guys'll give you hell for this," he said nonchalantly.

"Yeah, like to see it. I'll break some fucking heads."

Cutter chuckled and we lapsed into silence. I felt agitated. I itched to go up and try and do something, but I knew it was a bad idea.

"I need a cigarette," I mumbled and got up heading for the back door. Cutter let out a sharp whistle and I turned.

"Nice try, Man. Why don't you blow smoke out front? Where you can't go lookin' up at windows." He raised his eyebrows at me and I felt mine crush down in return, that hadn't been my fuckin' intention… I strode to the front door and went out. Who the fuck was I kidding? It had too.

I pulled a cigarette out of the pack with my lips and my lighter out of the little pocket in my jacket under my cut. I wanted to go for a ride somethin' fuckin' fierce but Faith was up there feelin' like shit on a kind of me and I didn't want to leave until I knew she was doin' better. Fuck, I'd hated shutting her down like that.

The door opened and shut as I sucked in that first drag and felt my nerves settle marginally.

"Hope you're done bustin' my chops, Cap. I'm not sure I can handle much more without putting my fist somewhere it don't belong."

"Oooh, baby! Sounds fun, but I'll pass." I turned sharply and squinted into the dim light of the porches overhang at Hope.

"Sorry," I grunted.

"Don't be," she sighed and leaned back against the door.

"How she doin'?"

"Physically, fine. Mentally and emotionally, a fucking train wreck."

"Look, Hope, you gotta believe me when I say, I didn't expect her to –"

"What? Like you?"

"Kiss me."

"Same thing at this point," she said, waving her hands ineffectually in the air between us. Her casted arm bulky, making what would have been a graceful movement on her part quite a bit more awkward, but Hope didn't seem to notice or care.

"When's that thing come off?" I tried to divert the conversation onto something else that didn't make me feel like a total tool bag.

"It's only been around a month, six to eight weeks they said. Don't change the subject."

I exhaled a plume of smoke and said, "No ma'am, wouldn't dream of it."

We were silent for some time and finally I asked, "She hate me?"

"No, but I wouldn't call you her favorite person right now."

"Ain't giving up on her, you know that right?"

"Ha! If you did, I'd have to whoop your ass again."

"Again? Oh, you think you can take me, huh?" I looped an arm around her neck and hugged her sideway, rubbing my knuckles against her hair; not near as hard as I would if she were one of the boys, but yeah. Hope had proven herself. She was, in all reality, one of the guys; which was only slightly weird as fuck. She fit with us, and it was like she was made for the Captain. She'd probably keep him busy for the rest of time with how much of a challenge she put up for him.

"I don't know what to do, Marlin." Hope was staring out at nothing, her dark eyes distant.

"She looks fine, like she's filling out and gettin' back to healthy, but her brain chemistry is still a mess from that shit. Not just what happened to her, but the drugs are still fucking with her. She's still in withdrawal. You gotta remember that. This is the hardest part, right here; ain't no cure for it but time. Time and no access to what made her sick in the first place."

Hope huffed a bitter chuckle and looked up at me, "At least there's that. She wouldn't know how to get her hands on it if she tried."

"Makes our job easier, but it doesn't do much for hers. She's still gotta live with the cravings and shit."

"Yeah. Yeah, she does."

We lapsed back into silence until finally, Hope sighed.

"Where do we go from here, Marlin? How do I save my sister?"

I took a thoughtful final drag off my cig, a long, pensive, deep one, and told Hope the truth; "I don't know, this is about as far as I got with Danny, but I do know one thing, ain't you or me that's gotta do the saving, Hope; it's Faith. At some point she's gotta stumble out there on her own. All we can do is be around to catch her, when and if she falls."

Hope nodded and asked, "You staying tonight?"

"She want me to?"

"She hasn't said either way."

"I need to go for a ride, clear my head. She got an appointment tomorrow?"

"No, day after tomorrow."

"What time?"

"Same time."

"I'll be here to take her."

"Okay."

I got on my bike and turned the waiting key, firing her up. It tore me to pieces leaving that driveway but I needed to think. Clear my head and blow this fucking town for a minute. I hoped Bobby had a cold fuckin' beer in his fridge, because I wanted some distance while at the same time, I didn't want to be alone. All that was going to do was let me replay the haunting image of those shattered aquamarine eyes as she turned away from me and that fuckin' window.

CHAPTER 16
Faith

Days. It'd been days since I'd tried to kiss Marlin like the idiot I am and he'd been keeping a careful distance ever since. I let the warm coastal waters wash in over my feet and watched it and the sand wash back out to sea. If I stood just right, and closed my eyes, I had the sensation that I was washing out with it. That even though I knew I stood perfectly still, I moved. A sense of motion without actually moving. I could dream, though. I could dream and wish that I were swept away, out to sea, away from all of these jacked up feelings that I was terrified to confront.

I sighed deeply and hugged my beach wrap tighter around my shoulders with one hand; even though I wasn't cold. It was hard to be cold in ninety degree heat. My other hand held the long skirt of the maxi dress I wore out of the water.

"Faith?" I opened my eyes and looked back over my shoulder at Hope who was coming up the beach, my mind drifting back to the day before yesterday when it'd been Marlin coming my way...

"What'cha thinkin' about so hard, Baby Girl?" He'd drawn himself up short, a few arm lengths away and the distance might as well have been an entire gulf between us. I'd swallowed hard, mouth suddenly dry and had tried to tighten up my resolve.

"Listen, Marlin…"

He smiled, "Uh oh, sounds serious."

I'd looked down at the water rushing away from my feet and closed my eyes, breathing slowly, heart pounding.

"It is, I mean, I am." I'd looked up and pinned him with my gaze, his smile sliding off his face, he'd reached out, but let his hand drop.

"What's on your mind, Baby Girl?" he'd said gently and I almost had hated that he still called me that, knowing that it didn't hold anything but superficial meaning.

"I don't think we should see as much of each other anymore. My doctor says I may be using you, the people around me, as a crutch. I need to not do that…" *Liar. Lie, lie, lie, lie; lies!* My brain had screamed at me, was still screaming at me, but I'd pressed my lips together and tried not to look as miserable as I'd felt. I still hadn't even told Dr. Shiendland about Marlin. She didn't even know he existed and had actually said the opposite, of what I was suggesting. She'd told me I should try and spend a little more time around some of my sister's friends. To remind myself there were good people in the world too.

"That so?" he asked and his expression had gone glacial.

I nodded, not trusting my voice. The truth was, I missed him. His closeness, the comfort he provided, but the new distance; him being there without actually being there… it was too much. I couldn't do it. I didn't want to do it. The deep sense of shame and self-loathing had been and still was taking over everything, and this was the only solution I could come up with. *Stupid, stupid, stupid!*

Marlin had nodded carefully, his lips twisting as if he were tasting something foul. He scraped his bottom lip between his teeth a couple of times and had pinned me with a look.

"It's okay, Baby Girl, I get it. You change your mind, I'm never far away."

I felt myself blanche, "I…"

"I'm not far, you hear me?" and he wasn't. I could see him back at the house, perched on the small retaining wall ringing the grand house's back patio. He was looking mine and my sister's direction and I quickly dropped my eyes from his distant form to Hope's anxiety ridden face.

"You okay?"

I nodded mutely, too exhausted, too worn to speak the truth, no matter how ugly it was.

"Talk to me, please?"

"Just enjoying the quiet, and that sensation, you know?" I looked down at the water rushing back in towards my feet, a different skirt clutched in my fingers than the teal and white chevroned dress of days earlier.

"Sensation?"

"Yeah," I felt my face break into a nostalgic smile, "Remember when we were kids, and mom took us to the beach and we'd stand in the water and feel it pulling us?"

Hope smiled too, "Yeah, we're a long way from the Pacific," she said.

"Feels just the same, anyways."

Hope put her good arm around my lean shoulders and we stared out over the water for a minute or two.

"Cutter and Marlin are grilling," she said and kissed my shoulder, "The rest of the guys from the club will be over for dinner. You going to be okay?" I nodded and touched the leather and metal band around my wrist.

"Bonfire later; how does that sound?"

"Okay," I murmured and let her steer me back towards the house. Cutter was, indeed, at the big stainless steel grill, and had it going. Distortions from the heat making the air above it shimmer. Marlin raised a dark glass bottle to his lips and drank deeply of it. Cutter turned his head and asked the blond man something, and I saw Marlin's lips part in answer, but his gaze never left me as Hope and I trudged across the sand towards them.

"Hey, Firefly!" Cutter greeted and I felt the ghost of a smile play across my lips.

"Hi," I replied faintly, but Marlin was raking his gaze over me. I was under the distinct impression that he was almost… taking stock. Making sure I was well. I inclined my head gently and let Hope tug me into the kitchen to wash and cut greens and veggies for a crisp summer garden salad.

I looked out the kitchen window above the sink, and there was Marlin, angled again, so he could watch me. I breathed deep and slow and focused on the menial task at hand and thought about it. I was surprised to find that his intense scrutiny didn't make me uncomfortable. In fact, it did just the opposite. I felt… relieved and safe. I glanced up and my breath caught, when his gaze captured mine. Stupid, so stupid, I cut my damn finger and jumped with a little cry dropping the knife with a clatter.

"Shit!" I swore and he was just there, dish towel in hand squeezing the cut.

"Nothing here?" he called out.

"Just walked in the door," another man I vaguely remembered answered.

"Easy, Baby Girl, let Nothing have a look," I looked up at the ceiling and blew out a breath.

"Oh, jeez, it's probably nothing. Just a little cut." I bit my lip and forced a smile.

"Hey, that's my name, now let me have a look at it and see." I glanced at the man who'd spoken. I remembered him, quiet, and sad. Dark hair and clear grey eyes. He took my hand from Marlin and peeked under the dish towel which was soaking red rather rapidly.

"Yeah, you got yourself good, but I don't think you're gonna need stitches. It's just a bleeder. Here, Marlin, keep pressure on it and I'll go hit the medicine cabinet. I'm sure the Captain has a boatload of crap to doctor her up with."

"I'm sorry," I stammered.

"Don't be, accidents happen, Bubbles," Hope said gently, she was staring at my hand in Marlin's and I was trying to look anywhere but.

"What happened, Baby Girl? Shaky?" he asked.

I nodded mutely for a moment before finding my voice, "I-I think so."

I knew he knew it was a lie, because a small smile played across his mouth. I closed my eyes and swayed on my feet a touch, flushing at the memory of the feeling of them on mine, however brief it may have been.

"Easy, Babe. You need to sit down? You getting woozy on me?" I nodded but didn't open my eyes. A gentle tug on my fingers and I stepped, trusting for that fraction of a moment, blind to wherever it was he wanted to lead me. I opened my eyed and looked down and felt myself blanch; I was *really* bleeding.

The man I recognized but had no name for pulled out a chair at the big dining room table for me, he smiled and ducked his head in polite greeting, "Radar, good to see you looking better," he smiled broadly and I couldn't help but smile back.

"Faith, it's nice to…" I wasn't meeting him, not technically, "…see you again." I finished, and his smile got bigger which in turn made mine jump minutely. Marlin sank into the chair across from mine and I closed my eyes tight.

"Raise her injury up above her head, and keep pressure. Might help slow it up," Nothing called and strode up to the table, dropping what he'd found across its glass surface. Hope's good hand fell on my shoulder and she called my name twice I think.

"I'm fine! I'm fine!" I said a little breathy.

"You don't sound fine," Marlin said cautiously.

"She can't deal with the sight of blood, hasn't ever been able to handle it," Hope told him.

I kept my eyes squeezed shut and let my sister and the men handle it. Hope kept making the same soothing noises that she'd always made when Char and I were kids and it was like coming home. It was strange that that would be the thing to do it, isn't it?

Packaging crackled and I didn't have time to dwell on it, because the cloth lifted from my hands and was immediately reapplied with a curse.

"Hope, why won't it stop bleeding?" I asked, and hated how my voice sounded high and a little frightened.

"Easy, no need to panic yet," Nothing said and sounded far away like he was concentrating on something, "If I don't get to panic, you don't get to panic, okay, Faith?"

"Okay," I replied automatically, and I heard Marlin chuckle. I breathed deep and my breath caught, his familiar smell of cigarettes, alcohol, and peaches reached me and had the most wonderful calming effect.

"There you go, atta girl," Nothing murmured and the cloth was pulled from my hands. It stung and I tried to jerk, but the hands holding mine steady for whatever Nothing was doing wouldn't give.

The back slider opened and Cutter chuckled, "What in the hell?" he remarked, "Firefly, you should see yourself."

"No, thank you!" I blurted and was met with a track of male laughter.

"It's the blood, blood and Faith don't mix," Hope explained.

"Ain't your other sister becoming a nurse?" someone asked.

"Charity is the crazy sister," I said and more laughter followed.

"Aaaand you are all done," I opened my eyes and Marlin lowered my hands, the index finger on my left hand was bandaged not only neatly, but wasn't bulky at all.

"Thank you," I murmured.

"Any time," Nothing gave me the ghost of a smile.

"Man, you are wasted on painting houses," Radar groused, examining Nothing's handy work.

"Drop it," Nothing said shortly and gathered up packaging off the wrought iron and glass tabletop. I stared at my hand and finally dragged my eyes up to Marlin's.

"You've got to be more careful, Baby Girl. I don't like seeing you hurt," he murmured. I startled and took my hands back from his.

"I said I was sorry," I stood.

"Not what I meant, and you know it."

I bit my lips together and nodded, returning to the kitchen, but I was shooed out by my sister, Radar taking up where I'd left off.

"It was a clean slice, not too deep, you should be good to take off the bandage and put a new one on tomorrow."

"Thank you again, Nothing."

"Don't mention it," he said, then as an aside, "You look good."

"Thank you," I murmured again, and with a look to my sister, jerked my head towards the sliding glass door. She nodded and I slipped out into the bright sun, the heat a shock after the air conditioned coolness of the house.

I turned to slide the door shut, but Marlin loomed in its frame. I nodded and made to slip down the back steps and into the sand. I nearly missed it when Marlin followed.

"How've you been doing?" he asked me.

I swallowed and tried to find my voice, "It's only been a few days, I don't really know how to answer that."

"Fair enough."

He walked along with me and I hugged myself protectively. Finally, I turned and looked at him plainly.

"Why are you here?"

"To have dinner with my brothers."

"I mean, here, now…"

"You lost some blood, making sure you're not woozy."

"I'm not woozy."

"Okay."

I stopped my slow march towards the sea completely and cleared my throat.

"You know I'm here if you need me, Faith."

"I… I gather. I just, need some space."

"I can respect that, Baby Girl, I just needed to say…" he looked me up and down and after a span of time murmured, "I'm sorry I hurt you."

"You didn't," I protested, but it was already too late, he was making long strides back toward the house and I couldn't help myself. I continued my slow progressive march towards the sea for that sensation of being carried away.

CHAPTER 17
Marlin

This was fucking stupid. Probably the dumbest thing I'd ever done, but I couldn't fucking help myself. I was sitting on my bike, outside Faith's shrink's office smoking a cigarette. Only Faith wasn't with me. She wasn't inside either. I was here by myself to talk to the good doctor, and maybe get an answer or two. See? Fucking stupid. A violation of Faith's privacy, for sure, but I couldn't fucking help myself. Not after talking to the Captain, not after Hope…

I looked up sharply as the door opened and stood up, dropping my cigarette to the ground and grinding it out under my boot. She walked right up to me which surprised me, and I half wondered if the cops were on their way.

"She doesn't know that I've seen you bring her here, but I assume you're here about Faith?"

She was a grand lady; older and reminded me of that dame in the double-oh-seven Bond flicks. The newer ones with that badass that plays him with two first names. Daniel something. Only reason I could remember that much was because of my little brother having the same first name.

"Doctor Shiendland?" I asked, just to be clear.

She smiled sweetly, comfortingly and said, "The one and only; now what can I do for you…"

"Marlin." Her eyebrows went up and she nodded.

"What can I do for you, Marlin?"

I frowned, "You don't know who I am?"

"No." She smiled again and waited patiently.

"You can't tell me why you told her she shouldn't see me anymore?"

"I can't tell you anything about my sessions with Faith. Mental health professionals, such as myself, are bound by a code of ethics, confidentiality chief among them. You seem like a very smart man, however, so might I ask, if I know nothing about you…"

"You didn't. How could you, if you don't know who I am?" I bowed my head and nodded to myself. Faith had lied. I wondered why.

"Let's talk about you, my dear boy. Walk an old woman to her car." Without missing a beat, she linked her arm through mine and gestured across the lot to a newer Nissan. What could I do but oblige her?

I turned with her on my arm and started the slow walk across the lot, asking, "What about me?"

"You must care for her a great deal to come all the way out here."

"Yeah, yeah I do."

"If I may?" I nodded, curious as to what she had to say, she stopped us up short and sighed, "It has been my experience with victims of human trafficking; that they hide their true feelings away, deeply, as these feelings are the one and only thing that these traffickers can't take from them. Now, of course, I am purely speaking from years of experience but I am sure you can draw inferences, no?"

I listened, rapt and searched the doctor's face, understanding dawning…

"Right. The more you care about it, the less you talk about it. The less you care, the more you talk, something like that?"

She patted my arm and beamed me a huge smile, "I can tell you care very deeply for Faith, and I can honestly say I have never met you or heard anything about you from anyone, ever before."

"You like her." I said smiling.

"Oh," she laughed, "I like all of my patients," she said with a wink and pressed the button on her key fob to unlock her car doors. I opened her door for her because I both liked and respected the woman. I was glad Faith was in her care.

"I shall see you on Tuesday," she said and I smiled, nodding and shut the door.

"See you on Tuesday, Doc." I called through the glass and shot the dame a salute. She smiled and pushed the button to start her car. I made strides back to my bike and settled on some wind therapy and some solid time to think. I ended up back at the marina, a bunch of the guys walking to and from the parking lot taking coolers down to the beach for the bonfire that night.

Spring break was in full swing in the little town me and the boys called home, so there more than a few fuckin' douchebags taking up the parking down at the marina where they didn't fuckin' belong. I wasn't about to chance having to whoop some guy's ass for touching my bike, so I went straight for the line of cinderblock garages.

When she was safely stored, I made a beeline for my boat to change into some more comfortable beach wear versus my hot as fuck riding leathers. I grabbed my guitar almost as an afterthought on my way back out and down to the beach.

"Hey, Marlin! What's up?" Radar called. Lightning straightened up from the cooler he was setting down by our pile of wood. I eyed our road captain, Pyro, doing his thing building his latest and greatest conflagration. It was a constant argument between him and Lighting on whether the pyramid or log cabin formation was more fuel efficient or which burned hotter or some shit. Me? I said, fuck it. Make a pile of wood and burn it. The one time I'd voiced my opinion aloud, both of those dumb motherfuckers had looked at me like I was bat-shit or something and had gone back to arguing. I hadn't put in my two cents since; all I could do was shake my fuckin' head when they started in together.

I set my guitar down against a washed up log we used as a backrest sometimes, until the next big storm took it out or relocated it on us. No one would fuck with it, but just in case, I looked around for Trike, our prospect. He caught my eye and I signed him the directive to keep an eye on it. He nodded and waved me off and I started lookin' for who I really wanted to see, and sure as shit, there she was, standing in the surf, aquamarine eyes distant and staring over the water.

"Hey," Hope called and came up next to me. She shaded her eyes with her arm which was, thankfully, cast free.

"Finally got that thing off huh?"

"Yeah, yesterday. I seriously need to work on my tan lines now."

It'd been a couple of weeks since dinner at the Captain's house and from what he and Hope told me, the nightmares were tearing my girl up.

"How was last night?"

"Bad."

"Saw her doctor today."

"Yeah?"

"Didn't know a thing about me."

"I figured as much."

"Not pissed at me?"

"You're trying to help her; I don't know what to do. *I can't* do anything. I just want the screaming to stop…"

"Yeah, me too."

Hope patted me on the arm and I looked over at her. She had this clouded look of helplessness on her face, and a look like I was her only fuckin' hope.

"I can't punch it in the face, I'm kind of fuckin' useless," she said and shrugged.

"Well, if there's a threat you can punch in the face, you'd still have to beat me to it."

"Game on," she said.

I laughed, and watched Faith from afar, as she dipped her toes in the surf and wandered aimlessly back and forth in the water in her shorts and bikini top, hugging her swim suit cover up around her shoulders like it was fuckin' freezing out here, when the temp was in the high eighties or low nineties.

She looked lost, but at the same time, physically she looked healthier. She'd put some weight on her; I could see it from here. Her bones no longer stood out prominently against her skin, and she'd tanned up some, too I ground my teeth a bit when a couple of college dudes turned their heads as they went by, but Faith, thankfully, was oblivious to it.

I went to help some of the guys out getting the grill started and food cooking, but my gaze never wandered off of Faith for very long.

I wanted to keep her safe, she needed to *feel* safe. She deserved that and much more, and I was in a place now, and I was beginning to think she was too, where I needed to take a more active role in her life again. This bystander bullshit was for the fucking birds.

"Heads up, Brother. Here she comes." I looked up at Nothing and then back the way of the water, and sure enough here she came. So fuckin' beautiful it made the center of my chest tight, although to some extent, I was betting that had more to do with the fucking tragedy of it all.

"How you doing, Baby Girl?" I asked her when she came up.

"Fine," she lied. I smiled and let her get away with it.

"Good to hear."

I fixed her a plate and had Trike pass it to her, she smiled at the prospect and thanked him for it and sat down between Hossler and my guitar. I turned back to the grill and did up some more meat, wondering how I'd managed to get drafted into grill master in the shuffle of things. Not like I minded. It was fresh caught fish on the menu tonight, and I had to head back to the Scarlett Ann when the shindig was over. Johnny and I had to shove off early the next morning to make a killing off some spring breakers. It was our busy season, and we'd spent the majority of the week on the water. So much so, that Cutter had to take Faith to her first appointment this week. The first one I'd missed. I had to chuckle when she'd come out and asked what I was doing the first time after our little… hell, I don't know what you would call it. I guess 'break up' is as apt a description as any.

Truthfully, Hope and I had argued about that one. I'd told her I'd given her sister my word on it and that was it, I was taking her. The Captain had to talk his woman down because she and I were about to get into a solid scrap over it. I damn sure would have still won. If taking Faith to her appointments was the one thing I could hold onto, then I damn sure was going to grab onto it with both hands. You could pry it from them when they were cold and dead.

I went and sat down beside my guitar and Faith startled, looking from it to me with a frown. I smiled like the damned Cheshire cat and she rolled her eyes, turning back to Hossler. Hossler laughed at me and gave me an acknowledging nod and I just shook my head. By now I was pretty sure Faith had somehow gotten it into her head that I didn't want her, which was just plain stupid and ridiculous seeing as she was all I could ever fucking think about.

I sighed inwardly and ate my fuckin' food, watchin' the sun set over the water and the bonfires start up along the beach. Pyro had gotten ours going and it was already throwing off that good campfire smell that I loved almost as much as the salt in the wind as we cut across the water.

Faith got up and went over to her sister, across the fire who was doing a shot with the Captain. She knelt by her sister and they laughed about something. I didn't hear, or care what. It just did my heart some fucking good to see Faith smile.

I set aside my plate, and Hossler took it, bringing me a beer and gesturing with hers toward my guitar.

"Play something for us," she bossed and I smiled. I picked up the instrument and settled it across my lap. Faith had perked up some, in interest and I shot her a bit of a roguish grin and plucked out a random scale to make sure everything was tuned up enough. Satisfied, I plucked out the first few notes of her song, *Hope Never Dies*. Her eyes went real wide and I smiled, I think it really flipped her switch when I started to sing it.

She stood slowly, those gorgeous gemstone eyes fixed on me and I didn't even try to hide it, or pretend. I sang my girl her favorite song and said with every bit of me, *I'm right here if you need me. I haven't gone anywhere.*

Her eyes welled and she turned away from me, to the ocean crashing on the shore down the beach, as if it were calling her just as surely, but I didn't quit. Even when she walked away to get a grip. Hope made to stand up, but the Captain pulled her down into his lap. I caught this in my periphery, because my gaze was locked solid on Faith, as she moved wraith like through the sand, a beautiful dream.

CHAPTER 18
Faith

    I could feel him watching me, even from way down by the water and I could feel my muscles relax, minutely. I cursed myself for being so damn weak that he could still make me feel so safe, just by the weight of his gaze. I looked at the fading pink scar on my finger and sighed. Was it strange that I almost treasured the thin scar now? As much as it had bled, it was also the last time Marlin had touched me, and countless times in the weeks since, I have closed my eyes and remembered the warmth of his calloused fingers around my own.

    God, I must be pathetic.

    I looked back and there he was, standing in his cargo shorts and motorcycle vest, barefoot in the sand beside where the rest of the club's men set up the grill and coolers. Pyro and Lightning had been amassing and walking circles around the pile of wood meant for the fire for the better part of an hour now, and I had to smile.

    "Whoa! Sorry."

    I bent and picked up the plastic disc that had landed by my feet up from the surf and held it out to the man my age it had gotten away from. I forced a smile that felt timid and handed it back to him. He smiled and took it.

    "Pretty eyes," he remarked and I was suffused by a bit of glow from the compliment.

    "Thank you," I murmured and he jogged backwards to his friends.

    I checked back towards our camp, for lack of a better word, but Marlin had relocated a few steps away, where he was now manning the grill.

    "You coming, Faith?" Hossler asked as she jogged, near breathless, out of the surf.

"Yeah, I'll be right there."

I soaked up some of the sun's last rays for a few minutes more before trudging my way up the beach towards the friendly club gathering.

I know he watched me. He was always watching, it seemed. There were nights I woke up screaming and after Hope and Cutter had gone from my new, smaller and more comfortable room, I would sit by the window. I could see him smoking, the orange glow from his cigarette unmistakable, despite how he parked under the shadows beneath the trees at the start of the drive. You would think I would find it creepy, or overbearing, but it was neither of those things. Not from him, not from Marlin.

I also knew my sister and Cutter filled him in regularly on my progress, and he still drove me to my appointments with Dr. Shiendland. I had put up a fuss. They didn't need to know the tears were of relief, rather than anger. I liked riding with Marlin. The wind and the sound of the engine drowned everything out into a comforting blur and hum of sight and sound that had quite the lulling effect. Everything was simple on the back of the bike. Everything was about being in tune with the man in front of me and the machine beneath me. I could appreciate the simple complexity of it all coming together until my mind was a pleasant, quiet space… at least until Dr. Shiendland went digging around in it. But that was what the trip back was for. Just enough to get me through until I could stand in the water where the sand met the sea. Until the water could wash all my horrible sins out to the depths and I could find my calm again.

The tranquility of the ride and of standing at the water's edge had replaced the drugs. It was my new, much less effective, high. Bar none, it was far better for me, both body and soul.

I made my way back up the beach and accepted a plate of food from the club's prospect. My sister, Hope, had explained it to me, and Hossler too, but I still found it to be confusing. It was almost barbaric in a way, how simplistic these men led their lives, but in that simplicity there was such beauty too. It was far less confusing when you knew your place, and almost familiar in a way. The structure, I mean. It wasn't threatening, but knowing your role and what was expected of you was… refreshing. I was sick and tired of the unknown.

"Hey, Girl! Have a sit." I sat down between Hossler and an abandoned guitar.

"Who plays?" I asked quietly but before Hossler could answer, Marlin took the seat.

We ate quietly, the sun dipping ever lower until it vanished below the horizon. I didn't see the green flash that Cutter had pointed out to me one night, but I was probably at the wrong angle for it.

The fires were lit and starting to catch, and Hossler turned to Marlin, "Play something for us," she urged and he smiled at me. I got up and went over to my sister who was laughing in Cutter's arms when the first notes of *Hope Never Dies*, drifted over the fire. I froze and turned, standing slowly, making eye contact with Marlin over the flames. When he opened his mouth and started to sing. It was like I couldn't move, like I was just frozen in place. I couldn't be sure, my eyes glued to Marlin as they were, but I think my sister was smiling.

I felt the sting of tears as my favorite song drifted to me, in that voice that had comforted me, cheered me, as the man who had seen me at nothing but my worst sang it to me. I was overwhelmed, overjoyed, and at the same time felt myself sink into one of my lowest lows all at once. I couldn't believe he had learned the song. That he sat there singing it to me in front of all these people like he hadn't just cracked open my chest in front of them all and touched the deepest, most private parts of me.

I turned and went for the water. It was too much, just too intimate in front of so many witnesses. My, god. I was just so *confused.*

"Hey, whoa! Easy!" I'd accidentally crashed into the same man from earlier, the one with the Frisbee.

"I'm so sorry!" I cried.

"Hey, it's nothing. My name is Brent, what's yours?"

"I'm sorry?" I shook off the heavy moment before and focused on him in the light from their fire.

"I could always call you 'girl with the eyes' but I was hoping for your name," he said gently.

"Oh, I'm sorry," I laughed, "Faith. My name is Faith."

"It's nice to meet you, Faith. Now, where's the fire at?" he smiled, and it was charming and normal and carried none of the so serious weight of Marlin's gaze which for the first time felt oppressive rather than protective. I touched the band around my wrist and thought of the boy, back in New Orleans. Brent's smile was a lot like his. Open and friendly, care free and innocent.

Desperate to lighten my mood I laughed and waved out over the fires dotting the beach, "Take your pick…" He laughed too and we began to talk.

"Now, you're way too pretty to be apologizing for everything, what's eating you?"

"Oh, nothing… Where are you from?" I tried. He flashed a smile, teeth very straight and white in the shifting firelight.

"Maryland originally, but I'm down here for spring break. I go to college in Indiana. It's my last year and I've been in serious need of blowing off some steam. Some fun, sun and relaxation. What about you?"

I scrambled around for an answer and Hope flashed into my mind, "Visiting my sister, she's back that way." I smiled and hoped he didn't pry too deeply and as luck would have it, he didn't.

"She as pretty as you?" he asked and winked and I hugged myself and laughed.

"Prettier, she's also got a boyfriend… not that she'd need him to come to her defense." I rolled my eyes. No, Hope was perfectly capable of taking care of herself and everyone around her. She always had been, even before our mom had gotten sick. I kept the sigh that wanted out under wraps and smiled with false brightness.

Brent smiled, "Feel like hanging for a bit, Faith?" he asked and I smiled, nodding. I was maybe two fires down the beach, closer to the water. I looked back over my shoulder and could see Marlin, still plucking the strings of his guitar, his eyes seeking me out in the darkness. His gaze wrapped around me and even though I was still rattled, I felt that familiar sense that no matter what, if I fell that safety net was there to catch me.

"Sure, I'd like that," I murmured and my fingers went back to the leather wrist band the boy had given me. Dr. Shiendland had told me the boy's last message to me was an important one not to give up on.

Not everyone is a dick, you have to believe that there are some good people still out there. Even if I'm not one of the best, I try not to be one of the worst.

"Great," Brent was saying, "Let me get you a drink..." I smiled at him again and attempted to wear my knowledge like invisible armor. The knowledge that none of these people knew me from Adam, none of them knew what I had been or about the drugs, none of them figured me for anything but a normal girl here to visit my sister.

"Sure," I nodded and smiled, Brent was handsome in his own way. He carried none of the rugged look that Marlin did. Instead, he was a clean cut and athletic type of strong. It would have been appealing to the 'me' of three years ago, but now... I glanced back again to the gathering around the fire and strained my ears to catch some errant notes from Marlin's guitar over the mini sound system that the college boys had set up.

Brent returned with an iconic red Solo cup in each hand and handed me one of them. I smiled and sipped the cold drink in mine. It tasted strongly of pineapple and coconut with a slightly salty finish which was strange.

I laughed a little, "Someone mix their rum up with Tequila?" Brent laughed and shook his head.

"There's no telling with these wise guys. So, tell me, where are you from originally?"

"California. Sacramento to be exact."

"Ahhh, so east meets west, nice! So I guess you're used to the weather here in sunny Florida. Isn't California about the same?"

"Sunny and warm, yes, the humidity, not so much, but yeah, I'm sort of used to the humidity by now. It can be awful, sometimes, but I guess that's what air conditioning is for."

Brent laughed again, a little more nervously this time and I sipped my drink, "Wow, look at us, is all we really have to talk about the weather?"

"Mm, safe enough topic as any," I returned and it was. I closed my eyes a moment and opened them, the firelight beginning to swim. Brent reached out and took my arm and I jumped.

"Hey, you alright? Maybe that drink was a little stronger than expected," he tugged on me lightly and I resisted.

"No, it's not that…" I dropped the cup in the sand as I was swamped with a dizzy spell. Oh, God. Oh, God help me, there was something in it… this wasn't right.

"Maybe you should come and sit down."

I put my arm out and staggered slightly and opened my mouth, "Marlin!" I called but I didn't know if it was loud enough to be heard over the music.

"Marlin!" I shouted, at least I think I shouted louder.

Suddenly arms wrapped around my waist and pulled; I was up in the air and panic seized me. I screamed, wordlessly and my mind screamed louder, *no, no, no, no, no! Not again, not again!*

"Hope! Hope, help me! Marlin!"

I kept screaming, everything'd gone blurry, the blood was rushing in my head. Male voices were shouting, an urgent voice near my ear, warm breath on my neck. I struggled, fighting like mad, but he had me, he was holding me and dragging me back, away, I was terrified, and just when I thought my heart was going to explode in my chest I was turned loose, pitching forward only to crash into leather and wall of muscle.

Arms went around me, and I was enveloped in the comforting scent of cigarettes, alcohol and peach shampoo.

"I've got you, Baby Girl. Arms up, around my neck; that's it." I was lifted, just like back in that house in New Orleans, and just like the house in New Orleans, I felt, deep down in my heart, what the true meaning of the word *safe* meant.

"I'm sorry, I'm so sorry…" I wailed.

"Shhh, you're good, Baby, I've got you. I promised you, no one would ever hurt you again; I meant it. You're okay now."

I buried my face in the side of his neck and squeezed my eyes shut against the dizzy sensation threatening to overwhelm me, but I didn't have long to think about it because as Marlin made strides to who knew where, I think I lost consciousness.

CHAPTER 19
Marlin

I kept my eye on her, she'd made her way down the beach; head bowed. She had run almost head long into a guy and I closely watched their exchange. I waited, I didn't want to jump in if it wasn't needed; she had to do some things on her own, after all. If she needed me I would go, but the guy reached out and steadied her and they began talking, so I let it be. Keeping my silent guardianship from a distance, the same way I'd been doing for weeks now.

Cutter got up and dragged Hope to her feet laughing a few moments later and I took my eyes off of Faith for a minute.

"Well, it's been swell, but the swelling's –er, gone up and I need to go fuck my woman," the Captain said to a round of rowdy cheers; Hope laughed and shook her head.

"Marlin, you got Faith?" she asked; worry deepening her dark brown eyes to near black.

"Hope, do you really need to even ask me that?"

She smiled, an almost rueful turn of lips and laughed softly, "No. No, I guess I don't."

"Go on, Captain. I'll take Faith back to the house, later."

"We'll be on the boat," Cutter said slinging an arm across Hope's shoulders and turning her toward the Marina.

"Call us if anything happens!" Hope called and I returned my eyes back to the blonde siren with the jewel bright eyes.

"You know I will," I muttered and played the opening chords of one of my old favorite Stones songs.

Faith was still standing by the fire, around two down from ours, talking to the college pretty boy. I watched as she hugged herself, and laughed at something he'd said. A moment later he returned with a couple of cups. They talked, she occasionally sipped, and it all seemed like pretty normal stuff.

I glanced down for half a second and when I looked up again, I could tell something was very wrong. Faith dropped her cup and had her arm out. She had looked down and away from the dude but her hand was out as if to ward him off. I was on my feet, passing my guitar into Hossler's hands and striding around the fire before he could even reach for her. When his hand closed around her wrist and before her first indistinct shout, I had broken into a run, brothers falling in beside me and hot on my heels.

I was barely a few paces away when she opened her mouth a second time and cried out for me, *"Marlin!"*

"Nothing!" I snapped out to the nearest brother beside me and he moved forward.

"I got her, take care of him," he said.

"You're mine, asshole!"

Nothing pulled Faith away from the little cockbite trying to take her, and I was on him. His little fucking frat buddies started to move in, but all of 'em were just as quick to step back when the rest of the club got there. I grabbed the little worm, cocked back and while his hands went around my wrist to keep me from choking the shit out of him, I let fly right into his smirking prettyboy face.

I dropped his ass, grounded and pounded him, and didn't let up until Faith's panicked shrieking voice broke through the angry haze of red that'd fallen over my vision.

"Help me! Marlin!"

I got off the man-child, moaning and crying like a little bitch in the sand and went to her. Nothing let her go and she lurched forward and away from him right into my arms; her soft, lithe form folding in against me and fuck it all, she was meant to be there. I put my arms around her and held her close.

"I've got you, Baby Girl. Arms up, around my neck; that's it."

She complied, sweetly, and with complete and total, well, faith in me that I knew exactly what my next move needed to be. I was taking her home, *my* home, where I could watch her. Where I could be sure to protect her. She sobbed into the side of my neck as I made strides in the direction of the Marina.

"I'm sorry! I'm so sorry!" her words were slurred around the edges and my suspicions were pretty much confirmed. It happened out here all the time and I should have seen it coming; fuckin' college spring breakers and their fuckin' date rape shit. Drug a girl's drink, get it on… motherfucker! I kept a lid on

"Shhh, you're good, Baby, I've got you. I promised you, no one would ever hurt you again; I meant it. You're okay now."

I talked to her, all the way back to the Scarlett Ann. When I got to my boat, I let Nothing and Radar board ahead of me. Faith had become so much dead weight in my arms when I'd hit the steps up to the Marina's lot, my anger about her having been drugged reached boiling point all over again. I stuffed it down, there weren't nothing I could do about it except seethe but I could do that, so I did it well. Nothing reached down for her, and him being the closest thing to our resident medic, I handed her up to him before boarding myself.

"Radar, let the Captain and Hope know what's up," I ordered.

"On it," the compact Hispanic man bolted up the dock and took the shortcut, hopping across moored boats, rather than going the long way around up and down the rows of docks separating mine and Cutter's slips.

Hossler handed me up my guitar and I set it aside and went where Nothing had gone, taking Faith to my quarters below decks. I entered my cabin which was sizeable enough you could walk around the queen sized bed with room to spare. He'd set her on it and was taking her pulse. Satisfied, he went about peeling back her eyelids and shining a pen light into them that had appeared from somewhere out of the inside of his cut.

"What's the word?"

"If I had to guess its GHB or one of its siblings. Can't know for sure without a blood draw and testing equipment I just don't have the access to. That shit ain't something the town, let alone me, has on hand. That's why we got such a problem with these fuckers doin' it here. Good news is, that the shit they use for this kind of thing is fast metabolizing. She'll wake up thirsty, with a headache maybe… probably with some memory loss for sure."

"Damn, I hope this don't set her back."

"Hard to say, Man. Hard to say."

"You might want to bail before Hope and the Captain get here."

"Cops are going to be on this for sure, Dude. You beat the brakes off that happy bastard in front of a lot of people, and you could smell the money."

"Fuck if I care."

"Yeah, me either, I'm sure the Captain'll sort it out."

"What am I sorting out?" Cutter demanded.

Nothing sighed, and gestured that Cutter had probably best follow him and get the full meal deal, because right on the Captain's heels was his woman. Hope burst into the room like a hurricane, the energy rolling off her, the air crackling with her rage.

"What happened?" she demanded and went for the side of the bed Faith was laying on. Nothing had put her on her side, in the recovery position in case whatever was in her system caused her stomach to heave. Hope stood by the raised bed and took her sister's had between her own.

"I was watching her, she was talkin' to one of the college boys and he brought her a drink. The second she showed anything was wrong I was on it."

"Jesus, Faith!" Hope sounded incredulous, but luckily her sister was out, and didn't have to hear it.

"Hope, don't blame her for tryin'. She was on the beach with all of us right fuckin' there. Nothing happened, she's gonna be fine. I swear to Christ, though… if Faith didn't have bad luck she wouldn't have any luck at all."

"We'll take her back to the house –"

I scoffed, "She's stayin' right here, where I can take care of her, besides, where you gonna get a cage to take her in? Not like she's fit to ride and I'm damn sure not gonna carry her all the way to the house."

Hope looked at me, her expression fractured and haunted, tears starting to well up.

"I am like the worst fucking parent ever at this point, aren't I?" she asked and sniffed.

"Naw, Sweetheart," Cutter answered from the doorway.

"She was all grown up when she was eighteen," I added, "Besides, come tomorrow, we can go back over the lessons about taking candy, or in this case drinks, from strangers. She's good. I've got her, and I promise I'm takin' care of her."

Hope nodded, and Cutter held out his hand to her, "C'mon, Sweetheart. I've gotta go be the President for a minute, we need to talk to our people and get the full Monty from all sides."

"We have an early set of customers tomorrow," I said.

"It's best just to let her sleep until whatever it is wears off," Nothing counseled.

"Fine, that settles that then, she can come out with me and my brother. Ain't no place safer for her."

"I'll try to be here for that," Hope said.

I nodded, "Johnny can suck it."

Plans made, Hope and the Captain left, Nothing gave me some instructions on what to check on throughout the night and he left soon after. I debated, for a time, what to do. I finally settled on leaving her as is, as much as I wanted to get her changed into something more comfortable than her cut offs and such, I figured preserving her modesty was more important this time around.

I smoothed some of her bright blonde beach waved locks out of her face; slack with her drug induced sleep and asked her, "Why didn't you just come back to me, Baby Girl? Why do you keep runnin', huh?"

I wouldn't be getting an answer to the question tonight, there wasn't no way, so instead, I got myself ready for bed. I grabbed a quick shower and some clean boxers. I usually didn't bother with actual sleepwear, so it was the best I had. Usually, I crashed out one of two ways, nude or fully clothed.

I climbed up onto the bed and settled onto my side behind my girl and pulled her gently back into the protective curve of my body. We had a lot to talk about she and I, and needed to come to some kind of understanding quick, because *this?* What we been doing? It wasn't working for me anymore and it damn sure wasn't working for her. I'd given her space. Tomorrow, I was going to be up close and personal, and push some of her limits. I just hoped like hell it weren't too soon.

CHAPTER 20
Faith

I woke slowly; my head full of cotton and dragged open my eyes half expecting that it had all been a dream. My sister, Marlin, and the daring rescue, no more than a drug induced hallucination… I pushed myself up in the comfortable bed and nearly wept when I realized I was in a room that looked awfully expensive. I'd been in high priced suites before and this looked to be one of them, only strangely compact. Not at all like a full sized hotel room, and there was no bathroom that I could see, just one door which was presumably the exit.

I groaned softly and covered my face with my hands at the sense of vertigo, as if the room were tipping. It took me several moments to realize that it actually *was*. I swallowed my stomach contents which were threatening to rebel and looked down. I felt myself frown in confusion. I was clothed. Not only was I clothed, I was clothed in the same thing as my dream.

I closed my eyes and breathed deep to steady myself, which is when I realized I could smell him. I could smell him in the sheets and along my skin. A light perfume of peaches, smoke and alcohol.

"Not a dream, Faith. He's real, it's real, you're safe," I whispered to myself.

When I felt steady enough, I got out of the bed using the three steps at the foot and buried my toes into the carpet surrounding it which was thick and soft. I hugged myself, self-conscious about my state of dress, still being in my rumpled clothing, but I didn't have anything else and I needed to pee – badly.

I sucked in a deep breath and opened the door and blinked in surprise. I was in a little area with two doors to either side. An expanse of living space was spread out in front of me, but I needed the bathroom so I ignored it for now, since it was empty. The door on my left was firmly shut, but the one on my right was the bathroom, so I slipped into it quickly and shut the door firmly behind me, flipping the little switch on the doorknob into the locked position.

I took care of my needs and spent more time than was required washing my hands and splashing cold water from the faucet on my face, scrubbing my fingers over it to rid my skin of the tight feeling. I'd been crying. It was a familiar sensation, but when I tried to remember why it was like the memories were an amorphous black cloud and would shimmer just out of my reach every time I tried to grasp them. I remembered having lunch with Cutter and Hope, I remembered riding behind Cutter to the beach, and Hope riding beside us, happy to be out of her cast.

I remember walking along the water line, and I remembered Marlin. I remembered Marlin singing *Hope Never Dies* to me and then nothing… just nothing. I dried my face with a nearby hand towel and worried my bottom lip between my teeth as I stared at myself in the mirror over the sink.

"What happened?" I asked the girl in the glass, but all she did was stare back at me, eyes too wide and startled in her pale face.

I took a deep breath and squared my shoulders, ghosting back over to the bathroom door. Another deep breath, I unlocked it and opened it up to an unfamiliar man standing it its frame. I let out a little startled shriek and jumped backwards in the small space, but I think I startled him just as much. He jumped too, and leapt back, his back crashing into the wall behind him.

"Jimmy!" He called out, "You better get down here!"

I folded back in on myself and cowered, I couldn't help it; it was almost an ingrained response to being trapped in a corner with a large man looming in front of me. He stood just outside the bathroom door, his hand pressed to the center of his chest, which heaved with him being out of breath.

"Sorry," he said, "You scared the shit out of me."

I tried to speak, but all that came out was a forced whimper. He looked familiar, yet he was a stranger to me. His light brown hair with golden highlights was cut business short, and was a little bit off from the rest of his appearance which consisted of soft, light blue, broken in jeans faded to near white along the tops of his thighs, and a vintage looking medium blue cotton tee with a distressed darker blue image of a swordfish leaping out of the water. A hook was in the corner of the creature's mouth and a fishing line leading back to the viewer that faded off into nothing.

"I'm not helping here, am I?" he asked and backed off a little further. When he moved I flinched and he sighed and swore softly and yelled out, "JIMMY!"

I sank down onto the closed lid of the toilet and bit my lips together. I didn't know where I was, I didn't know who he was and I didn't know a Jimmy. Marlin appeared in the doorway a moment later and shoved the other man aside, "I got it, Johnny. Go take care of the customers," he said.

I swallowed hard and the other man, Johnny, squeezed around Marlin and that's when it clicked.

"He's your brother," I murmured.

"Yeah, that's my dumbassed brother," Marlin smiled.

"You wanna come out of there?" he asked and I unfolded myself and stood up. Marlin stepped back towards the living area and I exited the small bathroom.

"Where are we? Why can't I remember?" I asked.

Marlin sighed, "What's the last thing you *do* remember?"

I stared at him and licked suddenly dry lips, "I didn't know you could play – or sing," I said finally.

He smiled, "It's a hobby, and that song? Only for you."

"Why?"

"What do you mean why?"

I shook my head back and forth and covered my face with my hands, breathing in and out slowly. Marlin sighed and I felt his fingers close around my wrist. I jerked my face out of my hands just in time for him to jerk me in against his chest. His arms went around me and his breath was warm in my hair, but all I could do was stand there stiff as a board.

"I'm so confused…" I moaned.

"Why? Talk to me, Baby Girl. I'm right here, and it's high time we *did* talk about it."

"Talk about what?"

"Let's start with why you lied to me, hmm?" His voice held no accusation and no reproach. It did, however, hold hurt which was rich, considering…

I tried to shove away from him but he was firm, and didn't let go.

"There's no running away from this one, Faith. I'm not going to let you go without an answer on this. I'm sorry I have to push, Baby Girl, but I need an answer. I need to understand why you did what you did last night."

"*I* don't even know what I did last night!" I half wailed, my eyes filling with tears, my heart surging in my chest and crowding my throat.

"Why'd you lie to me, Faith?"

"About what?" I demanded, the anger coming in a hot flood.

"About me. Tellin' me your shrink told you to stay away from me or some shit."

I froze, like a rabbit in a trap, I looked up at him slowly and the expression on his face was stony, but clearly hurt.

"I…"

"Don't lie to me now, Baby Girl. You do, and it'll be the last you see of me."

"I was giving you an easy out."

His brow furrowed down and he looked downright tempestuous, "It's time you showed me a little trust, you explain to me what you mean by that. I think I've more than earned it at this point."

I shoved away from him violently and he let me go this time, the tears rose hot and fierce and it all just boiled over.

"An easy out! Away from me! So you didn't have to pretend anymore," I raged.

"Pretend what?" he demanded.

"That you *liked* me. I get it, Marlin. I do, okay? I'm a junkie fucking *whore*. Sold for a few bucks a fuck. I'm disgusting, okay? *Okay?*"

He stood there, stunned, mouth hanging open, and I drove the knife in the last few inches, "I'm just your project to ease your guilt over your brother! You can't even stand to *touch* me!"

He put his hand over his mouth, like he was trying to stop himself from saying anything, but I could see the fractured ache in his bright blue eyes. He was stunned, speechless, and I felt hollow and empty. It had felt good to get it out, to get it off my chest but now I felt ugly and exposed. I was standing in front of him raw, and emotionally, as naked as the day I was born and waiting for him to finish what I'd started. I was waiting for him to tear me down the rest of the way.

He pulled his hand down, wiping his mouth, the stubble of the growth on his face rasping in the ringing silence left by my confession.

"Jesus-fucking-Christ, Baby Girl. Is that really what you think?" he asked and his voice was breathy and incredulous with stunned disbelief.

I nodded, mute and dismayed… I'd broken it between us; I could see it all over his face. There was no coming back from this, no way possible. It was all I was ever good at, breaking things. Breaking the people that I loved the most. Destroying them and how they viewed me until there just wasn't anything left to care about with disappointment after disappointment.

"Stop," he ordered sharply and I looked up. "Don't do that, Faith. Stop it, you're hurting yourself. Just, stop."

He strode forward and pulled me against him, crushing me against his chest, his fingers tangled in my hair, holding it back from my face and he pressed his lips to my forehead. My eyes drifted shut and I let myself take it in, knowing it was likely the last time he would ever…

"I've been trying so hard *not* to touch you when all I've wanted… Fuck. You have it all wrong, Baby Girl. You're all I think about. You're all I want. I just don't think you're ready for that, do you? I mean… Christ, I really fucked it up this time didn't I?"

I laughed and felt as if I were going mad, I felt my arms go around him and I held just as tightly to him as he did to me. We stood there in silence while the tears stained his tee and the water lapped at the hull, the boat we were on bobbing around, voices filtered down to us and I sniffed, changing the subject.

"Where are we?"

Marlin sighed, "Don't think this conversation is over, Baby Girl, but I gotta get back up there. We're on my boat, the Scarlett Ann; I've got customers up on deck. Hope is on board too, I'll have her bring you down the clothes she brought and when you're ready, you can join us up on deck. Okay?"

I nodded against his chest, "I guess it has to be," I said.

"That's my girl." He kissed my forehead one more time and let me go reluctantly.

"Stay here."

He turned me loose back into the bedroom and went back out toward the living room. He left the door open behind him, which I was grateful for. I didn't much like closed doors anymore. I went back up the steps and sat on the end of the bed, feeling lighter than I had in a long time, but at the same time, harboring that shadow of ugliness deep down inside. It was like I had purged and the foul little creature, the monster inside my head, needed time to recharge now.

I wondered if I would carry it forever. Probably, knowing my luck, which made me wonder, *why in the world would Marlin want me?*

I didn't know. Maybe he wouldn't now; we still needed to talk… I guess there wasn't anything I could do about it one way or another. I would just have to wait and see.

CHAPTER 21
Marlin

"You're up," I said to Hope and she got up off the lounger on the bow of my boat.

"You look pissed," she observed.

"Yeah, well, I honestly can't really tell at this point."

"Tell what?"

"Who I'm pissed at, her or me."

Hope smiled and knocked me in the shoulder lightly, "Welcome to my world of the last twenty-seven years," she said and I frowned.

"I don't get it; I thought you took over as 'mom' when she was nine."

Hope snorted, "Please, our mom was never really a mom. She was too busy trying to be our best friend. I didn't take over officially until I was eighteen, but I'd been doing it from the day mom turned up pregnant with Faith." She sighed and it was a heavy, thing.

"So, what I'm feelin'?"

"Yeah, welcome to what it's like to be a parent."

"That's not creepy at all," I muttered.

"Fine, I'll rephrase, 'welcome to what it feels like to be responsible for another human being.'"

I looked at Hope, long and hard, the wheels turning in my head. Maybe that was the problem. There was taking care of someone then there was taking responsibility over some one... Faith needed the first, sure, but she was a big fuckin' girl...

"You're thinking awfully hard," Hope stated sardonically.

I nodded, "Yeah, talk about it later. Right now, she needs a change of clothes and to stop hiding."

Hope looked me over, carefully considering, "This conversation isn't over, is it?"

"Not by a long shot, now I've got two of those and customers waiting. Johnny will make three if I keep delaying. He's gotta take a leak."

"Say no more."

Hope went down below decks and I went around to the stern where my brother and our two customers were chatting.

"Sorry, Johnny. Go ahead." I said and Johnny nodded, giving me a look full of weight.

"No problem, be right back."

He went through the door and down the steps, disappearing into my living quarters. I heard him and Hope exchange a hello and doors open and shut and the rest was quiet. This wasn't the most ideal situation, but then again, it never was, was it?

I sighed and plucked my sunglasses off the table I'd left them on and put 'em on my face. Our two customers were a couple of guys in their fifties and teachers from some high school up north. They'd left their wives back in town and had come out to indulge whatever bromance they had going on, having been buddies for however many years.

I checked their lines and made small talk with them, did my job, but I kept getting distracted, letting my gaze stray from the water and my customers to the stairs leading down into my home, waiting for that pretty blonde head of hair to appear. No such luck, it was my asshole brother who showed back up first.

"Thanks, Man," he grunted and took over as the social one, although these two weren't bad as far as some of the dudes I had standing on my deck. They'd at least fished before, although fly fishing on a river and deep sea fishing like we were now, were worlds apart as far as fishing went.

Johnny came back up and slapped me on the back of the shoulder, giving me a meaningful look that I couldn't readily identify its meaning before diving back in with the clients. I turned back when Faith appeared in a long, airy skirt and white tank top. The outfit suited her; modest but cool for the soaring temperatures out here. Hope came up behind her and gave me a dirty look followed immediately with a considering one.

"You girls want to head up to the foredeck?" I asked. It was going to be crowded back here otherwise and if one of the guys –

"Fish on!" one of them cried, and I bowed my head. Of course, why wouldn't they catch something at the precise fucking time she got up here? All I wanted to do was check with her, and nope, no, no and no. *Motherfucker.*

I went up to the grinning fool who's rod was bending under the strain of whatever was on the other end. Damn, he got a big one.

"Hope, Faith, gonna need you girls to head up to the front of the boat for your safety please," Johnny told them and nodding, Faith caught my eye, uncertainty radiating out from those aquamarine jewels.

"Go on, I'll be up when I can. Soak up some sun and try to relax," I grunted, while helping the dude with the fish on his line into the fighting chair. I could feel the tension in the rod, the dude was putting up a fight and his muscles trembled with exertion already. Still, he seemed determined and if the line didn't break, or if the fish didn't slip the hook, he had a good chance of getting it in so long as it didn't turn into a day long fight.

God I sincerely hoped it didn't.

CHAPTER 22
Faith

I was surprised that Hope wasn't angry with me, at least not about last night. She seemed fairly disappointed in me where Marlin was concerned but instead of one of her classic long lectures on responsibility and how to better behave to her standards, she simply sighed, hugged me, and told me I was on my own to sort it out.

That instilled a whole new kind of hurt and anxiety that I couldn't quite define. It was like she'd finally given up on me, yet she was still here, lounging in the sun beside me holding my hand. I felt crippled, debilitated, and lost worse than I ever had in captivity. I almost longed for someone to tell me what to do because it was so familiar. I needed familiarity… or did I?

I'd accused Marlin of acting like a crutch as my excuse to set myself apart from him and wow had that backfired on me. I'd hurt him; badly… as was evidenced by his inability to even look at me right now. Every time he had to come up here, to the front of his boat, he would only address Hope, and would try to pointedly ignore me. Of course, it wasn't like I could speak to him, so embarrassed was I about how I'd treated him. I hadn't meant it that way, sure, but that was the way it'd come across and as Hope had always told me growing up – that was what mattered. That people wouldn't always remember what you said, or what you did, but they would always and forever remember how it was you made them feel and I could see plain as day, I made everyone I came in contact with feel awful, despite my best intentions.

I huddled in on myself and stared out over the water, losing myself in the glint of the sun off its surface while the joyful shouts of the men behind us blurred into so much white noise. I had a lot to think about, and Hope pretty much left me to it. Finally, with a sigh, she put down her book and jiggled my hand.

"Lay it on me, Bubbles. What's going on up there?"

I startled as if coming awake and looked into my sister's sad, deep brown eyes, "I screw everything up Hope. I don't mean to, but I do. It's like everything I touch becomes poisoned and crumbles into so much ash."

Her face crumbled at that and I scrubbed my face with my hands, "See! That's exactly what I mean."

"Oh, Baby, you're just hurting is all. You've been through a lot and we're all still here, we just don't know what to do or how to help you."

"I don't think there *is* any helping me," I said dully.

My sister sighed and looked about as helpless as to what to say as I'd ever seen her. She finally licked her lips and sat up, facing me.

"I've lectured you, come down on you like a ton of bricks and have just generally been this overbearing parent figure your whole life. I was hard on you because I wanted better for you; better for you and Char both," she bowed her head and shook it, taking a deep breath, "Charity took to the discipline like I did. Like a fish to water, but you? You're a free spirit like mom and all I was doing was driving a wedge. I can't take that back, I don't know how to fix it… Then you were gone and all I could do was work my ass off to get you back so I could have the chance."

She looked me up and down, searching my face, "You're still you in there, Faith. I believe that, and I don't want to mess up again. I don't know how to do this."

"Well," I sniffed, "It was always your way or the highway."

She laughed, "Damn fuckin' straight –" she stopped herself. When we were younger she would have called me a hooker, just joking around, but now, now I guess it was the truth. An awkward silence ensued.

"You're *you*, little sister. Don't let yourself become what they tried to make you. If you wouldn't let me do it, why let them?"

I blinked and tears spilled out. It was one of those perfect moments where what she said made perfect sense. She was right, and I wasn't about to argue her logic. I reached for my sister and she reached for me and we hugged fiercely. We were a broken little family of three and far from okay, but at least now we had a chance to make it right. That, and if I had ever doubted it before, those doubts were dashed. My sister Hope loved me with a whole lot more than I could have ever imagined. She'd come to the rescue, had never stopped looking, even when I had all but given up; she hadn't and that spoke volumes. We may not know how to relate to one another, but we were sisters and that was a bond that would never ever break. This whole ordeal was proof enough of that.

We talked a lot after that, and it didn't go unnoticed that Marlin found a number of small tasks to come to the front of his boat where we were at. Checking on us, I think. I wanted to get my hopes up that maybe I could fix things with him too, but I'd had those dashed so many times in the last couple of years, I found myself fighting down their rise at every turn.

Eventually there was triumphant shouting and cheering from the back, and I found my fingertips grazing the leather and metal wristband around my wrist, wishing it were a time piece. We'd been out here for a really long time. Hours and hours it felt like, and Marlin appeared again.

"We're headed back in, might want to pick up some. The wind is bound to kick up once we start moving," he gave me a lingering look, and the hurt and reservation in his sky blue eyes left my heart sinking. I swallowed hard and nodded softly.

"Okay."

He disappeared as suddenly as he'd come and Hope knocked her shoulder into mine, "It'll be okay. You just need to talk it out. These guys don't know when to quit and won't let anything lie for very long. They like to get things sorted and done fast so they can get back to enjoying life."

"How do you know?"

"Because I'm with their leader, and that's the way he likes it. Marlin is his second in command and I've never seen them disagree, so I think it's safe to assume they're alike in a lot of ways."

"How did you find these guys again?"

My sister grinned as she picked up around our area and the boat's motor rumbled to life, "You sure you're ready for the whole story? It's a wild ride."

I nodded, "We haven't talked about it much."

"Okay, so I was looking for that bitch ass roomy of yours that you went to New Orleans with in the first place... She dropped off the radar pretty much the exact same time you disappeared," she made a face and I did too. That was because the bitch had drugged me and sold me to those fucking animals.

"So anyways, I hired a PI and he tracked her last known whereabouts to..."

I listened to my sister. It was a long story, but by the end, I felt a little more put back together. She had gone to such extremes to save me, all of them had, and I just didn't understand it. I traced the leather cuff around my wrist and thought about something the boy had told me, *"We aren't all bad guys... men, I mean. There are some of us out there that have our head mostly on straight. I'm sorry I wasn't exactly one of them."* It was the last thing he'd said, before he'd gone out the door and I'd sat in the rank dark of my little cell, clutching his gift in my hands.

We were pulling up to the dock, two of The Kraken's men standing on it as we did. They looked nervous. Hope and I stood, my sister at the ready while I? I shaded my eyes from the bright Florida sun reflecting off of the boat's sleek white walls and deck.

"Marlin!" one of them called as we got close, he was stocky and Hispanic, his name was on the tip of my tongue and had to do with a piece of equipment...

"Radar! What's up, Buddy?"

"We need to talk, Man," his tone sounded ominous and I found my hand reaching for Hope's. Marlin eyed his brother in leather and nodded.

"Good deal, give us a hand and we'll get to it."

The other man on the dock I knew better. Nothing leapt aboard and nodded in our direction before he set to work helping the men with their gear. They'd taken a lot of pictures with their fish, but ultimately had thrown the catch back into the sea, tired and with a hole in its lip, but otherwise unharmed.

Radar and Marlin wandered up our way, speaking in low and insistent tones, just enough for Hope and I to hear, and the news wasn't good.

"… was some kind of Senator's kid or some shit. You beat the brakes off that fucker and he deserved it, for sure, unfortunately the cops are involved in this one and they can't go away. You need to head out and take Faith with you. They ran her name and she's got a warrant out for her arrest," Radar was telling him. I felt myself pale.

"I do?" I asked quietly, "What for?"

"Jumping bond in NOLA. You never answered for your prostitution charge, which was a misdemeanor; the bail jump is a little more serious."

Oh. Hope turned me to face her by my shoulders, "One thing at a time, Bubbles. You don't get to panic, not yet."

I nodded, but my eyes were affixed to Marlin, sorrow welling in the center of my being for having been so *stupid*. For having gotten him into trouble because I couldn't hold my shit together. He stared back at me, his face unmoved, his expression shuttered and calculating, he ran his bottom lip between his teeth and eyed Radar.

"Captain's orders?" he asked.

"Head out to the Locker, he's stalling the local PD. He needs Hope here to plan but he figures a day, maybe two out there, long enough for the politician and his douchebag son to skip town and go back where they came from…" Marlin was nodding as he listened to Radar talk, and Johnny was on the dock smiling and sending off their fishing clients. Nothing was standing with Johnny and when the two men left, he and Johnny were exchanging words. It all blurred together making me a bit dizzy to think about.

How could I be so toxic? I asked myself, sinking down to sit on the edge of the nearest lounger.

Hope was nodding, bags were being brought on board and my mind was whirling and spiraling uncontrollably.

What did I do, what did I do, what did I do…

"Faith…" I looked up sharply into Marlin's face and he knelt down in front of me, he reached out and grazed a thumb through the tears I hadn't even realized I'd started crying.

"We'll get it sorted, just like Hope said."

I nodded numbly and he stood, and my sister knelt down giving me a hug, "It's not the end of the world, Bubbles. Just another bump in the road called life. We'll handle it. You going to be okay?" I nodded bewildered and she hugged me again, I hugged her back and before I knew it, she was gone and the boat was moving; my sister on the dock with Radar watching us go.

I didn't even know *where* I was going. Shouldn't I know that?

Shit.

What was wrong with me?

I was sick and tired of every little nuanced thing feeling like it had life or death consequences. It was like I was constantly living in that moment, the one where after you've tripped and you don't know if you are going to catch yourself or not. It was like I was there, trapped in that small sliver of time where your heart is dropping and your chest is seized up and you just *don't know* all day long. I seriously just wished it would stop, but I didn't have a name for it, or any idea of *how* to make it stop.

Nothing sat down beside me and handed me a bottle of water, "Drink this then take this." He dropped a little round yellow tablet into the palm of my hand.

"What is it?"

"A valium. It'll stop the anxiety attack, and if it doesn't, it'll at least help slow it down. Maybe make you feel like you can at least breathe again."

I blinked slowly, the little round pill taking up too much of my vision.

"Is that what this is?" I asked.

He nodded, and I looked him in the eyes, he flinched when our gazes met and I blinked, "How do you know?"

His grey eyes slid from mine, off to the side and he pushed to his feet, "Because I have it too, where do you think I got the valium? Take it or don't. I'm just trying to help," he went around to the back of the boat and left me staring at the pill in my hand. Finally, I took it. Popping it into my mouth and swallowing it down before I could change my mind about it.

Nothing was like Marlin; a sweet man, who had done everything to help me and nothing to hurt me. I stared at the wristband around my wrist and closed my eyes, hoping that the pill would at least stop my heart from speeding like it was. I bit my lower lip and stood, finding Nothing and smiling a little sadly.

"Thank you."

He looked me over and nodded, "No problem."

"Where are we going?" I asked.

"We call it The Locker, but it's not exactly, there's this thing we built, out in the water. A place to stay a day or two at a time when the shit gets too deep, like now, and we need to take cover or just get the fuck out of dodge for a few days."

"What, just out in the middle of the ocean?"

"Not exactly. It's inside swimming distance of one of the Key islands if you're ballsy enough. You and Marlin will be good there until the Captain can come out. He needs time to deal with the cops and for the shit storm to die down."

"This is all my fault," I said and gripped the railing, letting the wind carry my hair into my face, hiding my shame for the moment.

Nothing nodded, "Pretty much," he agreed and I felt it like a needle prick to my heart, "But it doesn't make a difference if it were you, or Hope, or Hossler or one of the other girls attached to the club. The result would have been the same. Hell, if we'd seen it and it was just another Spring break girl, he still would've got his ass beat. We don't like that shit in our town. Period."

I looked at him, and his dark hair, just long enough to fall into his eyes, did. He didn't bother to push it back he just bowed his head and spoke honestly, "Truth is, I don't think I've ever seen Marlin move that fast. The prick deserved to have his ass beat, sure, but because it was you? That son of a bitch got off light, because after everything you've been through, that fucker deserved to die."

He left me then, standing there open mouthed and robbed of speech, as the wind buffeted me and the sleek sport fishing boat cut through the waters turned blue with their depth. We bounced through the small waves for a while, and eventually reached a structure, set out from a small and seemingly abandoned little island.

It was square in nature and mostly wood, with at least two stories to it. The top had a platform on it, and stairs leading up one side. The platform looked like it was for viewing the stars, and underneath it, open on one side looking out over the water, was a seating area. Backed benches were set in a horseshoe shape around a low square table, the seating area decorated with patio furniture cushions in oranges and yellows.

Marlin made the jump from the boat to the floating structure, "Looks like we had some partiers," he called back then added, "Locks are in place! Johnny, help me clean up before Faith comes aboard."

It was Nothing who made the leap across to the floating box, and disappeared behind one of the sides of it, there were a couple of nooks to either side of the ground floor, one held a small kitchen the other a showerhead and what looked like a small, boxy toilet. I sat on the edge of the boat and watched the men with fascination for a moment as they moved around this thing, then with a little apprehension when I realized that we would be *living* on it for a day; maybe two.

I picked myself up and gathered the long skirt of my maxi dress and made the unassisted leap from the side of the boat to the lower most platform of the Locker, which I had no idea why they would even call it that.

Marlin appeared almost immediately, "Whoa, hey, you shouldn't be over here just yet, there were people out here and they left some needles and shit behind."

I looked up at him and nodded, biting my lip between my teeth, "I thought I could help, if I'm going to be staying here too."

He looked me over, appraising and finally nodded, "Let Johnny hand you some of the bags and gear and put 'em down here."

I turned back and Johnny was reaching out, plastic grocery bags laden with things presumably from Marlin's fridge or freezer in them. I reached out and so it went until I had a neat pile of things around my feet. It was a flurry of activity and it felt good to be a part of it rather than just a sidelined observer.

All too soon, black garbage bags were being passed back to Johnny and Nothing made the leap back across onto the *Scarlett Ann*. Farewells were given and I watched them go, sighing softly to myself. I suppose it was time to face the music.

I turned and Marlin was looking at me, I waited for him to say something, but he just stood there, bags in his hands looking me over for the longest time.

"Hungry?" he asked finally and I was surprised to find that I was. I nodded mutely and he jerked his head to the side.

"Come help me put this shit away and I'll fix us some dinner."

I nodded and picked up a bag with food in it and followed him to the side with a small kitchenette.

"Stay here, I need to get the generator running to power the fridge and freezer." He left me after unlocking the padlock and letting the hasp loose on the freezer then the fridge in the narrow space and soon the rhythmic grinding sound of a generator running filled the quiet.

"It's old, but it'll cool off quick," he said returning around the back of the wall.

I nodded again and he sighed, "I'm mad at you Faith, but it ain't nothing that'll last. Let's eat, we'll talk and get it figured out."

I sniffed, eyes welling and nodded when all I really wanted to do was drop what was in my hands and hug him. I felt grateful that he wasn't giving up on me and I would give anything in that moment to say or do the thing that would erase the hurt, but I knew there wasn't anything I could do. I'd opened the box and let it out into the world and once it was out, there was no putting it back in.

A gentle touch to the side of my face that I didn't see coming through the curtain of my hair left me flinching. It didn't go away though, Marlin's roughened thumb so gently, so softly grazed my bottom lip as he tipped my face up to look me in the eyes.

"I get it, Baby Girl, you've got a lot going on in there. We ain't never been the best at communicating and I aim to fix that, but first some dinner. Go on up top, I'll meet you up there and get the grill fired up."

I nodded mutely and slipped out and around to the side with stairs, taking them in my bare feet to the platform at the top. There was a gas grill bolted to the ground in one corner and the raised platform was all wood. It was beautifully put together but sadly marred with people carving their initials into the wood. In some places, it looked as if girls had painted designs, crudely done, with nail polish. Other things were drawn and written in black permanent marker.

"It happens," Marlin said with a shrug of one shoulder. "We got lucky this time. All the locks are in place and checking things out, everything is in order. Just some partiers came across it. We've had to chase a few off from time to time. It isn't a big deal."

"It looks like you all put a lot of effort into this place," I murmured.

"Yeah, a couple of summers back, one of the boys came across this video on YouTube. This place called the Manta Resort out in Africa somewhere. We built this. It's a replication structurally and was expensive as hell to build, but the whole club did it."

"Why do you call it the 'Locker' though?"

"Davey Jones' Locker, its code. Law enforcement, hell even the Coast Guard would be hard pressed to find this place, and if they did? We would probably just build another one or tow it to another location." He explained all of this while hooking a propane tank to the grill. Rising in a surprisingly fluid motion and looking back over his shoulder at me as he got the grill started.

"Fish okay? It's the only thing not frozen."

I nodded, and he nodded back carefully. He made several trips back and forth from the little kitchenette up to here and I helped where I could, which wasn't much. Marlin had a thing about people in his kitchen or invading his space when he cooked. Eventually he sent me back down to sit on the couches they had graced with cushions from some storage locker or other.

I sat on the bright orange, canvas wrapped foam in the shade and had a cold drink pressed into my hand as I stared sightlessly out over the water. Soon, Marlin set two plates of grilled fish and vegetables down on the table and eyed me with a grave expression.

"Eat," he said softly.

I did, and it was good, but in some ways it almost felt like a last meal.

Why and how did I always get myself into these awful situations without meaning to?

CHAPTER 23

Marlin

She looked both somber and deathly afraid and I could tell it was eating her up inside. The fact that she was so distressed made me wonder. I don't think Hope had it right; it was Hope's opinion that when Faith was growing up, when she was caught doing something wrong or whatever, Faith was more upset about being caught than any of the actual damage she did. That wasn't what I was seeing here. Every time I caught her looking at me she would turn those jewel bright eyes away, made brighter by her fight to suppress the tears. I think Hope was projecting more than a few of her own issues onto her younger sister, and that Faith was climbing the walls on the inside with anxiety over what she'd done. Not because she'd done it, but because it'd hurt, and damn did it ever. I was surprised to find how much.

The worst part was, that hurt was more over the fact that she didn't trust me yet. Not enough to be plain with me, at any rate. That blew, but could it really be considered unexpected? I mean shit, look what she'd gone through.

We finished our meal and I rinsed the plates over the side for now, before setting them in the kitchen. I refreshed her glass of iced tea and mine out of the pitcher I'd brought out of my fridge on the *Scarlett Ann* and held out my hand to her. She looked up at me, blinking from behind a curtain of her long blonde hair, and tentatively took my hand. I took her up top where we could watch the sunset and the rainclouds roll in.

"Will it be bad?" she asked looking at the clouds in the distance, the flicker of occasional lighting forking through them.

"Nah, a lot of rain, some thunder and lightning, but wind shouldn't be too bad. Just another thunderstorm in Florida."

She turned and looked at me and her expression was fuckin' heartbroken. I sighed and took her into my arms which felt fuckin' good with how long I'd been fighting it.

"I owe you an apology, Baby Girl," I held her close and she looked up at me sharply.

"I don't understand..."

"Oh, don't get me wrong, you owe me one too, but we'll get there in a minute."

She looked so confused that it was hard for me not to laugh; I managed though, "I'm sorry I ever made you feel like I didn't want to touch you." I murmured, and she searched my face in silence for several long moments.

I smiled but it was a sad thing and told her, "This is the part where you apologize for puttin' words in my mouth rather 'n just talking with me straight."

She closed her eyes and sagged in my arms, resting her forehead on my chest she said, "I'm so sorry for everything, for that, but mostly for hurting you... I don't mean to hurt anybody, I'm... I'm like a poison. It's just; it's just what I do, no matter how hard I try. I can't help it."

I held her tighter against me and sighed out, "Breaks my fuckin' heart to hear you talkin' about yourself that way," I told her, but the only answer I got was her breaking down into wracking sobs.

I didn't know what to say, so I just didn't say anything. Instead, I just held her, rubbing uselessly along her back over her soft jersey dress while she sobbed brokenly into my bare chest under my cut.

There was taking care of someone, then there was being responsible for them. I switched off that urge I had to tell her 'shh' or 'don't cry' and just let her have this. I didn't even lie to her and tell her it was okay, because it wasn't, but she didn't need any of that. Right now she needed to cry and let all the negative out.

"Gonna be honest with you, Baby Girl, I don't know what I'm doing here. I just know it's the right place for me to be. I get that you're hurting, but I don't know the first thing or way to go about healin' that hurt if you don't talk to me."

"I don't know what to say!" she wailed and that was the problem, right there in a nutshell. She was so worried about pleasing everyone else she couldn't do for herself anymore. You can't pour from an empty cup, and Faith had been trying for a long time, going by what she and Hope had told me about their arguments when she'd been growin' up.

I sighed and drew her back so that she could see me eye to eye, "Don't you ever filter yourself to me, Faith. You understand? I'm not going to get pissed because you feel one way or the other about somethin'. There is no right or wrong way to *feel* and you won't find me tossin' your feelin's aside. You just gotta *talk to me*, Baby. I can't promise I'll be perfect when it comes to all of these things, but I can promise to try."

"Why?"

"Why what?"

"Why would you even want to?"

"What, try?"

"Yeah."

"Better question, why d'you seem to think I shouldn't?"

She was silent, eyes searching my face, the turmoil in them clear. I waited her out patiently and finally she caved, her expression crumbling and becoming sort of desolate.

"Look at me," she uttered, "I'm a mess. I can't hold myself together and after… after everything, what could I even do?"

"How do you mean?"

"Who's going to hire a whore?" she asked harshly, "And a junkie at that?"

"You ain't either of those things, Faith." She looked at me sharply, with an incredulous '*are you serious!?*' look painted across her lovely face. I traced my thumbs gently across her cheeks and smiled.

"The way I see it, just because you were forced to do something, even for as long as you were, it don't make you that thing. You aren't a whore, you aren't a junkie, and you're only a victim for however long you choose to be."

She scoffed, and I kissed her, which changed the sound from incredulous to one of surprise. She pressed her hands against my chest and I stopped, just like that, drawing back. She blinked up at me and I asked her, "Are you okay?"

"Yeah, why'd you stop?"

I looked down at her hands and she dropped her eyes, staring at them for a considerable amount of time. Finally, her hands raised, along with her eyes. She twined them around my neck, burying her fingers into the short ponytail at the back of my head and gently drew me down. I didn't resist her, and gave her what she wanted, touching my lips softly to hers, less demanding and more giving this time.

She opened under my touch and it was beautiful, her body finally relaxing, her breath sighing out against my lips gently. I let her kiss me, and simply gave her what she was asking for, I didn't push, I didn't take more or try to find an angle, I simply took what she was giving and was grateful that she let me in.

The kiss ran its course and we pulled apart gently, the breeze ruffling her hair as the sun began to dip lower. A flash turned our attention out to sea and the band of gray clouds closing in.

"Will we be okay downstairs with the side open like that?" she asked.

"We can watch the storm for a while, sure, but we're sleepin' below deck."

"Oh."

She stood with me, watching the sun set, and the rain showers move in and it was one of the first times I think we were both at peace, or on the same page, really. Her voice, when it came again was small and quiet.

"I feel safe with you. I have ever since you picked me up, in that house."

"Yeah?" I asked.

She nodded, "The only time I can remember sleeping without the nightmares creeping in on me was back in the orchard. Remember?" she looked up at me and smiled wryly.

"How could I forget? Feels right having you in my arms." I gave her a little squeeze.

"I'm really sorry," she said and I nodded.

"I know, Baby Girl. I can see you are."

"I'll do better, I promise."

"I suspect you will, just promise me somethin' okay?"

"What?"

"If you can't talk to me, you feel uncomfortable or whatever, just tell me so and promise you'll talk to someone about it. Be it the doctor lady, or one of yer sisters. You can't do it all by yourself. Ain't no one can after all of that."

She looked pensive for a minute, eyes distant, before she nodded finally, "That's reasonable…"

"I also know it's hard as fuck for you, isn't it?"

She looked up at me sharply, and I pressed on, "You been told your whole life what's what and how to act and you just lock it all down, bottle it all up, then you're kidnapped, sold into sexual slavery, they get you hooked on some of the nastiest shit to keep you shackled and in line… Baby, it's no wonder you have a hard time speaking your heart and mind. You been nothing but punished for it for a long, long, time."

Her eyes welled and she nodded, before quickly averting her gaze toward the dipping sun. I sighed, and gathered her close, holding her tight as she gave a muffled sniff. A tension that she just about always carried had eased out of her some and I pretty much figured I'd just hit the damn nail on the head. It was a shit way to live and she'd been living that way for so long… I couldn't even. I'd grown up similarly, but at some point I'd just stopped giving a fuck what my ma and pop had to say about things. Their religion hadn't really done anything for me or any of my brothers that I could see, 'cept'n for giving us a boat load of guilt about any given subject.

Faith cuddled into me and I wrapped my arms around her tighter, kissing the top of her head as she stared sightless and thinking into the setting sun, the cloud front moving across the water in our direction until the breeze carried with it the damp, ozone scent of imminent rain.

"Come on, Baby Girl. Time to go down and take cover," I murmured into her hair. She nodded and let me lead her by the hand down the steps. At the bottom, I rounded the corner and got my keys out of my pocket. I unlocked the padlock holding the hatch shut and opened it up.

"It's dark," she said.

"Afraid?"

"Are you with me?"

"Always."

"Then no."

I smiled and she took the ladder carefully down into the bunk. I went down after her, shutting the hatch tightly against the coming rain. Our stuff was already down here, but with the growing dark, it wasn't like you could see it. Hell, it might as well be light tight already.

"I can't see, Marlin," she uttered softly, and I could barely see her myself.

"Stay there, Baby. I'll move this stuff off the bed and then I can hold you."

I shifted our bags of clothes to the floor and dug around in the top of mine. I went to her and she jumped at my light touch. I trailed fingertips down her arm and put my tee in her hands.

"Can't see a thing, Darlin'," I led her around to the side of the bed and put her hand on it, "Go ahead and change."

I felt my way around as cloth whispered in the dark and turned back the fresh bedding that'd come from my boat. I took off my cut and felt for the hook in the side of the headboard, and hung it up. The shorts I let hit the floor. I tugged up my boxer shorts and got into the bed. Faith stole in beside me and I held myself at the ready.

"Make yourself comfortable, Faith, however you'd like."

She lay her head on my chest, and cuddled in close and I dropped the sheet and light blanket over the top of her.

"It's cooler down here," she uttered.

"Yeah, it is," I kissed the top of her head and held her, and it felt right. Like this was where she was meant to be, in my arms each night, where I could keep her safe from the world that seemed pretty much dead set on stealing any light she had left. Truth be told, I was beginning to wonder that she still managed to hang on to any at all.

"What're you thinking?" she whispered into the deep night.

"How you've been hanging on for so long, and how you really shouldn't trust anybody anymore. How it's both kind of amazing and beautiful that you trust me."

"I do," she looked up, I could tell by the movement of her head against my chest. She pushed off of me and a second later her lips touched to my chin, she giggled a bit and hit her mark on the second try, her lips soft and silky against my own.

She settled back down after the slow, relatively chaste, kiss and sighed as if content. Wasn't long after that we was both asleep.

CHAPTER 24

Faith

Shifting light dancing across my eyes is what woke me. I put up a hand and opened them slowly, gasping. I hadn't really taken into account the fact that by climbing down into the sleeping quarters of the Locker that we would be going below the water. It had been dark in here the evening before. So dark, I hadn't seen the windows making up three of the four sides of the box.

I sat up slowly and stared into the blue, the fish swimming past the thick glass. It was beautiful. So peaceful, so... just... *beautiful*. I didn't have the words. I stared, and stared, and felt a tranquility fill my heart. The light that had come through was sunlight through the waves up top, casting those shifting light patterns that you would see at the bottoms of swimming pools. Like marble veins carved from light, shifting with motion gently.

An equally gentle touch at my back caused me to jump; I looked down into Marlin's bright blue eyes, vivid from the color of the deep blue around us.

"Good morning," he said, voice rough with sleep.

"Hi," I murmured.

"You sleep okay?"

I smiled; I knew my best sleep was when he was close and when I knew he watched over me. I felt self-conscious saying anything out loud to that effect. It sounded cheesy or corny, so I simply nodded in answer to his question. I looked down at him, where he lay against the white cotton sheets and swiped some of the golden strands of his shoulder length hair off the side of his face, where they'd caught in the rough stubble along his cheeks.

He was such a ruggedly handsome man. Strong, skin golden with the kiss of the sun, so deep a tan that it held an almost permanently reddish hue. I pushed myself up to my knees and threw a leg over his lean hips.

"Whoa. Hey, Faith, I just woke up," he warned, a hint of panic in his tone and I smiled. He didn't need to warn me about his erection. I knew it was there, just below the sheet. I also knew I was in a place where I wanted it. I wanted *him*, and the thought of having him inside me sent butterflies swirling in my stomach, the good kind. I felt calm, and it felt good to be confident, and in control. It felt good to trust him because I knew, if I couldn't handle it, he would stop.

I pushed the sheet down behind me and his hands found my hips over the tee-shirt, but I was feeling brave, and the first thing I did was haul it off over my head. He gasped, the cotton jersey knit slicking against my skin, warmer where his hands rested until his work roughened fingers and palms rested against my bare skin. I shivered at the delicious sensation and his grip on my hips tightened. I met his eyes and he stared me in mine, refusing to let his gaze wander.

"You're sure?" he asked, and I covered his mouth with mine.

"Do you have a condom?" I asked softly, knowing that it would still be months before I had a clean bill of health. I was sure. He looked at me, and I could tell he wasn't, so I reached behind me and let my fingers close around the scorching stiff length of him, poking out the front of his boxers. It didn't bother me that he had them and I was nude, not enough to make me want to move off of him and take them down. I wanted him with a gnawing ache in my center, and I could feel myself, slick at the apex of my thighs. *I wanted him so damn badly.*

"Oh, god, Faith," he groaned into my mouth, his hands tightening around my waist, he scrambled at the headboard and tore open a foil packet, rolling a rubber down his length for me. I raised myself up and sank onto him slowly, working him into me a little at a time. He wasn't huge, but he wasn't small either. To me, he was perfect; my body coming alive around him like it hadn't in a very, very long time when it came to sex.

I don't know if it was because of the way he stretched me, or if it was the smoldering light of pride, love and perfect trust that made his eyes glow fiercely in the deep blue light. I didn't care, I simply buried him as deeply inside me as he could go, my eyes sinking shut as he found the end of the line, and nudged it gently. God he really was a perfect fit. I bowed my head and flattened my palms against his chest, the light smattering of crisp hair under my fingers adding to the sensory overload, until I was simply drowning in everything that was Marlin.

His scent, his touch, his warmth, and I think even his love. You couldn't put up with someone as broken as I was and not love them, could you?

I met his eyes and bit my lower lip, rising off of him and sinking back down slowly, he gave an impassioned moan and closed his eyes, turning his head as if to savor my slow gasping breath.

"Feels so good," I moaned and he looked at me and smiled.

"Good, take your pleasure, Baby Girl, I love to see you move."

His hands caressed over my hips, smoothing up and down my thighs. Encouraged and emboldened by his touch, his words, and the look he was giving me, I let my inhibitions fall away the rest of the way and rode him, placing my hands over his and guiding them to my breasts. I wanted him to touch me, I wanted to make him feel as good as he was making me feel and as wonderful as riding him was… I was stuck, just on that maddening edge unable to go over.

"God, I'm so close," I gasped in a frustrated whine and Marlin chuckled softly.

"Let me help you with that," he whispered seductively and trailed his hands down my body delving one thumb between us where our bodies met.

"God*damn*, you're so wet," he growled and the warm glow of pleasure that suffused me grew incrementally, just that much more. He found my clit with his thumb, wet from my body, and teased it gently, rubbing it back and forth. I spasmed around him, tightening up my core, my body reacting to the light touch and with a wail I shattered above him, bending, back arching into a curve that must have looked extreme but felt so incredibly fucking good.

I came hard, and by some trick of his thumb, or the way he thrust his hips gently, he kept me coming for what felt like a blessed, glowing, eternity until it built and built and all became too much and laughing, shrieking, I threw myself to the side, away from his probing fingers. He slipped out of me and I mourned *that* loss, but he was, by all accounts, some sort of rascal. A pirate beneath his veneer of civility, and if it was one thing a pirate loved to do, it was plunder.

"Not done with you yet," he said with a playful smile and sat up, he got between my knees, and I got a look at him for the first time, long and glistening from where he'd been inside me. He grinned and shucked his boxers off, giving me both a little time to cool down and because they looked uncomfortable, stuck to him as they were.

"You good for more, Honey?" he asked me and I nodded, a little unsure with him being on top, but willing to try.

"You need me to stop, or do something different, you just say," he said gently and I nodded again.

He was so perfect. So attentive to my needs it was mind boggling. Always asking before taking, always making sure I was alright with whatever he did and I could see him making mental notes as we went along, for next time… and it thrilled me that he would even want there to *be* a next time.

He knelt between my thighs, and grasped my waist, making sure to give me enough room to breathe, not caging me, and giving me a significant look, and plenty of time to deny him before he slid himself back into me. I arched again and he grinned, and set a faster but still gentle rhythm.

I gazed at him with a mixture of adoration and lust and he bent, enveloping me in his bigger, far more muscular body, but instead of feeling trapped, or caged, I felt safe; protected. He kissed me and I kissed him and holding his long hair back from our faces I told him, "I want you to come, I want you to feel as good as I do."

"I already feel as good as you do, Baby Girl, maybe even better," he murmured back and I think my heart melted. He closed his eyes and listened to my lilting pants and cries like it was the sweetest music he'd ever heard. With an impassioned grunt, he thrust hard one last time and came deep inside me, which made me cringe slightly. I didn't know if I liked that sensation. It harkened back to dark places and the careless men who'd used and…

"Easy, Baby," he uttered, pressing a hand tenderly to the side of my face, "Look at me, Faith, look at me."

I looked, "I won't do that again, I didn't know. It's okay, you're okay, look at me, see me."

I nodded, "I see you," I whispered.

"I see you, too, Baby. I see you too." He was breathless, I was breathless, and we stared at one another in the blue light from beneath the ocean, safe in the little room from the world up above in a little world of our own making, both of us coming down from our first time together. He leaned down and kissed me, holding me near and I closed my eyes, a grateful tear or two escaping down my temple that my shattered mind and heart had allowed me this one thing, without too much of an incident.

"I love you, Baby Girl," he whispered suddenly into my ear and my heart shattered all over again, bursting with joy.

CHAPTER 25
Marlin

She gave this lighthearted, but broken laugh and wrapped her arms around me, pulling me down against her harder. I flattened her to the mattress and kissed the side of her neck. There wasn't any taking it back and I didn't want to. Things like that didn't just slip out if you didn't mean them. It was on par with drunken truthfulness, and truthfully, this right here weren't much different. I *was* drunk. Drunk on the woman in my arms, on the pleasure we'd shared, on her trust and her bravery in letting me share her body, to touch and delight and take delight of my own.

"Okay, come on. I bet you'll like this," I whispered smiling and curving my arms around her, delving between her hot, flushed skin and the sheets, I brought her up with me.

"Where are we going?"

"Baby Girl, we are out in the absolute middle of nowhere. Ain't another man, woman, or child for miles and miles. Let's go jump in."

She gazed at me, apprehension in her posture, and the set of her eyes, "Can we really?"

"Just you and me, and no one to tell us what the fuck to do, what do you say?"

Her face broke into one of the most beautiful smiles I'd ever seen and she let me hoist her up onto her feet. She went ahead of me, and I snagged a couple of large bath sheet towels out of the pile of crap from my boat sitting in the corner. She climbed the ladder and I got a gorgeous view as we climbed up.

Faith threw back the hatch and climbed out into the sun the rest of the way and I followed her. She gave a little look over her shoulder and without any warning, dived smoothly into the sea.

Fearless, beautiful, like some kind of water nymph that was born to it and headed home. I dropped the towels and dove in after her, coming up for air to find her treading water and laughing.

The sound sent shivers down my spine, so clear and beautiful, so *her*, I couldn't hardly stand it. She tipped herself into a back float and gazed up at the sky, her hand reaching out and finding my own. I joined her and we floated and made comments about the clouds in the sky, trailing by fluffy and white. We spoke of dreams, both before and what they were now for her and I felt the need to make every damned one of them come true for her, no matter what the cost.

I wanted for her, so bad, like I've never wanted anything before in my life. We swam for an hour, two hours? Who knew how long, before I finally helped her to the ladder and we climbed out. We dressed, I made her lunch, and we lounged under cover, out from the hot sun on the shaded, waterline deck with the couches. I think we napped, her resting against my chest, legs tangled, because it was the Captain, kicking my foot lightly that brought us both awake with a start.

"Time is it?" I asked sucking in a breath.

"Late afternoon," he sighed, "I'm hungry. Let's cook, let's eat, and let's talk. We got shit to discuss and it ain't all pretty."

Faith stirred against my chest and I looked past the Captain into a set of very dark, very lovely, and very *worried* eyes. I sighed, this was going to be a fuckin' tightrope and a half to walk, and I couldn't say that walking gently had ever really been my strongest suit.

"You okay, Bubbles?" Hope called out to her groggy sister and I felt Faith tense up like she was in trouble or some shit at her sister's voice. Too long, a conditioned response, things needed to change and the cycle needed to be busted, but how to do that and mitigate the damage? I guess there weren't no easy way, so I did what I thought was best. I drew fire.

"Hope," I grated and her eyes flicked to mine, "You doubt me to be anything less than an honorable man?" I demanded and she jerked back some, like I'd slapped her with a cold fish, right in her kisser. Faith's breaths came sharp and too close together for my liking and I tightened my hold on her to reassure, hoping that's what it did. Hope was looking me up and down; silent, calculating.

"Answer the fuckin' question, if you please."

"The fuck, Mar?" I shot the Captain a glare enough to quell him and he nodded, raising his hands, recognizing it for what it was. A brother correcting an out 'o line fellow brother, because that's almost what Hope was, wearin' the club colors like she was.

"No, I know you're a good man, Marlin. I wouldn't trust my little sister to just anybody."

"You think I'd hurt her?" I demanded.

"No."

"Then the fuck you comin' up here asking after my girl like I did?" Hope startled and Cut looked mutinous for a half second, before tacking, his mouth turning down; eyebrows going up, giving a tilt of his head as if he'd changed his mind about what he was going to say.

"You serious?" Hope demanded, and she looked like she was starting to amp up. Faith gasped and I held her just a little bit closer, steadying her.

"As a fuckin' heart attack."

The Captain chuffed a bit of a laugh and put in his two cents, "'Bout fuckin' time," he said, "Now can we all get back on the same fuckin' team and get back to what needs doin'?" he asked.

It was Hope's turn to look positively mutinous for a second bus she was looking over Faith. Her expression softened and she jerked her chin at her sister, "You okay with this, Faith?"

Faith swallowed hard, "Yes," and it was written all over her that she expected screaming or yelling to start. Hope saw it too, her shoulders dropping; she dropped onto the couch across from us and huffed in a deep breath letting it out slowly.

"As long as you're safe, and happy, that's all I want for you," she told Faith calmly, and she meant it, too.

"I am," she whispered and sat up slowly.

"Good, now can we please get something to fuckin' eat and go over this?" Cutter demanded.

"Keep your pants on," I grumbled.

"Oh fuck him," Hope waved her hand dismissively, "He's just hangry, feed him and his attitude ought to improve. It's been a long fucking day for us, trying to clean up this mess."

Faith closed her eyes and her shoulders dropped, Hope looked over at her, "Not your fault, Bubbles. If anything, it's ours for being so damned overprotective. The harder I tried wrapping you up, the more I tried to shelve you to protect you from everything, the more you fought growing up." Hope lifted one shoulder in an inelegant shrug, "Why should now be any different? Should have changed tactics a long time ago."

Faith very nearly held her breath, looking from one to the next, to the next, her gaze finally settling back on her sister. We all sort of waited to see what she would say.

"What," she cleared her throat, "What happened?" she asked and it was as good a change of subject as any, so we took it, at least the Captain did.

"I think I got Marlin off the hook for the most part," Cutter said and I raised an eyebrow at that, "Faith is another story, there ain't nothing for it. We gotta go back to NOLA so she can appear; get this mess sorted out in front of a judge."

Faith visibly wilted and I smoothed my hands up and down her arms, telling her, "Not like you ain't going without us, Baby Girl. If the Captain says it's gotta be done, it's gotta be done, but ain't no fuckin' way you're gonna face any of it without all of us at your back."

Hope smiled, "What Marlin said."

"Don't you worry about a thing, Firefly. We've contacted a lawyer out there; a dude Ruth knows. The Voodoo Bastards wouldn't steer us wrong after the solid we did each other. We'll ride out tomorrow, get this shit sorted and be home by midweek."

The Captain looked at each of us in turn and we all sort of slowly nodded, there really weren't nothing for it. I wanted this all cleared up and in my Baby Girl's rearview as fast as possible. I sorta couldn't believe we'd all forgotten about the outstanding charges. It was a call from the police that'd cracked this wide open for Hope in the first place. A bolt from the blue, fuckin' kismet, a gift from God, whatever the fuck you wanted to call it; that's what it was.

"Now if y'all don't mind, I'm fuckin' hungry. Gimme the goddamn keys to the freezer, you jackass." I laughed and dug between me and Faith, pulling the keys out of the pocket of my board shorts, and unclipping them from the ring designed to keep them there while I was in the water.

I tossed them to the Captain who swore, "Thank you fuckin' *Jesus!* You know, a little respect every now and again wouldn't be misplaced..." he ranted to a soundtrack of both Hope and Faith's laughter. Yeah, the bastard knew we all respected the shit out of him and then some; otherwise he wouldn't *be* the Captain.

We cooked, we ate; we stripped the Locker down and locked her up. The whole while Faith moved silently, wrestling with whatever demons she had over returning to that godforsaken place. We got the *Mysteria Avenge* underway. It didn't take much, there was another thunderhead moving across the water in our direction, the direction back to town, and despite the fact I owned an ultra-modern sport fishing boat, I loved to sail with the next Mariner. Cutter and I hauled anchor and ran canvas, tacking windward. The sails filled pretty quickly, and with the Captain at the helm we were underway pretty quick.

I went to Faith who stood at the starboard bow, the wind sweeping her hair at her back, blowing it in front of her. I went up behind her and let her know I was there with a gentle, "Hey, Baby Girl," but she still startled. I pulled her back against me in the circle of my arms and just enjoyed the wind and the salt and her warmth tucked against me.

"How you doin'?" I asked her.

"Scared."

"Yeah, I get that. Anything I can do?"

"No, I don't think so."

"You tell me if there is?"

"I promise," she said turning so she could lean on me, her arm snaking around my waist. I held her, and she held onto me and we sailed back to the marina, both of us lost in our own heads.

CHAPTER 26
Faith

We walked along the beach from the marina, towards Cutter's house. Marlin had asked if I wanted to walk and I had. It felt strange being on solid ground after almost two solid days on the water; I was missing the rolling motion of it. The ground not pitching underfoot was strange.

He held my hand as we walked; that felt strange too, although it was a good strange. A warm, glowy sort of strange that I never wanted to end. He stopped about midway up the beach from the long line of houses and pulled me up short. I turned, and he was regarding me, a grave expression on his face.

"What?" I asked softly.

"I don't want to lose you back down the rabbit hole of awful at this setback, Baby Girl. I like your smile and the laughing? Well, that's good too."

I smiled because of his words and it felt good. I wasn't sure how to tell him what I was feeling but I owed it to him to try.

"I'm scared. I don't want to go back there, and I don't know…" I looked out over the water, the sun beginning it's slow descent in the sky. We should still have some daylight when we made it back to the house. Hope and Cutter had taken our bags. Nothing had met them at the marina with his station wagon. He'd been perfectly willing to drive us, but I needed some time before going inside. I loved it out here in the sun and the warmth.

"Talk to me, Faith. Whatever you need to say, I'm here."

I looked up at Marlin, "I'm afraid they'll lock me up. Afraid that those men, that they'll find out and come get me. I know that's stupid…"

"Hush, ain't nothing stupid about it. Shit happened, bad shit that

I wouldn't wish on anybody and you're perfectly justified feelin' the way you do. There's a difference though; I'm gonna be there. Hope's gonna be there. The Captain, the rest of the crew; we're all going to be there and you ain't alone. Ain't none of us going to let you go or lose you without one hell of a fight, Baby Girl."

"Why?" I asked him, because I seriously couldn't fathom what he was telling me. I mean, I hadn't exactly gone out of my way the last few months or so to connect with any of his other brothers. When they talked to me, I usually smiled as politely as I could and tried to get the small talk over with as quickly as possible.

"I'm not sure you understand what being my woman means to men like us," he said gently, cupping the side of my face. His thumb grazed lightly over my bottom lip and I resisted the urge to flick out my tongue and taste him. Instead I closed my eyes and enjoyed the simple touch.

"I don't, I guess… I mean, not really." I wasn't entirely comfortable with the possessiveness of how he said it and having just made the promise to communicate better, I said so.

Marlin laughed gently, "It's true, I'll give you that. We talk like a bunch of barbarian hill men, but really, it's just us breaking something very complex into terms that any fuckin' idiot can understand."

"Okay, can you dumb it down even more for me then?"

"Nope, don't have to. You're not an idiot, Faith. I'll just give it to you straight," he put us back in motion, walking gently, and slowly beside me, his arm curving around my shoulders, protectively tucking me into his side.

"Okay," I agreed, "I'd like that. Give it to me straight."

"Not sure where to start, so how about you ask me somethin' to get us going."

"I can ask anything, and you'll tell me, just like that?"

"I promised you I would, didn't I?"

He had. He'd promised to stop wrapping me in imaginary cellophane. That he would stop shelving me when it came to decisions that regarded me and I was so incredibly grateful for that. So incredibly tired of the lot of them talking about me and what to do about this or that when I was standing right there.

"Gonna ask me something or what?" he said, snapping me out of my own thoughts. I felt my cheeks flush and laughed nervously.

"Sorry, a lot to think about, um, I guess my first question is, why would the rest of the guys do anything for me? I mean, I haven't exactly been outgoing or even nice in some cases."

"I told you, because you're my woman."

"Okay, and what does *that* mean, exactly? Like, I'm your girlfriend?"

"To the bunch of civilians here around town, yeah. But they don't have any appreciation for what that means to us. Faith, I know this is a lot, but from the minute I picked you up I felt somethin' for you and those feelings, they've just been getting stronger. Now I didn't mean to put any kind of pressure on you, sayin' what I said back at the Locker this morning…"

"That you loved me?" I asked so softly I was afraid he didn't hear it. My heart sank, and I stuttered to a stop in my tracks. He looked at me and this odd, sad little smile took up half of his generous lips. Of course he hadn't meant it; it was just a thing to say in the heat of the moment. I looked away, out over the water but he touched my face and brought me back around to look at him.

"No, don't do that…" he uttered.

"Do what?"

"Make up your mind what I did or did'nt mean, what I did or didn't say for whatever reasons in your head and accept them for truth. There's only one person who decides my truth and that's me. That's the heart of livin' the life in an MC."

I searched his face, and took a deep breath, holding it, dreading the answer, I asked the question, "Then tell me your truth, did you mean it?"

"I love you, Faith. I have for more 'n a minute. I realized it when you told me that doctor lady said you shouldn't see me no more. It's the only explanation I had for why it tore me up so bad on the inside."

Guilt settled around my shoulders, a weighted shawl of sadness mixed with regret. I let out my breath I'd been holding and returned my gaze to the water so I didn't have to see his face when I took my leap of faith and spoke my truth...

"It hurt thinking I wasn't worth anything to you. That I was just some sad, pitiful, broken head case that you were trying to help because of guilt, or whatever."

Again with those gentle, rough fingers tipping my face forward and back to look up at him. Again with those searching blue eyes, so bright with an inner fire that I ached to warm my cold, broken heart against.

"That weren't ever my truth, but I could see how it could be the one you believed. A misunderstanding, Baby Girl. May have been our first but probably won't be our last." He punctuated this statement by bringing his lips down to mine, kissing me gently but firmly, stealing my breath away on the sandy shore.

I ached with such an awful regret for that; for not trying to talk, but the fear was so great that I couldn't have, even if I had wanted to. I was so tired of being shot down and I was so afraid that it was true, and I didn't want it to be and it had almost been better *not* knowing for sure because then at least I could hold the illusion that it was possible, at least for a short while yet.

Tears spilled along with my explanation and Marlin held me to him, an arm across my back, one hand cradling my head to his chest as he swayed me from side to side, comforting me, calming me as my anxiety had me coming apart.

"It's okay, Baby Girl, but that's exactly *why*. Why my brothers will protect you. In our world I've as good as gone and made you my Ol' Lady. That means you're mine. My property; which I know sounds awful to a citizen like you, but if you give me the chance to finish explaining, I will."

He searched me out with his eyes, giving me the choice and I shut my mouth and nodded.

"Okay, so there's *things* like my boat, or my clothes. Then there's my *property*. That's a whole other ballgame. For us, we could care less about a boat or a house, or a cage to roll around in. They're just things. You lose one of them, fuck it," he shrugged, "You just go buy another or rebuild or do whatever."

"Okay, and property?" I asked quietly, understanding beginning to dawn.

"I will kill a motherfucker for you. I would lay down my life, my limb, tear my still beating heart out of my fuckin' chest if it would keep you safe and happy. You're mine to defend. The only things I won't give up for you is my club and my bike."

Again my heart filled to bursting with joy and elation, but I tried to keep enough of a lid on it. I twisted my lips hard to keep from smiling and nodded in what I hoped was a sagely fashion, "You would give up the bike over my dead body," I said lightly.

"Oh yeah?" he asked, grinning.

"Mm, I like it too much."

He threw back his head and laughed; a deep, rich and generally overpowering sound that lifted me up even more. He gathered me into his arms and took me off balance, so I had to lean into him to keep from falling. I laughed, and he walked backwards a bit in the direction of Cutter's house and we kept moving.

"I wouldn't want you to give up either of those things," I said after a time.

"Yeah? Why not?"

"Because, I feel safe with you and I think I am beginning to realize, if what you're saying is true, that it doesn't stop with you. That I'm safe no matter where I am or where I go because if it's not you, one of the other men in the club would come, would be there for me."

He positively glowed with pride, "That's exactly it, Baby Girl."

"That's what Hope's vest means, isn't it?" I asked. "It's like that with her and with Cutter."

"Yep, that's exactly what that means."

"Except Hope can take care of herself," I frowned with confusion.

"So Hope's cut isn't the same as what, say, I would give you. If you wore my rag, and you don't have to, it would mean a lot to me if you would, but if you're not ready or okay, then you really don't got to, I…" I put both of my hands over his mouth and pressed to get him to stop talking, laughing lightly that I could make this big giant of a biker spew such stuttering utter nonsense.

"Stop, just stop!" I cried.

"What would be the difference between mine and my sister's what did you call it?"

"Cut."

"Yes, cut, what would be the difference?"

"Yours wouldn't have the club's colors. It was put to a special vote and that's why she got it. She's Cutter's Ol' Lady, but she's more 'n that."

"Colors? You mean the octopus patch?"

It was his turn to laugh, "Kraken, yes, the kraken dragging down the ship."

"So what goes there?" I asked.

"Nothing, it's usually just left empty."

I made a face, "Well that's boring! You should really consider putting a flower or something pretty there. You know, for the girly girls."

"Baby, we're bikers, it wouldn't look all that badass and besides that, we don't usually attract girly girls and when we do, they ain't much for staying."

I thought about that and nodded, we were probably a good ten or so houses away from Cutter's by now and I sighed inwardly. It was still hard being around a lot of people for me. One or two was about my limit for comfort. I looked down at my hand, fingers linked with Marlin's. Maybe things were different now, though. I mean, I wasn't exactly single, now was I?

I thought about things hard while Marlin idly swung our linked hands between us and came to a decision.

"I'll wear it, if you want me to," I said softly.

"My cut?" he asked like he almost didn't believe what he was hearing.

"Yes."

"Property patches and all?"

"I'm yours, aren't I?" I asked.

"As long as you want to be, Baby Girl, and not a moment more. You tell me to fuck off, that's what I'll do."

I stopped in my tracks, the back stone deck, of Cutter's house was visible and there were a bunch of The Kraken on it. Some were looking our way, most had a beer or a joint in their hand. The movable metal fire pit had a cheery fire started in it and I realized it was growing dimmer out here.

"I don't want you to go, Marlin. I can't think of anyplace I would rather be than with you." I looked up at him and his mouth came down on mine, urgent and passionate and I returned the kiss gladly, feeling lighter than I could ever remember.

Cheers, whistles and howls went up before Cutter's voice raised, "Knock it off you fuckin' animals!" he called and there was laughter, but not at me and I couldn't care.

"I love you," he repeated against my mouth but I couldn't bring myself to say it. Not yet, because I couldn't help but feel like in some ways I was using him and that wasn't love, or right at all. At least not according to the way my sister had raised me.

I shoved that unpleasant mix of feelings aside, tucking myself into Marlin's side as we walked up the beach, towards the house and his brothers, at least in arms, or leather, or whatever. Vowing silently that I would talk with him about that soon, before he could start to worry that everything was totally one sided. I'd sworn to him that I would talk to him; that I would communicate. I trusted him at his word that he would be the calm and rational person he'd displayed thus far and that if he weren't; because no one was perfect, that nothing would be beyond our fixing because everything he had had me agree to, had sounded so perfectly reasonable.

I huddled into his side, shyly and we moved among the rest of the guys, each of them smiling, and telling me they were glad I was okay. Some simply smiling bigger and giving me a wink. All of them warm and all of them putting me further at ease. Displaying everything that Marlin had told me. It put me at ease, knowing that this might really be for real and not too good to be true like so many other things I'd encountered in my life.

It was probably the first night I had spent among them where I truly felt at peace, despite knowing that it would all be shaken up with the long ride back to Louisiana that was supposed to happen the next day.

CHAPTER 27
Marlin

I held Faith close in the dark, and l knew she was awake. She was thinking so loud I could almost hear it and had been at it, staring at the rain pattering against the glass, the blue flashes of light from thundershower illuminating those glittering gems of her eyes. The party had wrapped up pretty quick when the rain had started coming down. The bikes had all been moved, parked in the stone garage on the other side of the house in anticipation of the rain before it'd come, so the guys had all just come in and bunked down where they could. My bike had apparently been brought in the crash truck. Johnny had used my spare set of keys for Cutter and my brothers to get into my garage back at the marina. Sometimes Johnny had some actual fuckin' sense going on that didn't revolve around just him. Who knew?

"What are you thinking about so hard, Baby Girl?" I'd asked, and she shook as if waking from a dream.

"I feel a lot of things… I'm still trying to sort everything out and I feel almost guilty that I haven't said 'I love you too.'"

"I don't expect you would, or even that you do, and that's okay."

"It's not, though. I mean, I feel *safe* with you, I feel *relieved* and *protected* and *good* when I'm with you… but does that all equal love, or does it equal 'I'm using you?'"

God, it made me smile to hear all that; it really did, despite her second guessing last remark.

"So what if you are, Faith? Would it make you feel better if I told you that I'm perfectly okay with you using me if it makes you feel safe, relieved, protected, and good? As far as I'm concerned you just told me that you feel *loved*, and that's been my goal for something like the last month."

"But that's not fair to you," she tried to protest.

"Is so, so don't sweat it."

She scoffed, "How is it fair to you?" she demanded and I kind of liked this little glimpse of confidence I was getting. It meant she really was comfortable with me.

"Because if I do for you everything that you're sayin'; that makes me a *man*, Sweetheart. It means I'm doing everything right *as* a man and that puts me on top of the fuckin' world."

She exhaled and did what she did that morning, hoisted herself into a sitting position, throwing a leg over my hip and straddling me. Her hands rested lightly on my chest over my heart, which I admit, beat faster when I saw her like this. She looked down at me, my tee slipping off one of her delicate, slim shoulders, her hair framing her face and tumbling loose.

She was achingly beautiful in the subtle, deep night lighting, even though she was regarding me with a queer look on her face. She leaned down, holding my hair back from my face, hands gentle on the sides of my face, even as her hair curtained us from the rest of the room. Her lips met mine and I kissed her. I couldn't help that my cock stirred between us, and I had a moment of anxiety that it might turn her off or scare her off of me.

I must have tensed up or something because she drew back, searching my face with those typically jewel bright eyes, but the lighting, or lack of it in here, did something to them, turning them ghostly and near colorless. They were clear, just held none of that aquamarine hue I loved so much.

"Sorry, Baby Girl, I ain't got much control over things like –" she placed her fingertips against my lips to silence me.

"I know," she whispered and I cursed myself silently. Seemed she'd been fine with it, but my saying something about it wasn't okay by her. Too damn late to take it back now. I needed to learn to live in the moment with Faith and let our bodies do the talking when she instigated anything.

She slipped off my lap and tumbled elegantly to my side, cuddling back in and laying her head on my chest. Her arms took up a defensive posture against her chest and I sighed, wrapping her up in my arms, smoothing a hand up and down her back.

We both closed our eyes, listening to each other's breath and the rain pattering down against the window glass. The perfect soundtrack to lead into a deep, restful sleep.

**

The next morning I woke before she did, her head pillowed on my bicep, head tucked beneath my chin. My free arm was curved protectively over her body but I was stiff as hell for not having moved all night. When I tried to extract myself gently, Faith's eyes flew open; that glorious color returned full force with the daylight.

"Morning," I murmured, voice rough with sleep and need for a cigarette. I'd run out the day before but I'd snagged a pack off my boat at the marina last night. They were callin' my name. It was almost as good as that first cup of coffee to be honest.

"Hi," her soft lyrical voice was soft with wonder like she almost couldn't believe I was here or that she'd slept the whole night through. Truth was she hadn't, not really. She'd started whimpering and twitching in her sleep, heralding one of her nightmares coming on and I'd done the only thing I could think of. I'd held her and sung *Hope Never Dies* to her. By some fuckin' miracle that'd calmed her shit right down and she'd sunk right back down into sleep, pulling herself tight into me, her fingers curling in my hair. I chalked it up as a total win.

"What time is it?" she asked.

"By the smell, time for us to get our asses up, dressed and ready to ride. Breakfast is on down there." She lifted her head and took a deep breath, smiling; bacon made me smile, too.

Up, showered, dressed for the road, and seated at the table in record time. I pulled Faith into my lap; the giant table in the dining room only held eight where the patio table held a dozen, so all but one seat was taken by a brother. Faith hid behind a curtain of her hair, blushing furiously at the stares and grins and I wrapped my knuckles on the wooden table.

"I know you fuckers are jealous, I would be too in yer place, but knock it off with the fuckin' staring. You're makin' my girl uncomfortable."

Wild laughter met my demand and Faith turned that much redder. I swear, she blushed any harder it'd be to her knees. Hope set a couple of plates down in front of us loaded with bacon, cheesy eggs, and toast and we ate but *good*.

Piling out the front door, rucksacks and road gear in hand and over shoulders, I saw we had Stoker along for this ride in addition to Beast, The Captain, Hope, Radar, Lighting, and Atlas. Damn near the whole crew was here. Trike, our Prospect, and Gator who was nursing an ankle injury, were over near the crash truck. Pyro came out the house's front door and Nothing was pulling in on his bike, new tires on it. *Shit*, that made pretty much the whole gang then.

"Alright, listen up!" The Captain bellowed and all eyes went to him. He part and parceled the information we needed out and we listened. Faith fidgeted nearby and Hope caught my eye, giving me a chin lift. I raised an eyebrow and she nodded and I tuned back in to what the Captain was saying.

After he shut his yap, Hope came over and handed me the cut I'd requested. I shook it out and had a look, smiling. 'Property Of' was loud and proud on the top rocker, 'Marlin' across the bottom and in the center? Where our colors would be if she were a brother, well it wasn't *quite* a rose, but it was something. A marlin fish arching out of the water, fierce. I'd asked the guys last night and they all thought it was a fine idea. No fuckin' idea how she'd pulled it off so fast, then I realized, it wasn't a patch but rather embroidered right into the leather. Must have been one of those shopping mall embroidery kiosk deals. Didn't much care, it looked great and bonus points? The front of the cut was just as good. 'Faith' was displayed on the name flash, and opposite on the lower portion of the cut, just like I'd asked, was a red and black A&E band logo patch.

"It's beautiful," Faith said and I looked up from the cut in my hands and over at her, turning my head I held it out for her to slip into. She did and turned obediently, and I zipped up the front. It was ladies cut, again like I'd asked and the sides accentuated her feminine curves. Faith had pretty ample breasts as compared to

Hope, and the cut, worn with just a tank or nothing at all would display them to perfection if she were ever so inclined. I know I hoped to see the day her confidence returned enough for it.

The guys stood around clapping and cheering for a minute and Faith spent a few minutes blushing fiercely before the Captain told us all, pretty much to stow it and to fall in. Hope was riding herself, not that any of us saw any different coming out of her, and we did as commanded, firing up, following hand signals and getting in our places in the procession.

I was a little afraid for Faith, both for the long ride and the destination, but being surrounded by all the guys, she seemed a little more at ease with having to go. She had her shades on, so it was hard to read her face but what I could see didn't hold lines of tension and she didn't grip me any harder or softer than she usually did which was a good deal.

The ride was long and pretty punishing with the heat, humidity, and all the riding gear. We were sweatin' in all that black leather, and the wind didn't really do *shit* to cool you off when it got up above ninety degrees. I think all of us were draggin' some serious fuckin' ass when we pulled onto the rural highway through Jefferson Parish, heading into the city.

The plan was to bunk down with the Voodoo Bastards tonight, and meet with the lawyer in the morning. That plan, however, was shot to shit the second we got lit up by the Jefferson Parrish Sherriff cruiser that'd fallen in behind the line. Of course, we weren't doin' nothin' wrong; we never did when we were ridin' pack like this. It was always best to keep a low profile, and by that I mean minding your P's and Q's in regards to speed, signaling, and what have you. Was hard to be considered anything low except 'life's' to citizens when you thundered down the road however many strong.

We did what we were supposed to by citizen law, and pulled over. The douchebag cop sat in his cruiser running plates, so a lot of us got off our bikes and stretched the stiffness out before the second cruiser pulled up. I guess I couldn't blame the one cop. When you pulled over a bunch of bikers for no good reason, then you probably wanted more cops to back your play. Faith stood with me, Hope, and Cutter and looked pretty much scared to death.

"They're going to hassle us, take all our information and then they're going to take their sweet time running all of us," Cutter said grimly, I knew it as well as he did, so did Hope. The procedure is pretty fuckin' routine. Hope was on her cellphone in a flash when the second cruiser pulled up along the line of bikes and parked at the front. Some of the guys had theirs out as well, to start recording.

The door to the cruiser up front popped open and the deputy got out. Faith looked up at me, lost and afraid…

"If they run my information, they'll know about the warrant and they'll arrest me, won't they?" she whispered.

"Yeah Baby Girl, but it'll be okay…" I was cut off by the deputy.

"Identification, all a y'all, right now; let's see 'em," he demanded and he already had his hand on the butt of his gun. Jesus-fucking-Christ. I handed him mine and Faiths, he took Cutter's and Hopes.

"Hang that up!" he barked at Hope and Cutter who were each on their phones. Hope defiantly read off the dude's badge number to whoever was on the other end of the line before hanging up and sticking her phone in her back pocket. Probably one of her cop friends if I had to guess.

Cutter was on the phone with the lawyer that the Voodoo Bastards crew had set us up with. The deputies split the licenses between them and ordered us that we all stay where we were while they returned to their cruisers to run them. A third one pulled up across the street and we were all left standin' with our dicks waving while they went to running us all down.

I pulled a cigarette from my pack and lit up. Faith stood stoic, disappearing inside of herself, tears starting to drip down her face as the terror took hold. She'd told me she remembered enough about gettin' arrested the first time to know she never wanted to have it happen again while she was sober and here it was about to happen and there wasn't fuck all I could do about it.

"Gimme your cut, Baby Girl," I murmured and she looked up at me stricken.

"For safe keeping, Bubbles," Hope promised her and she was taking hers off and handing it to Cutter. I raised an eyebrow at her and she looked determined, so I kept my fuckin' trap shut. The Captain did likewise.

"It's okay, Bubbles, I promise. Nothing is going to happen to you," Hope hugged her sister from the side as the dickcheese deputy came back.

"You," he grabbed Faith by the arm and she yelped; a half fearful, half pained sound and I felt myself growl and take a step forward.

"Watch it," I grated at him and Faith looked at me, helpless, lost, but also concerned.

"It's okay, Marlin, I'm okay," she said, voice strained, words coming too fast. Tryin' to be brave and failin' miserable at it.

"Up against the car, Sugar," the deputy said, smug. He pushed Faith up against the front fender, grinding his cock into her ass.

"Hey!" I barked and hands were on me, my brothers holding me back from lunging forward.

"Female officer!" Hope shouted at Faith, "Demand a female officer, Faith!"

"I-I-I d-demand a female officer!" Faith stammered out, and the deputy scoffed.

"Ain't none on duty and you're wanted on a warrant on account of you're a whore, so I don't see why you should protest havin' a man's hands on you none."

He said it clear as fuckin' day, all cheerful with a side of condescending; the cocky *bastard*. All of us fell quiet, holding our collective breaths stunned...

"You son of a bitch!" I burst out, when it registered what he'd said; I mean we were all so fuckin' floored that it took time to sink the fuck in. I lunged at him and my brothers held me back. Shouting from all sides and that motherfucker had my girl pinned against his fuckin' cruiser, his hands gliding over her in the raunchiest, most vile fuckin' farce of a pat down any of us had seen.

Hope looked at Cutter and they exchanged looks. I think I heard her say something to the effect of "Here goes my career," before *she* marched forward and popped the son of a bitch right in the fucking face. She immediately leaned over the cruiser beside Faith; palms flat to the faded metal before one of the other shit bags slammed her down hard, cuffing her with unnecessary force.

Cutter stood impassive in that way that told me he was going to end somebody's world and I stopped struggling, breathing hard, all of us watching as they shoved first Hope, then Faith cuffed in the back of the patrol car. None of us had any words, and the rest of us, we were all free to go after having our licenses tossed at us.

"Trike, Gator, load Hope's bike into the back of the truck," Cutter ordered in that creepy sort of detached calm way of his.

The guys had let me go, my jacket and cut hanging on me askew. I jerked my arms and the leather settled where it belonged.

"What the fuck we gonna do, Captain?"

"Meet with the fuckin' lawyer back at the Voodoo Bastard's. He's meeting us there. Likely they'll be arraigned tomorrow. They just gotta make it through the night." He turned and looked up and down the rows of bikes.

"Nothing! Beast!" he barked, "Set up shop outside the jail until they trespass you, then call it in and fall back. Be a presence, make sure they know our women are going to be missed and it'll be fuckin' noticed if they're abused."

"Aye, Captain!" They both shouted in unison and they got on their bikes, taking off after the line of cruisers that were starting to distort in their retreat up the road with the heat patterns raising off the blacktop.

"Radar, you get all that?" I asked.

"Oh yeah, we got it all from like four different angles," he answered.

"Good, fuckin' make it go viral." Cutter ordered.

"On it, Captain."

"Fuck me swingin'," I uttered, leaning over, hands on my knees.

"Too, right," Cutter agreed.

Too fuckin' right.

CHAPTER 28
Faith

I bent over my knees and keened. I couldn't stop crying. Hope kept talking to me, I could hear her voice controlled and even, I just couldn't make sense of what she was saying through the mad jamble of panic going on inside my heart and head.

"Shut the fuck up!" the policeman bellowed from the front seat and I shut up, like flipping a switch. *If you don't do what they say, they will just rape you longer and hurt you more.* The voice in my head was both practical and cruel, and worse… it was right. I looked at Hope and mouthed 'I'm so sorry,' but all she did was shake her head at me. Her dark eyes stormy and unreadable.

I stared out the grate in front of the window at the scenery whizzing by and felt lost. Marlin had let them take me, but he couldn't stop them. I knew that. If he had, he would just be in trouble too and they would have separated us anyways. His brothers had done the right thing in holding him back, but a part of me feared I would never see him again.

I looked at Hope, both of us were handcuffed and neither could do anything to comfort the other, but leave it to my big sister to figure out a way anyways.

"'Mere Bubbles, lay your head on my shoulder."

I did what she told me to do and I felt better. She kissed the top of my head and whispered, "It's okay, I'm here. I'll always be here. You just do what I do, say what I say. Okay?"

"Okay," I whimpered brokenly and hated that the sound had come out of me.

"You gonna give us some hot lesbian action back at holding?" The deputy asked from the front seat and Hope scowled.

"Break your nose?" she asked. He scowled into the rearview.

"No, bloodied it good, and you're gonna pay for it too."

"Knew I should have gone for your balls, but if you're making threats against defenseless cuffed up women, then I guess I made the right call the first time. You don't have any."

"Fucking little cunt, I'm gonna fuck you real good," he threatened and I felt myself blanch.

"Gonna have to find it first," Hope shot and I kicked her foot with mine.

"Hope, stop!" I hissed, afraid.

"Don't worry, Faith. He can't, and won't, do anything," she said and sounded absolutely sure of herself. I bit my bottom lip and we made the rest of the drive to the jail in silence.

We were processed, and it wasn't *as* bad, because there were female officers in the jail and they, shockingly, acted professional. More professional than the deputies who had brought us in, but they were there too, for a while. Soon after our arrival, a man in plain clothes from New Orleans showed up. He spoke to one of the jailers in a deep rumbling Cajun accent and introduced himself as a detective.

"Joe!" Hope called out when she'd seen him, and she jerked her head in my direction. I looked at Hope and she gave me that silent look like everything was going to be okay. Her deep, dark, eyes saying without words that this Joe was on our side. I nodded and he asked me to stand up and to go with him.

I debated and he said low so no one could hear, "C'mon Cher, no one's gonna do nutin' with a big city type here. Hope can take care of herself. Let's go talk." I got up and followed him and he took me into a little box of a room with a table and two chairs. I sank into the one he pulled out for me, shaking.

"Now, I'm a friend of your sister's," he said gently, "An' I'm gonna keep you in here as long as I can for her and away from those officers that brought you in…"

We talked and he was kind, though we did have to go over difficult subjects surrounding my captivity. When he brought me out, hours later, the sun had gone and Hope was still sitting, leaning nonchalantly in the same row of DMV-like seats, her hands cuffed in front of her like mine were. She had a split in the corner of her lip, and her eyes sparked fury, but she seemed otherwise unharmed.

"You alright, Cherie?" Joe asked her and she nodded. I sat down next to her.

Joe nodded, and sucked his teeth considering, he caught one of the officers by her sleeve and demanded, "What happened here?"

The female officer made a face and looked pointedly at one of the male officers across the room, "Resisting Babbineaux."

"Uh huh, put 'em in holding together. Might calm her shit down some."

"Both of you come with me," she walked us to a cell across from us and opened the big metal door. Thick glass left us visible to the room and she locked us inside. Hope stuck her hands out a slot in the door and the cuffs were taken off, then she motioned for me to do the same.

I looked around at the stark, white walls, the stink of desperation filling my nose and finally looked at my sister as the handcuffs came free and I withdrew my hands from the little portal.

"I don't understand…" I moaned and hated how scared and defeated I sounded.

"I know, there was no time to explain, it happened all on the fly, come here." She dropped onto one of the benches ringing the room and I sat down beside her.

"Here's what's up, Bubbles. I had some problems with these assholes when I came to get you. They'd let you go with those dicks before I could get here and it pissed me off. I felt like I'd gotten so close, but yet was back to square one, you know?" I nodded, and listened to my sister, rapt.

"So when they pulled us over, I knew they didn't have a reason. I also knew it meant you were going to get picked up. I called Joe; he was one of the detectives that raided the place where you got picked up the first time. I knew if I could get him down here to interview you, that it'd put these fuckers on notice. I'm glad I did it too." She sniffed, eyes welling with angry tears and my heart gave a fractured ache.

"When that son of a bitch put his hands on you, I knew you were going to need more than just Joe here to watch your back. Felt really good to punch him, just sayin', and I'd fucking do it again in a heartbeat. Nobody, and I do mean *nobody*, disrespects my girls in front of me like that without paying some kind of price."

"Oh, Hope," I grabbed my sister and hugged her fiercely, tears sliding down both our faces. I sniffed and she laughed a little brokenly.

"What do you need me to do?" I asked, making the decision that I needed to be an agent of my own rescue for a change. That if my sister were going to be brave, possibly even throw her career away for me, that at the very least I could pretend to be strong just long enough until we were both clear of this mess.

As if she'd read my mind that was almost exactly word for word, what my sister told me: "Just be strong, Bubbles. Okay? Just be strong for us and trust us. Believe in us that we'll get you out of this mess."

I nodded and linked fingers with her, "What about you?" I asked, not fully satisfied with simply worrying about my own hide.

"Don't you worry about me, Little Sister, I've got this and what I can't handle up front, the guys have got my back and will help me handle when I'm in a better position to do it." There wasn't one iota of doubt or worry in my sister's voice. So strong was her conviction, that I let myself believe, despite all evidence to the contrary, that things were going to work out and everything was going to be just fine.

CHAPTER 29
Marlin

I felt caged and I hated that I could feel this way knowing that my girl was the one behind physical bars, *with those fuckin' animals.* I was smoking like a fuckin' chimney listening to the Captain and that lawyer of Ruth's talk it out. I didn't sleep; instead I parked my ass on one of the picnic tables out front of the compound's doors staring out at the green slats in the chain link. The bikes parked to either side of the cement slab of a drive gleaming softly in the diffuse light of the half-moon hangin' high in the sky.

Cutter dropped onto the table beside me, propping his booted feet on the bench, much like me. I sucked in a drag and dropped my cig into the coffee can full of 'em at my hip.

"How are you not goin' fuckin' crazy?" I asked him.

"Hope can take care of herself and then some; I ain't got nothin' to worry about 'cept gettin' your girl out intact. You been doin' good with her, you two been findin' some happy in each other. It's nice to see."

"Thanks," I said and sighed out. "I'm just worried about how far this might set her back."

"Won't know that until we get her out tomorrow."

"Think the lawyer has a shot at making that happen?"

"Pretty sure."

"And Hope?" I asked when the Captain became more guarded.

"Probably not, she assaulted a cop. There's more, the Russians have those hick fuckin' cops in their pocket. Ruth says they're bad business and might not give up now that the girls are here and they have a scent to follow."

We searched each other's faces for a long, drawn out minute and Cutter asked, "You still good buddies with that orange grower?"

"Bobby? Yeah, what 'cha thinkin'? I should take Faith out there instead of the home front?"

Cutter was nodding scraping his bottom lip between his teeth, "Yeah, at least until all of us are back in town."

I nodded, too; saying to him, "You know Faith ain't gonna wanna leave Hope here, locked up by herself."

"So don't give her a choice. You saw her, Bro. It's too soon, she ain't gotta be nor *should she* be strong. You feel me? You need to get her the fuck out of here at the first opportunity and get her back on track and makin' progress again. 'Sides," he slid of the table and stood on the cracked concrete, "If Hope is anyone's responsibility she's mine, bein' my woman an' all."

I nodded, that more than anything told me how much it bothered the Captain that Hope was locked up with her sister. Even though he'd agreed with the course of action, it didn't make it any easier to be on the outside, separated and all thing's said and done, helpless. Helpless didn't sit well with men like us.

"I'd better call Bobby," I said, sliding my phone out of the inside pocket of my cut.

Cutter jerked his head in a sharp nod, "You do that," he said and slapped me on the back of my shoulder before heading in.

I thumbed my way across the screen through menus and pulled another cigarette from my pack, sticking it between my lips and thumbing the wheel on a cheap plastic lighter. I lit the cancer stick and breathed deep as the deep trill of the ringer droned in my ear.

Shit, I was gonna get his fuckin' voicemail.

"Yeah, hello?"

"Bobby?"

"Jimmy, hey, what's up, Man?"

I thought for a moment and finally breathed out, taking another drag on my cigarette I said, "I need to ask you, probably the biggest favor I've ever asked in our lives…"

Bobby was quiet for several tense seconds before wherever he was, the noise in the background disappeared and he said, "What's going on, man? You got my attention."

I explained it all. I'd been avoiding telling him much about Faith since the morning, weeks ago, he'd found us sleeping in his orange grove. It wasn't my usual thing to do and he knew it. We'd been friends for a real long time.

He listened and when I finished he said the only thing I could and would say if our roles were reversed.

"Yeah, Man. Think nothing of it, come on down. The guest room'll be ready and waiting for as long as you need it."

"Thanks Bobby, it's just until the MC gets back with Hope and we're in a better position to handle things."

He snorted, "You like to forget that I was your brother long before any of them other fuckers were."

I winced, he was right, and he'd had the opportunity to be one of The Kraken back in the days before Cutter had been our Captain, but for some reason Bobby and the dude that'd been P. before Cutter had never seen eye to eye. Bobby walked before making it out of his hang around cut and was never one to let go of a grudge. I was just both lucky and blessed that he had enough sense to remember just *who* his grudge was with for the most part. He sometimes let his grudge against Mac, the guy who'd started the club, bleed onto my club colors, but it never went further than the occasional biting comment.

We'd done everything together growing up; I think on a deep level it hurt my best friend that he didn't share this with me too.

"Thanks, Man. You don't know how much I owe you for this."

"I look forward to meeting her for real this time."

"Just, you know, you gotta be careful sorta; she spooks real easy."

"I get it man, we'll talk more when you get here."

"Could be a long stay depending on how things go…"

Again he made a rude noise, blowing me off, "It'll give us time to catch up some seeing as I haven't exactly made the time to come down your way. I need a new foreman… bad."

"Hey, Marlin!" Radar called from the open doorway.

"Shit, Bobby, I gotta go. I'll see you soon. Get a six pack in the fridge."

Bobby laughed, "There's *always* a six pack in my fridge in case you stop by. See you soon."

"Yeah, see you soon." I hung up.

Radar gave me a chin lift that indicated I needed to come inside for a piece of business or other so I stubbed out my cig and got up, stretched and made my way back inside.

There was some more politicking to be done before we bunked down. I hated politics, but I couldn't deny I had an eye and a practiced mind for 'em. You had to back in the days under Mac. I think it's why Cutter had put me up for VP. I never quite did fully understand that move but the Captain was a guy that was wise beyond his years and pretty fuckin' fair. We followed him for a reason.

The night was long, sleep was short, and we pretty much found ourselves riding for the courthouse at first light. We knew, thanks to Ruth's lawyer guy, when the girls were going to be arraigned and we needed to be there. The lawyer was pretty much sucking the club's last reserves bone dry, but it'd been a unanimous vote with the understanding among the club that more money was always easy to acquire. We had our ways; we just hadn't had to resort to 'em in a while. I guess we would as soon as we got back home, I was okay with that. I would work eighteen hour days for the rest of my fucking life if I had to, just to make sure Faith stayed free and could really put this behind her once and for all.

Enough was enough already.

CHAPTER 30
Faith

The courtroom was stark, and I couldn't be near Hope. They seated us apart from each other, but when I saw them all in the gallery I didn't mind so much. One side of the seating area was devoid of anyone, but behind the short wall that the defense table was in front of? Well, the first few rows of professional looking people in their suits and jackets, briefcases and file folders overflowing and in some cases spilling out onto the floor immediately gave way to densely packed benches full of bikers. The first two rows were familiar faces, from Florida, Marlin's among them. His blue eyes searching each face in turn until his gaze landed on *me*. At that point, his stare became locked, though his expression was neutral and carefully guarded.

Past the men of The Kraken were an even rougher looking lot, though the orange bandanas and yellow and white accent colors that I had grown so used to seeing, instead gave way to purple and gold. They wore their jackets and tee shirts but their leather vests, or cuts, remained conspicuously absent. I bit my lower lip and scanned the room. The bailiffs seemed tense and it dawned on me, that in here, they may not have been allowed to wear their cuts. It was clear that the police didn't like the club, but I wasn't sure why. They hadn't done anything wrong, but then again I suppose it was like any other thing. The cops in the jail where Hope and I spent the night saw me as 'whore' and not even human. My sister, I guess they lumped in with the MC, which they were convinced was a gang... even though they didn't act like one, at least not like any of the ones I'd grown up around in California.

I didn't know the difference, and I didn't care about it either... I just wanted to go home and I was a little surprised that in such a short amount of time, that I felt like Ft. Royal *was* home.

It'd only been a few months… two months? I'd lost track.

"All rise…"

I stood because everyone else stood, even though we were set apart in a little box to the side, much like a jury except the actual jury box sat vacant across the room and held more seats.

I didn't listen to the goings on, or the others as they each, one by one, stood and were led by a jailer to their lawyer's side. Well, I didn't pay attention to the first woman; the second was my sister as they were going in alphabetical order by last name. I paid attention to *her*.

"Still, it was an assault on a police officer; I'm not inclined to treat that lightly." The judge said, and I felt hollow inside. Hope stood stoic and didn't look surprised in the slightest.

"Your Honor," her lawyer began and laid out a very convincing argument, even going as far as to show the judge a video of our arrest on a cell phone, which the judge didn't look at all happy about when she viewed it.

"As much as I would like to grant Ms. Andrews bail, the best I can, *and will*, do is grant her an expeditious trial date. Given what you have there, I am certain either a reasonable plea agreement can be reached or any good judge worth their salt would acquit. I'm sorry, Ms. Andrews, but my hands are tied by law in this state." The judge did indeed look sympathetically at my sister as she picked up her gavel.

"Remand," she said shortly and tapped the gavel's rest and she seemed weary a bit.

I stared at Hope wide eyed as she was led from the courtroom, right past the box I was sitting in. She smiled at me, dazzling and said as she passed in a harsh whisper, "It's okay, Bubbles. The guys will take care of you. A few weeks and this'll all be over."

Wait, a few *weeks*? Had she just said a few, *weeks!?*

I shifted in my seat and kept quiet even though I desperately wanted to cry out, wanted to jump up and run to my sister and hug her and cry and tell her how sorry I was and that this was all my fault and that I'd failed her again, except I knew deep down in my heart of hearts I hadn't. I had been so good by the side of that police car. I had done everything he'd told me to do and I had tried so very hard not to scream and not to cry. I had cried, but I'd held it in for the most part.

Hope had taken it upon herself, knowing full well the consequences, to hit that evil bastard, landing herself in this situation. I watched the jailer lead my sister out of sight and stared blindly after her for long moments afterward. I didn't hear anything being said, barely registered the gavel ringing sharply. When I turned, it was to see the men in purple and gold and some of The Kraken too, calling out, berating the judge and the lawyer for Hope not getting bail. Cutter stared after where Hope had gone too, a stony expression on his face and a glint of fury tempered with determination in his warm brown eyes.

Marlin stared at me still, and I met his gaze. A spark, something real even as it was intangible passed between us and my rising panic at wondering what would happen to my sister calmed. Marlin was calm, Cutter was calm, both of them stoic and steady which meant they had a plan and if they had a plan the best thing I could do was hold on. The best thing I could do was stay calm, hold on, and do nothing to jeopardize whatever they had in place. I trusted Marlin. I trusted him and my sister Hope implicitly, so that meant I needed to stay calm, I needed to not fall apart, and so I simply concentrated on slowing my breathing using exercises Dr. Sheindland had taught me and waited.

The roaring in my ears took much longer to subside than the men in the gallery. All it took was one word from Cutter for The Kraken to fall silent, as for the rest of the men, a heavy bald man, probably a few years younger than Cutter, said to knock it off and just like that, they did.

The judge was not amused, you could tell by her expression, and I hoped that when it was my turn, it wouldn't hurt me. I mean, she'd know I was with them. Not only did I still wear my riding leather, she'd watched Hope hit the deputy that'd been groping me, she'd seen me in the video.

"*Breathe,*" Marlin mouthed at me, and I resumed Dr. Sheindland's exercises.

"Faith Dobbins, one count failure to appear…" I shut out the bailiff's droning voice as I was hauled to my feet by one arm roughly, by one of the jailers.

The gavel made sharp reports again even as the gallery erupted in more than a little outrage, but the judge didn't pay them any mind; she addressed the jailer and when I looked up, I could see why… it was one of the other deputies that'd been there when I'd been arrested. Thankfully, not the same one who'd put his hands on me.

"Got my partner put on leave," he breathed. "You're going to pay for that," he threatened though no one else could hear it over the judge, her gavel, and the men in the gallery. He led me over to the same lawyer who was taking up position at the podium built into the defense table and I blinked stupidly at him. He smiled and it was a reassuring one.

"Just a few minutes more, they'll take you back to the jail and process your release, I promise."

"Mister Jeffries, go ahead," the judge ordered.

I could see why his suit was so expensive. He was good, *he was really good.* Before I knew it, he had launched into explaining that I was still in treatment. He even had documents to back it up, handing them through the bailiff to the judge. Copies of records from both a doctor whose name I didn't know and Dr. Sheindland. The first doctor had supposedly treated me in Kentucky for heroin withdrawal, as well as a host of other physical problems as a result of being held captive, before I'd joined my sister in Florida to receive treatment from Dr. Sheindland. When the judge had asked what Dr. Sheindland was treating me for, he summed it up rather succinctly by stating I was being treated for 'a host of mental trauma as a result of a textbook case of human trafficking.'

It made me ill just thinking about what he was saying, but it was the truth. He wasn't lying, and I couldn't deny or argue any of it and in this case, the truth, finally and really *did* set me free. The judge ordered me released on remand and the lawyer filed several motions, which essentially notified the court of his intent to handle both the charges of supposedly skipping my bond, and the initial prostitution charge without my need to be present, as the trauma of the last day or so left me in dire need of returning to Florida and treatment with my doctor.

My head was spinning, everything was so confusing, and I am sure I was getting some of the finer details wrong, but I didn't have time to think about it because they were taking me away. A different jailer; a woman this time, and Marlin was standing and calling out that he would be there and then I was out the door waiting in a long line of seats three people down from Hope. I was trying to relearn how to breathe, my sister leaning forward and back trying to see me, calling out that it was going to be okay, as the anxiety attack swallowed me whole and the floor rushed up to meet me.

I blinked open my eyes to a paramedic, or EMT? There was a difference wasn't there? I remember Charity telling me there was a difference and to try not to get them confused; it was considered rude…

"There she is! Hi, Baby! How you doing? Better now?" The woman of the pair was patting me on the back of the hand.

"What happened?" I asked.

"Had a little panic attack is all, you'll be alright." She smiled brightly at me and I nodded.

"I get them sometimes," I admitted.

"I don't know why, Baby. You're free! You're gonna be going home as soon as they take you back to the jail and get your things."

I looked around, "My sister, where's my sister?" I asked.

"Oh Honey," the male of the team said, "They had to clear the hall when you fainted, it's protocol. You feel like you need to go to the hospital?"

I shook my head, "No, I just want to see my sister."

Paperwork, a lot of paper work and people standing and milling about, a lot of questions and finally, *finally*, they led me to the van to be transported back to the jail. I hated it the first time, and this time wasn't any different, only this time… I rode in it alone. Except I wasn't alone. I could hear the roar behind us. A distinct sound, that many motorcycles, riding in a pack. I could hear them and they stayed with me, all the way back to the jail.

It was comforting, knowing that I would never be alone again.

CHAPTER 31

Marlin

She'd fuckin' fainted. They'd let her lawyer know, let him go back, but hadn't let any of us back there to see her. They'd rushed the prisoners back off to the jail and let medical people do their thing; the lawyer had stood off to the side and reported everything to Cutter. She was okay, a panic attack, she was refusing to go to the hospital, a county van, windowless… follow it, now, yes now, we'd started the bikes and trailed it all the way back to the fuckin jail.

They had her processed and out the fuckin' door in thirty minutes flat. Some kind of fuckin' record if you asked me. Maybe her fainting dead away had been good for *something*.

She stepped out into the bright afternoon sunlight and shaded her eyes and I went to her, pulling her tight against me, kissing the top of her head, hating the stink of institution in her hair. She was trembling, but being so brave.

"They wouldn't let me see Hope," she uttered brokenly, "I mean I saw her, but they wouldn't let me talk to her or say goodbye. They said visiting hours weren't until Saturday."

Fucking assholes, and here I was going to be one by whisking her away; *shit*.

I put an arm across her shoulders and led her gently to the bike where all my brothers were sitting astride theirs; baking in the fuckin' finest heat and humidity Louisiana had to offer.

I took her personal effects from her and slowly put her back together a piece at a time as we made our way. First I stopped her and slid her sunglasses on her face to protect her from not only the blinding fuckin' light beating down on us, but the retina scorching light beaming back up at us from the white cement we traversed to get to the parking lot's curb.

Next I slipped her slim wallet back into her jacket pocket and when we got to the bike I helped her finish suiting up, getting her back into her chaps while she stood shaking from her nerves being wracked so bad, I could almost believe they'd put her back on that stuff were it not for her clear gaze back at the courthouse that'd screamed that she was putting her life in my hands and she trusted me with it.

Last thing I did before mounting up and taking off with her was to get her back into my rag, zipping up the form fitting leather over her already zipped jacket. It was hot as fuck and the wind wasn't going to do too terribly much to cool us, but I wanted her safe. Especially knowing what me and the guys were about to pull.

"Mount up, let's get the fuck out of here," Cutter said, and didn't sound at all happy about it. Not that I blamed him; if Faith were still in there, I'd've been sleeping out here on my bike.

We got moving, falling into formation and headed for the highway; only when the boys went to get on heading east, back to the heart of the city, I broke off and went west. Faith gave a surprised shout, her head whipping in the direction where the rest of the boys had gone but I caned it, twisting down hard on the throttle, the bike jumping beneath us and startling my girl right into what I wanted her to do. She held on tighter, held on for dear life, as I blasted up the onramp and into the flow of traffic, making for home at breakneck speed. I wanted this fuckin' state in her goddamn rearview for good.

A couple three hours into the ride the sky looked threatening, so I pulled off on the side of the freeway and under an overpass. Just as I suspected it would, it started to rain; a thundershower one of those short cloud bursts more common Florida. They only lasted about twenty minutes or so, so I decided to let it pass before we continued on. There was no sense in us being soaked and really no point in digging out rain gear, unless it lasted longer than I thought it was going to. I rolled us to a stop and I shut off the bike. She got down, the roar of the rainfall outside our shelter, coupled with the traffic still passing by made it deafening.

"Waiting out the storm!" I shouted, and she simply stared at me.

Her eyes wide and her hands trembling lightly where they rested at her sides. I stepped into her space and took off her helmet and mine, setting them on the bike's seat before cupping her face in my hands. I smoothed my thumbs along her jaw, luxuriating in the feel of her hair across my fingers as she stared mutely up into my face.

I didn't speak. There was something here, something magic about this moment and I didn't want to ruin it by talking. She stared up into my eyes with that perfect trust from the courtroom but the hurt was still there in the way they shone in the dim light under here. I dipped my face down to hers and kissed her, a light brush of lips, a query, asking if it was okay that I do so when really, I felt like it should be a desperate plea for her not to be pissed at me for taking away any choice she had in the matter of her stayin' near her sister.

Her breath brushed my face, slight and relieved. She kissed me back, her lips moving carefully, tentatively, over my own. I pulled her into me and she molded so perfectly against my body. Her kiss tasted like forgiveness even though I'd yet to voice an apology. It was difficult to explain… While I was sorrier than she could know for not giving her the choice, for swooping in like the barbarian I could sometimes be, and just whisking her away… I *wasn't* sorry for doing it. It'd needed to happen. She couldn't stay; she'd have unraveled completely inside a day. Hell, she was still trembling, still likely to come apart in my arms right here, right now, on the side of the road.

She clung to me, as much to take shelter from the storm and traffic whizzing by as anything else and I let her. I would be her shield for a lot more than that. The kiss deepened, becoming a wild, passionate thing, that left me with a raging hard on in my jeans and leather that I couldn't do anything for. We broke apart, naturally; her aquamarine eyes hooded and her body language much more relaxed than it'd been before. As if I'd somehow calmed her with my touch. It was a good feeling. Like I'd reached the pinnacle of what it was to be a fucking man.

The weather abated and we rode until just after dark, I didn't want to subject her to any more today which meant we stopped somewhere near Panama City in Florida, being that I cut into the panhandle to get us back into our home state sooner rather than later. We were about halfway to Bobby's but I wanted to get her a shower, a change of clothes and a little rest before we took on more people. She looked like her rope was about ready to snap.

We hit a cheap motel, one of the big name ones that had locations all across the country. I tended to like them better when I was travelling solo, because they were cleaner and had higher standards. This time it was because I had higher standards too. I didn't want to bring Faith into some fleabag place. She'd probably seen enough of them for twenty life times. I regretted having to bring her to a motel at all, but the need for rest and a shower outweighed the desire to press all the way on down to Bobby's.

I doubted she had it in her to make the ride as much as I doubted she'd had any kind of restful sleep when she'd been locked up the night before. She stumbled with fatigue when she got off the bike and I'd had to reach out an arm to steady her. I got off myself, and we checked in, the chick behind the counter eying us suspiciously. She took both my driver's license and Faith's ID, which it was a good thing her sister Hope had had her passport; it'd made replacing Faith's ID weeks back much easier.

She handed over her shiny, new, Florida identification and the clerk glanced between it and Faith several times until Faith tucked herself into my side from the scrutiny. Ironically, that seemed to satisfy the clerk and I realized that the scrutiny wasn't likely what Faith had thought it to be. The well-meaning clerk had seen a fragile looking woman with the big bad biker and had leapt to the conclusion that she wasn't with me of her free will. It'd happened to a few of the guys and their women before. We were just another casualty of citizen preconceived notions and judgment, until she'd taken shelter in my arms. It both filled me with resignation and elated me at the same time. A weird mix of emotions that I shoved into a footlocker and kicked aside.

I wanted to get my girl a shower, and some restful sleep. I made it a point to be extra polite to the motel's clerk in an effort to speed things up and prove the bitch wrong in equal measure. She seemed unnerved by my smile, and by the quiet use of 'Ma'am' to address her and I was glad for it in a twisted kind of way. Any time you could kill that kind of negative with a positive was a good thing in my book. The world was a shitty enough place without adding more to the dung heap.

I put an arm around Faith's shoulders when the clerk slid the key card across the counter at us. I took it and tipped my head, picked up my bags at our feet, and made a point to say thank you one more time before I steered Faith back out the glass doors. I steered my girl up the stairs to the right of us and down the long line of tightly shut doors to the one that would be ours. She was trembling lightly, and I had to imagine that motels and hotels in general weren't the best place for her to be in light of recent events.

I made a strong mental note, that if I ever took her on the road or on a trip somewhere, that a bed and breakfast would be the way to go about lodging. There were plenty of 'em in Ft. Royal which is what gave me the idea.

I shut the door firmly behind us and shot every lock and bolt available. Faith stood by the bed, staring at it, though her gaze was far away, someplace else. I sighed inwardly, and considered what to do, what to say to bring her back.

"Baby Girl," I tried gently, and she startled.

She turned those beautiful aquamarine eyes up to mine and I lost whatever else I was going to say. Turns out I didn't need to *say* anything. Those eyes of hers filled to the brim, silently, and she dove at me. I caught her, and she buried her face in my chest and the wave crested. Faith crashed onto my shore, the sobs shaking her, wracking her still too-thin frame and it turned out, she didn't need any words. She just needed me to be there. She just needed to be held and to empty it all out, and that? That I could do.

CHAPTER 32
Faith

"Shhh, it's okay, Baby Girl, it's okay."

He was always so gentle with me, and this was no exception. He held me close, fingers buried in my hair, massaging my neck at the base of my skull. I expelled my anxiety, sadness, fear, and anger in the form of tears and shuddering sobs against him and he simply held me fast and let me do it. He let me cry it all out and sooner rather than later the storm was past.

I looked up at him, into his kind and caring eyes while he slicked the moisture off my face with his thumbs. He searched my eyes and whatever it was they held and finally smiled. He looked as tired and drawn as I felt and I realized the depth of his worry, and how hard it had been for him while I'd been… away.

"I don't know about you, but I could use a shower and some decent sleep. Can I interest you in both?" he asked gently and I nodded, too drained to speak.

"Okay," he murmured and unzipped my leather vest for me. His blunt fingers were gentle as he divested each of us of clothing, one piece at a time. Always keeping us even, one piece from me, one piece him, back and forth until he was just in his boxers and I in my bra and panty set.

He led me gently by the hands into the small bathroom and started the shower, smiling gently, but also a little sadly, he asked me, "Do you want to shower alone?"

I shook my head. After yesterday, I wanted to be close to him, he made me feel safe like nothing and no other, and I craved that almost more than I had ever craved the drugs they'd put in me.

"Okay, Baby Girl, okay," he murmured and drew my forehead to his lips. I collapsed my body into his arms, my hands resting against his chest, my ear over his heart. He was so warm, and the room was cool from the air conditioning unit. He let me go to start the shower and slipped out of his boxers before gently undoing the catch on my bra at the back. He let me hide against him, stepping into the tub before me so that he might steady me as I stepped in. As soon as he jerked the curtain closed he let me resume my hiding by tucking myself close into his body, though he turned me into the hot shower spray to keep me warm.

"No, let me," he murmured when I reached for the little packet with the bar of soap in it. He picked it up and tore the plastic with his teeth, sliding the sliver of a bar into his big hands. He soaped them and ran them gently along my throat, across my chest and shoulders, down my arms until my fingertips grazed his palms. My eyes had drifted shut at his pleasurable touch and they opened to a sparkle of joy in his eyes, a mischievous little boy smile on his lips.

"I love that I can do that," he said.

"What?"

"Make your eyes close; make you lose yourself a little…"

"Make me forget?" I asked, his smile grew into a pleased grin.

"Do I?" he asked.

"You know you do."

"It's still nice to hear it, Baby Girl, it's still nice to hear it."

He turned me so my front met the spray and massaged the soap into my shoulders and back. I very nearly melted beneath the soothing touches designed to ease my tension and fear. He was purely comforting and yet sensual without being overtly erotic. In short, he was being oh so careful of me and I both loved him for it and became extremely frustrated with myself over being so… broken.

I sighed under his gently prying fingers as he worked out the stiffness, kinks, and knots of the tension I very nearly always carried with me lately and found myself wanting for a deeper, more significant exchange between us. I turned, of my own volition this time, and kissed him fiercely, the rough stubble of his few days' growth tickling my palms. He pulled me tight against his body, the water sluicing through my hair, slicking it back from our faces.

I sighed out, comfortably, happy, and safe and Marlin did everything right, right up until he stopped me from wrapping my fingers around his length.

"Easy, Faith. I don't want that right now, not here anyways."

His cock was hard and hot where it was trapped between our bodies and I looked up at him, confused.

"Your body says otherwise," I said and he chuckled.

"Yeah, well my dick has a mind of its own, and he likes to forget that *I* call the shots."

I pursed my lips and breathed in, remembering my promise to communicate and to ask and answer... I took the leap, afraid of the possibility of rejection, "Why not?" I asked. His answer surprised me.

"When I make love to you again, it's not going to be in some cheap, crappy, motel room, Faith. You get me?" he asked softly. I stared up at him, shocked by the vehemence of his tone. "You deserve better than this, and tonight isn't about sex. Tonight is about me taking care of my woman after the shitty night you had last night and the even rougher day you had today. Tonight is about getting that place off of you and out of your hair, of holding you close and keeping you safe."

The shower was suddenly loud in the resounding silence that ensued, echoing off the tile walls in the small space we were in. I stared up at him, mute with shock, his hands kneading lightly up and down my back. I was glad for the water, disguising my tears. I didn't want him to think I was sad or unhappy. It was quite the opposite, actually. I couldn't ever remember a time I felt so happy. What I didn't expect was the overwhelming sense of *guilt* that came with it.

All I could think was *this man deserves so much better than me*, and it broke my heart that I couldn't provide him with that. That all I would ever be was this broken, sad, pathetic, hopeless *thing*. That he would eventually grow tired of me and my bullshit baggage.

I pulled myself close to him and he held me, and I took a little solace in the here and now. Shoving all that down and aside as a problem for another day. I knew I would have to face the music eventually, but for now... I could let myself have this for just a little while, couldn't I?

Marlin took his time with me and I my time with him. We bathed each other, gentle and careful, kissing when the urge overtook us, but he remained steadfast that there would be no sex tonight, and though I found myself aroused, I was grateful for his fierce adherence to simple tender care for tonight. I didn't think I could bear to have sex in a motel room. His perception was dead on in that case. I'd felt a creeping nausea when we'd first come through the door though it'd melted away beneath his touch and had, I think, gone somewhere down the shower drain.

When he'd turned off the water, it had begun to run cool, and coupled with the air conditioned ambient temperature of the room, I had begun to break out in goose flesh from the chill.

He dried me with equal consideration and care with which he'd washed me, wrapping me in a towel and holding out one of his clean tee shirts for me to slip into. It barely grazed the tops of my thighs below my panties, which he held out a clean pair of those for me to step into as well.

He quickly pulled on a pair of his boxers, adjusting himself with a slight grimace, which I don't think he realized I caught. I felt bad for him, but he made no further outward signs of discomfort, nor would he let me do anything to assuage his frustration. Instead he kissed my forehead and gently steered me to the bed, turning out the lights before climbing in after me.

Marlin gathered me back, against his chest, wrapping me in his strong arms before burying his nose in my hair, behind my ear. A sweet, gentle, kiss he placed there before letting out a contented hum. I fell asleep far faster than I wanted to after that. So tired that I was very nearly out the moment my head touched the pillow.

CHAPTER 33
Marlin

I let Faith sleep late, hell, I slept late, too. I still woke up before her, but she was sound asleep and lying on my chest so sweetly, I wasn't about to move her. Instead, I relaxed and simply enjoyed the sensation of her soft warmth against me. Her body was snug up against mine, in that way that was so trusting, so beautifully, innocently, sweet; that I could hardly believe my luck. I'd wanted this since forever, had almost had it a time or two, so I'd thought. Really only came close once. God, I loved her belief in me. It made me feel like a man in every way that counted. It made me want to fight hard and harder to be the man she believed me to be. I thought I'd done a pretty good job up to this point, but there was always room for improvement in anything a man did and taking care of his woman? Well that was no exception; so, I let her sleep.

I let her dream, and I smoothed my fingers through her hair while she did it. Didn't seem like it was one of her bad ones and the good was few and far between for her, so why not? I lazed in bed and relaxed and neither one of us had stirred until the phone had gone off with the 'get the fuck out' disguised as a curtesy call. We'd dressed in fresh clothes, had geared up for the ride and had gone as far as the nearest Denny's for breakfast before hitting the road again.

That'd been a little over five hours ago. We'd stopped once for fuel, and again a time or two for Faith or myself to use the restroom, and truth be told, I wasn't exactly pushing us hard. It was hot, and I don't care how much citizens thought the wind cooled a rider, you wear that much black leather in Florida heat and humidity, you started dyin' in a big damn hurry. The stops to pee were just as much stops to hydrate and try to cool down as much as they were anything. I saw another long shower in our future when we got to Bobby's; a cool one this time.

We pulled down the dirt lane leading through the orange grove and to his house, sometime around dusk. He heard the bike, and met us out on his wraparound porch. His country house was the real deal and had been in his family for something like four generations now. A bright, cheery yellow with white shutters and trim. It'd been in magazines a time or two when his parents had been in it, and his dad had been alive. His mom lived with her sister somewhere out near Tampa now. Bobby's siblings had long taken off for other states. He'd been the only one to get his dad's farming genes and loved this place like nobody's business.

I pulled off to the side of the front steps leading up onto his porch while Tango, Bobby's yellow Lab did his best imitation of bounding down to see us. Dog was so old, I was surprised he was still kickin'.

Faith got down, and I could tell she was road weary. Bobby caught it too, eying her carefully before setting his jaw in that way, arching an eyebrow in my direction, asking without words if it'd been a rough day. I turned down my mouth and cocked my head to the side to let him know that just about *every* day lately had been a rough one, but this one hadn't been overly so. I took off my helmet and stood up, swinging my leg over the seat and groaning a bit. Sometimes I felt like I was getting too old for these long rides, today was one of those days.

"Jimmy," Bobby greeted and we clasped forearms and pulled each other in for a hug and a slap on the back.

"Hey Bobby, thanks for taking us in on such short notice."

"It's not a problem, hi Faith," he stuck out his hand, "I'm Bobby. We haven't been formally intro'ed, but this here is my farm and you're welcome to sleep *inside* the house while you're here this time."

Faith blushed to the roots of her hair and shook Bobby's hand quickly before letting go and taking a half step back, both of her arms winding around one of mine in one of the most adorable displays of shyness I don't think either Bobby or I could hardly stand it.

"Thank you," she stammered awkwardly, "It's nice to meet you."

"Likewise," he smiled at her, his best most genuine good 'ol boy smile that usually had the girls dropping their panties saying they wouldn't be needin' 'em anymore. Instead, the smile earned him Faith tucking herself closer into my side. I smiled at that and Bobby grinned.

"Y'all hungry?" he asked and I nodded.

"Starved."

"Well, c'mon in! I'll get somethin' goin' on the grill out back."

"Sounds good," Faith said and smiled in an attempt to not seem rude. I'd filled Bobby in, and he didn't pay no never mind to her being so shy. I'd told him it'd take a good long while for her to warm up to him, if she ever did.

We had dinner and beers, made some small talk, but Bobby could tell we were wore out and didn't push it. Instead, he cleared plates and told us he was going to watch some TV before hitting the hay, and we were welcome to join him. Faith smiled wanly, and I declined for us before she had to.

"Right then, see y'all in the morning, then. Jimmy, you know where the guest room's at. Make yourself at home."

"You got it, Man. Thanks again."

"No problem."

Faith very nearly sagged with relief when I took her gently by the hand and led her upstairs. I took her down the hall to the bathroom and got the water running in the tub, stripping us down a piece at a time like the night before. I didn't know about her, but I was up for a soak, and Bobby had these giant ass old fashioned copper tubs in the house. The kind that were deep, and big. The kind that they just didn't make anymore, and apparently they were something Faith had never seen before because she couldn't stop staring at it, as if it were too good to be real.

"Never seen a woman fall in love with a bathtub," I said casually.

"What, am I looking at it the same way I look at you, or something?" I froze and looked up from where I was gathering her fitted tee in my hands to draw it over her head. I felt a slow, lazy grin overtake me, but I chose not to say anything. Instead, I undressed us and got into the tub, shutting off the tap. I held a hand out to Faith and she climbed in after me, situating herself in front of me, laying back against my chest carefully.

God, this must be what heaven is like.

My arms around her, she trailed fingertips beneath the warm water along my arm, and I had to smile to myself. Yeah, I was pretty sure this was heaven. I heaved a long sigh and I'm not sure why, but I sang to her; her song, *Hope Never Dies.*

She melted against me, and turned her head so it was pillowed half on my chest and half on my shoulder. I closed my eyes and the next thing I knew, the water was cold and we were both jerking awake at a hard thumping on the door.

"Y'allright in there?" Bobby called through the wood.

"Yeah, Man!" I laughed, "We fell asleep!"

"There's a bed for that y'know. See y'all tomorrow."

Faith rolled her head back and looked up at me, blinking owlishly, she shivered beneath the tepid-at-best water and I chuckled.

"I think we're both tired."

She nodded and winced as she moved, stiffly, to let me up. I pulled the drain and stood with her and reached for the towel rack, wrapping her in it first. We were prunes, and she was cold. I dried her off and she stood hugging the towel around her. I dried off, double timing it, so I could chivvy us a couple doors down to the guest room. I shut the door behind us and lifted the bedding so she could crawl in. I got in right behind her and she didn't hesitate to cuddle up to my side. I got comfortable and her body heat combined with mine had us warm enough and drifting off pretty quick.

Truthfully, we both passed right the hell back out again. It was nice, it was comfortable, and the next morning showed up too damn quick. Faith slept on, but I needed to make a run back out to my boat for a few reasons. Knowing she would be safe enough here, I laid out some clothes for her for the day and took myself downstairs. Bobby was in the kitchen and passed me a cup of strong, black coffee.

"Morning!"

I took the cup and nodded, grunting out a half assed, inarticulate reply.

"So, what's your plan for today?" he asked and looked entirely too pleased at my rough state. I was used to getting up early, fishing being my trade; I still didn't have to like it.

"Have t' head back to m' boat. Pick up some more clothes and shit for the both of us, talk to my brother… I might have to head back to work even though we'll be stayin' here, if that's cool."

"That's cool."

"Can't really bring Faith around Ft. Royal for much more'n a visit until the rest of the crew is back."

"I get you; remind me again what's up?"

I did, explained about the Russians and the whole bit. Bobby sniffed, and nodded.

"She's safe enough here, I'll keep an eye on her."

"Anyplace you don't want her poking around?"

"I'll give her the full tour when I see her up and moving around, set some boundaries for safety around the equipment. Shouldn't be bad, though. I'll tell the workers they'll be seeing her around and I'll also tell 'em to stay in their lane. She'll be fine."

I nodded carefully, and Bobby eyed me, "You got it bad for this chick, yeah?"

"Yeah."

That was all that needed to be said about it, too.

"I'll bring back some fish outta my freezer," I told him and he nodded.

"Sounds good."

I downed my coffee and headed for my bike, I knew Faith was safe enough with my best friend, but that still didn't mean I liked leaving her here like this one bit. I shot a text to her phone with where I was headed and to call me when she woke up so she didn't worry or have to contend with wondering if I was coming back. I figured she'd be freaked out enough.

With a heavy sigh, I fired my bike back up and made for Ft. Royal, I wanted to get back here sooner rather than later.

CHAPTER 34
Faith

I woke and it was so quiet, there was no distant crash of waves on the shore, and there wasn't any hum from the A/C unit. It was so very still, too, which meant I wasn't on the boat, either. I pushed myself into a sitting position and heaved out a breath.

No, I wasn't in familiar surroundings, but I *was* safe. I was on the orange farm and if Marlin wasn't here in the bedroom, knowing him, he wasn't likely far away. I got up and had to smile. He'd laid out my favorite, long, summer dress and sandals for me. He'd even remembered clean underthings. I dressed quickly and sighed out. It was warm in here. Too warm, almost like the house didn't have A/C, but what home in Florida didn't? Also, it'd been much cooler the night before. I wondered if Bobby had turned it off.

I let the dress fall around my body, the soft, breathable, jersey knit, fit well in the chest, but didn't cling badly to the rest of me. The teal and white chevron pattern was flattering, too. I picked up the light, white lace wrap that I liked to wear with it and slid my feet into the white sandals that waited for them. I went downstairs, figuring that I would find Marlin in the kitchen, but the house was deserted.

Panic began to swell in my breast and I forced it down, my fingertips finding the metal and leather cuff around my wrist. I opened the door to the house and pushed on the old, wooden screen door, letting myself out onto the porch. It was oppressively hot out here too, only marginally less bad than inside but that was due to the slight breeze rustling through the trees which marched in lines away from the house.

It was as if the house had been built, and orange trees had been planted in the back yard, but then the owner decided that he wanted more. The next thing you knew, there were rows of trees in all four directions, though they'd had the foresight to leave a little bit of a front yard, not only for kids to play on, but also an expanse to park cars on.

Marlin's motorcycle was conspicuously absent, and so was Bobby's battered old truck. I bit my bottom lip and listened, and hearing distant voices, picked that direction to walk in. I stayed out in the middle, between two rows of trees, so I wouldn't be missed, and took my time making my way towards the talking and laughing I could hear.

"Whoa! Hey, look who's up." Bobby smiled and waved at me from further up the row, and I slowed. I didn't see Marlin with him, or among the other men standing around the back of his truck.

"I was looking for Marlin," I called softly.

"Ah, he went back to his boat to pick up a few things for y'all. He should be back soon, he's been gone for a fair bit."

I smoothed my face into a mask of neutrality; I didn't want to show any of these men that this news upset me, or how afraid I was. Besides, if Marlin entrusted Bobby with my care, then I was reasonably sure that I could, too.

"You hungry?" Bobby called and I nodded carefully. He looked me over, considering and said to one of the men standing near the front of the truck, "Miguel, grab me the blanket off the front seat, would you?"

The man complied. He was older than Bobby, by quite a bit, maybe fifties or sixties, and a deep, deep tan from too much time in the sun. He smiled at me and handed Bobby, who was clearly his boss, the blanket. Bobby laid the blanket across the tailgate of his pickup and then held out a hand, motioning for me to come closer. I took stock of the situation.

Bobby, sure, but there were five other men standing around with him including Miguel. All of them appeared to be a worker of some sort in overalls with tank tops underneath, skin gleaming with a coat of sunscreen. Some wore heavy carpenter like pants and tees. I chewed my bottom lip in consideration and Bobby smiled.

"Boys, give the lady some room," he said and all of them looked at him quizzically but stepped further out from the truck. I sighed inwardly, and felt terrible. I gripped the leather cuff around my wrist and forced my feet into motion.

"There you are," Bobby said with mild strain as he caught me around the waist and lifted me, setting me on the blanket on the bed of the truck. I squeaked and tried to remember to keep my breathing under control. He eyed me and handed me an icy bottle of water out of a cooler in the back of his truck.

"Am I not supposed to be out here alone?" I asked.

"Nah, you're good," he said and his smile was warm with adorable dimples that would have made my sister Charity go on for hours. He pulled the red trucker hat off his head and scratched the top of his sweat-soaked, dark brown hair before replacing it. He reached into another cooler and handed me a half a sandwich wrapped in waxed paper.

"Thank you," I murmured.

"You're good, you're good," he repeated, though he was studying me rather intently. Some of the other men were, too. I shifted uncomfortably and with shaking hands unwrapped the sandwich.

"Lunch time is over boys, head on back to work," Bobby said quietly and the men nodded and began cleaning up.

"Thought you was gonna sleep all day, Darlin'."

"It was too hot, I woke up and couldn't go back to sleep."

Bobby swore, "A/C went out again. I'll head back to the house to fix it in a little while. First, I figure I should go over the rules of this place with yah." He chuckled, "You ain't done nothin' wrong Sweetheart, just some things to go over for your own safety."

"Oh, okay."

He told me if I went walking and found some men, to let them know I was there. He also told me to stick to the middle of the rows like I'd done, and to steer clear if I heard or saw any machinery operating and to watch and listen for yellow jackets. They liked the fallen fruit from the trees and could be aggressive; he didn't want me to get stung. He told me that I was free to go wherever I'd like and he pointed out where the groves gave way to a pond and a swimming hole, but warned me to look out for alligators. I didn't imagine I would see myself swimming after *that* bit of knowledge.

We were silent for a long time, and I finished my sandwich and half the bottle of water. Bobby wandered over to one of the trees and reached up into the greenery, "Ever had an orange fresh off the tree?" he asked. I shook my head and he pulled, the branch bowed for a second and snapped back up into place, the leaves rustling. He held a bright orange globe of fruit in his big hands and briskly, started to peel it. Citrus kissed the air and I breathed deep, the bright scent.

"Nothing like it really," he said and broke the fruit in half, handing me some of the smiles.

I peeled one off and ate it, the juice bursting in my mouth, cleansing my palate from the residual sandwich flavors. It was good. Probably the best orange I had ever tasted and I smiled, laughing a little. Bobby smiled, but soon the smile slipped and I sobered.

"Tell me something, Faith."

"Yes?"

"How do you feel about my friend, Jimmy?"

I eyed him carefully, and he eyed me back just as hard... considering.

"I, I care about him very much."

He nodded carefully, "But?" he asked.

"But he deserves to be happy, and I don't think I can possibly do that for him."

"Why would you say a thing like that?"

"He's told you, I'm sure."

"Yeah, but I want to hear it from you."

I put another bite of orange in my mouth instead, and chewed thoughtfully.

"What difference does that make?" I asked.

"You talk about it with anyone?"

"My doctor, and Marlin... sometimes."

Bobby nodded, "Don't trust me yet. I get you, that's okay," he was nodding but he wasn't looking at me, when he did, he pinned me with his hazel eyes. I swallowed hard and felt like my throat was going to close up with fear.

"Never seen Jimmy look at any girl like he does you. Never had him ask me to take care of one like his life depended on it neither. He's got it bad for you, Faith, and he's been my best friend since ever. Do me a favor and don't rip out his heart."

"I don't want that," I said, genuinely distressed by his words.

"No, I don't figure you do," he replied softly. He handed me a paper towel and I wiped off my hands, the juice from the orange making them sticky. "Do me another favor?" he asked.

"What?"

"Don't sell yourself short, neither. You seem like a nice girl and I get that bad shit happened to you, some really bad shit, but don't let it define you. Only you get to do that. Love yourself, then love my boy back. You get me?"

"I don't think I do," I told him.

"Hey, Bobby!" We both turned our heads at the shout of one of his workers; he was tromping through the aisle of trees in our direction from the front of the truck.

"You think about it, Darlin'. If you still don't get it in a day or so, we'll talk again. In the meantime I gotta deal with this," he helped me down to the ground. "Wander where you'd like, just remember to be safe." He gave me a wink and walked down the aisle a ways to speak to the approaching man. I stared after them for a moment but I knew when I'd been dismissed. Hard not to know after living with Hope, the mistress of dismissals.

I wandered among the trees, up and down the aisles and thought hard about what Bobby had said to me. It was clear he cared a great deal about Marlin, which I could understand completely. Marlin made it so very easy to love him, but that still didn't mean I was good for him. Not with everything wrong with me, that would be wrong with me for a long time to come.

I sighed out, I think I knew what Bobby meant by loving myself, I *was* hard on myself but it was hard not to be. I felt like a curse, like a blight upon the lives of the people closest to me, but I just couldn't bring myself to do anything about it. I also couldn't decide if that were incredibly brave or an act of complete cowardice. Everything about me felt so upside down and inside out and I didn't know what I could do to straighten my ass out.

Living inside my head was like being scared and tired at the same time. I felt like I should be *doing* something, *anything* to be useful, but terrified I would screw it up if I tried and equally terrified of the repercussions from that failure. Like now, I wanted to be alone, but I suddenly felt incredibly lonely and suddenly wished that Marlin were here, walking beside me like he so often did along the beach. Silent, but a presence, a comfort like a candle in the dark. It was like I cared so much about these things, but at the same time, I didn't really have the energy to care and it all amounted to me being so numb I couldn't be moved.

I gently wiped a stray tear as the yellow glimmer of Bobby's house loomed through the trunks and canopies of the trees to my left. The white trim glaringly bright in the Florida sun. I stopped and looked for a long time, at the shiny chrome and black motorcycle with its colorful blue Marlin fish painted on the tank. Relief flooded me, followed by soul crushing disappointment that he hadn't left a note, or *anything* that he'd gone. I swallowed hard and continued my walk, stopping again to watch him, sitting on the front step of the porch, cigarette between his lips as he texted or played a game on his phone; squinting at the screen.

It was overwhelming, how deeply I felt for this man. Overwhelming, and terrifying, but at the same time, something I so desperately wanted. He'd said he loved me, and I knew he meant it. I knew he meant it to the very bottom of my soul, but he'd left without saying a word, *knowing…*

I picked my way carefully through the trees and across the grass in his direction, his nose buried in the phone as he took a long drag on his cigarette. I would go inside. I wanted to be near him, but I didn't want to cry, I didn't want him to know how much I felt like I needed him and that his going like that, without saying anything, had rattled me so badly, so I would slip past him and go inside.

That's what I would do.

CHAPTER 35
Marlin

Her shadow fell across me as I shot yet another text to her phone, to see where she was at. I looked up and squinted, until she moved into the sun to block it out. Her face was reserved, with that tightness around her eyes that told me she was struggling with something. I looked down to where my hand unconsciously curled around her calf, rubbing soothingly up to her knee and back down.

My girl's toenail polish was chipped, I noted, and I couldn't remember the last time she and Hope had gone to get pedicures together. I didn't know if it warranted the risk of being out and about with the folks that'd taken her hot on our trail. I'd spent longer than I'd wanted to in Ft. Royal. The word was out to keep watch for rude dudes with tattoos, particularly any bearing Russian or Eastern European accents. I was going to have to commute, and keep working the boat. The best I could do for *that* was to make the ride slick backed and make sure I wasn't tailed but nothing was ever truly one hundred percent.

Taking Faith into town just for a pedicure seemed like a bad idea, but still… maybe it was something I could fix. I looked up at her again and smiled.

"You doin' okay, Baby Girl?" I asked.

"No."

I cocked my head to the side at her frank answer, and took my hand off her leg, waiting for her to finish.

"What's going on?" I asked.

"You just left; you didn't wake me up or say anything."

"I texted your phone, I figured you could use the sleep." She frowned and looked perplexed. I raised an eyebrow, "What's that look for?"

She didn't answer, she blew past me and went into the house, and I got up and followed her. All the way up the stairs, down the hall, into the bedroom where she snatched her phone off the bedside table and looked at it. Her face immediately crumbled and she started to cry.

"Hey, hey, hey! What's this now?" I asked and dropped onto the edge of the bed beside her, wrapping my arms around her shoulders and kissing her temple.

"I've been so hurt and mad all day, that Bobby had to be the one to tell me that you'd gone and it's not fair to you that I didn't even think to check this thing."

I tried not to laugh, that would just upset her more and honestly, she was right too, in a way. She'd been without a phone, conditioned after a fashion, to never go near one on threat of pain and heartbreak I couldn't even imagine. A couple of months doesn't fix that kind of thing, or bring the whole having a phone to the forethought at all. Plus, one of us was usually with her, so it wasn't like she got a lot of calls anyways. Nine times out of ten when we wanted to reach Faith, when we weren't right with her, we called the person she *was* with, be it me, Hope, the Captain or whoever. This was as much our fault for trying to wrap her up in bubble wrap and keep her on a shelf as it was any fault of hers.

What's that saying? The road to Hell is paved with good intentions. We were looking at a prime example of that now. I held her, and she cried, and I felt guilty as fuck that she'd been stewing in anxiety all day because I couldn't do better than a fucking text. I knew Faith had been resistant to the idea of taking medication after all the shit they'd pumped into her, but something had to give. She needed to talk to her doctor and we needed to put it in her hands on if she needed to take something or not, but she at least needed to do something about the anxiety and panic attacks. She couldn't live like this much longer; it was a serious road block to her recovery. I wasn't looking forward to the conversation but it was one that needed to be had.

We ended up laying down, and she cried herself to sleep. It broke my fucking heart, and tugged at every one of my heartstrings in all the worst ways. I couldn't sleep, so at some point I disengaged myself enough to sit up with my back to the headboard while she slept, standing guard, keeping watch, or whatever.

I put my headphones into my phone and hit up YouTube, watching videos on how to do a pedicure until I was pretty sure I had everything I would need memorized and could do one in my sleep. Faith had a therapy appointment set for the next day. That was nonnegotiable, the one thing I *needed* to take her to until the guys got back with Hope. There was no tellin' how long *that* was going to take, but me and Faith were good to be like this, here at Bobby's, until we had Ft. Royal fully stocked with the rest of the Kraken to protect what was ours.

I'd fixed the A/C when I'd gotten back, which hadn't taken very long, but Bobby seriously needed to invest in a new one, this one wasn't going to hold out forever. It was keeping the heat and humidity down to a tolerable level, but it didn't stop Faith from shifting restlessly in her sleep. I would touch her, a little touch, like smoothing her hair back from her face, or a light caress down her arm, and she would sigh out and settle again. I liked that I could do that for her. That she somehow slept better when I was around, even when I didn't touch her, like she knew I was there.

Eventually I was tired enough to lay down with her, so I cuddled up to her back, an arm hooked over her waist and closed my eyes, breathing her in. I was going to have to wake her up eventually, so that we could grab some dinner downstairs. I was pretty sure she'd eaten something that day, even though she forgot to more often than not, Bobby would have seen to it. It was our way.

Imagine my surprise when it was the man himself shaking both me and my girl awake. He chuckled and gave us a wink, "Must be nice, sleepin' the day away."

"Yeah, fuck you man, I work for a livin' just the same as you."

"I don't," Faith murmured unhappily.

"Not yet, but then again, you're my girl and I'm supposed to take care of you."

She looked me over and licked her lips, but remained silent, the wheels in her head turning.

"C'mon downstairs and get something to eat."
"Find the fish?" I asked.
"Right in the icebox, fresh catch?"
"Yeah, Johnny caught it this morning."
"Sweet."

Faith remained silent, and let me lead her downstairs, right behind Bobby. We went out back, where he had the grill and a picnic table with chairs around it. Faith asked what she could do to help and Bobby asked her to set places. Satisfied that she could pitch in, she moved wraith like between the kitchen and the outdoors, setting a nice spread. She made a salad without being asked and looked like she was going to have a heart attack until Bobby thanked her, assuring her he wasn't pissed about it. Jesus, a little over a fuckin' day in that shithole and it was like she was right back to square one.

"What are you doing tomorrow?" she asked me softly, as she stood to clear plates. I helped her out and Bobby watched us, leaned way back in his seat, beer perched on top of his thigh. He took a pull off it and raised his eyebrows at me.

"Taking you to Dr. Sheindland in the morning for an appointment," I stopped her, and put the plates in her hands back down atop the table, drawing her in close to me. I was cheating here, and I knew it, asking her in front of Bobby, but Faith was ever polite, and wouldn't disagree or make a fuss in front of another person. "Think you can do me a favor?"

She looked up at me quizzically, and raised her eyebrows. I smiled, and took it for what it was, an invitation to get on with it.

"Let her prescribe you something," I pulled her hand from my waist and raised it to my mouth, kissing her palm, "You don't have to take it, unless you really need it, but let it at least be an option. No one's gonna force you to take something you don't want to."

She looked away from me and away from Bobby, aquamarine eyes distant as she stared sightless in the direction of the groves. She didn't look at all happy, so it surprised me when she reluctantly nodded.

"I don't think I can do it on my own anymore without help, I just don't want to be addicted to anything ever again," she sniffed and I nodded, pulling her in and holding her close.

Bobby got up, and went inside silently, after we traded looks over the top of Faith's head. He took the plates along with him, and a second later you could hear the water running in the kitchen. I sighed out and held Faith tight who was going through this internal struggle the likes neither Bobby, nor I, could even begin to fathom. This trip back to NOLA had scrambled her system hard, set her back something fierce, and I don't think she could even put a finger on exactly why that was.

We ended the evening on the porch, Bobby and me with beers in hand, Faith with a tall glass of sweet iced tea. I brought my guitar out and wondered idly where she'd put her iPod. I hadn't seen it for a couple of days. I played idly for a while, nothing in particular, keeping to music on the soothing end of the spectrum while we relaxed and watched the stars come out. Faith and I traded a knowing look, and with a smile, I obliged her and played *Hope Never Dies* for her again. She closed her eyes, and some of the tension and stress eased out of her.

Tomorrow I would take her up to her Doctor, and see if the grand old dame would call in a script for her so I could pick it up while she was in her session. I'd go pick that up, and the other supplies I would need to see if I could make life a little better for my girl for a minute. It'd been way easier than I expected to get Faith to agree to take something, which meant that she was in rough shape on the inside. I had to hand it to her; she was pretty much the mistress of hiding it. Of course, she'd had to be and she'd had long practice.

Some wise old Chinese fucker had once said, 'The journey of a thousand miles begins with but a single step.' He wasn't wrong, it was just, with times like these, and all the seeming stumbling blocks in place, these first steps were all up hill. Here was to hoping the universe would see fit to mellow the fuck out where Faith was concerned and let her remember what it was to breathe again. Fuck knows, I would do whatever *I* could to see that happen.

CHAPTER 36
Faith

My session with Dr. Sheindland had gone well that morning, and when I'd come out, Marlin had been waiting for me, and had pretty much whisked me right back to Bobby's orange grove. It was hot, so I'd changed back into my dress and at Marlin's urging had brought out my iPod to listen to while I took a walk.

He had opted to stay behind and help Bobby with a more permanent fix to the air conditioning unit attached to the house. I listened to Ashes & Embers and strolled for *hours*. I had taken one of the antidepressants and one of the antianxiety pills that Dr. Sheindland had prescribed for me when we'd gotten back to the house. She was right, I didn't *have* to take them forever, and there really was nothing worse than heroin when it came to kicking a drug habit and I had already done that well enough. I'd already been through the worst anyone could go through, and I felt stronger, validated somehow when she'd said that if I could survive what I had already been through, then I could, quite literally, survive *anything*.

I felt a little less awkward, more put together, and it helped that I heard from my sister. Marlin had insisted I carry my cell phone with me when I walked, as much for safety as to get used to owning one, and when it rang, I had answered it to a collect call from the Jefferson Parrish Jail.

"Hope?"

"Hey Bubbles, sorry it took me so long to call."

"Never mind that, are you okay?"

"Yeah, the food sucks, these bitches…" my sister paused, "Both in uniform and jumpsuits ain't got nothin' on me and my court date is in a week and a half. The lawyer the boys sprang for is worth the money, believe me. I would have had to wait here a couple of months otherwise. How are you doing?"

We talked, I told her I saw the doctor that morning and that I was taking some medicine and she, surprisingly, made approving noises over that. She told me to call Charity in the next couple of days, and said that our youngest sister had opted to stay behind at school to get a jump on her studies through spring break, to get herself graduated that much sooner so she could come down here to be with us.

"Are you sure that's a good idea?" I asked.

"By the time she gets down there, I'll be back and so will the rest of the guys. There won't be anything to worry about, Bubs, trust me. Char is in a work study program, if we had her come down now, it'd screw that up, but sis, you need to call her more. It's freaking her out and tearing her up that you don't talk to her when you guys used to be so close."

"I'm sorry…"

"Hey, no, this isn't me tellin' you off or getting mad, Faith, believe me, I really do get it."

We lapsed into silence and I nodded, realized my sister couldn't see it, heaved a sigh, and told her, "I'll try to call her soon."

"That's my girl, listen, I have to go, but if you need anything or want me to call, just call Cutter and he'll tell me, okay?"

"Okay."

"I love you, Bubbles."

"Back at you, Buttercup."

"Talk to you soon, Sis."

"Okay."

We ended the call, and I felt marginally better. Hope had sounded unfazed by the happenings, and that made me feel, well, hope that things would actually be okay. My sister didn't know it, but I had so much of my namesake in her. She could do anything, just look at me. I'd believed she would find me, and she did. I may have lost my faith that she would in some of my darker days, but Hope came through. This was no different; she would come through and come home.

I stopped and looked up into the bright blue skies that matched Marlin's eyes to near perfection and had to smile. This was home. I hadn't felt a sense of home in a very long time. It was nice to have that again. I drew in a deep breath and let it out slowly. It was nice to be able to *breathe* again. I had a long ways to go to be completely free, but for one of the first times I felt like I was on the right path, and not only that, I felt like I could make it and the feeling wasn't *fleeting*.

I decided to wander back to the house. Marlin and Bobby should be done with the air conditioner by now, and I was fairly certain that they could both do with something to eat. I know I could.

As I entered the front yard, my suspicions about Marlin being through with the work were correct. He stood barefoot on the porch, hair dripping onto his bare shoulders from a fresh shower. He wore only a pair of faded, work worn jeans and I felt a throb of desire, a deep ache of appreciation that stopped me in my tracks so that I could simply drink the sight of him in. He pulled a hair elastic off his wrist and pulled his hair into a short man bun, catching the ends of his hair in the elastic to create a loop. It wasn't something I'd ever seen him do, and I had to admit, the look suited him.

He caught sight of me standing at the edge of the grove and his smile lit him up from the inside out. It was so startling, I had to turn and look just to be sure it was *me* that elicited the reaction, but of course I was out here alone, and it was only me he was looking at. It made me blush, and butterflies took off in my stomach, rising in a cloud and tickling the inside of my ribs, causing my heart to stutter in a giggle. Joy flooded my veins, more addictive, and better than any synthetic drug and my feet carried me forward even as my mind mourned not being able to capture this moment for a little longer.

I gathered the long skirt of my maxi dress in my free hand, my other occupied with my phone and little iPod. Marlin reached out and popped the earbud out of my one ear, and took the items from my hand, twisting to set them in reach on one of the porch railings.

"Hey, Baby Girl. Have a good walk?"

"I think so," I said smiling, and it felt natural, the smile.

"Good, c'mere, there's something I want to do for you." He took my hands in his and led me over to a rocking chair he'd brought out from inside the house. "Sit for me," he murmured and trusting him,

I did. He knelt and slipped off my sandals one at a time and I looked at him quizzically.

"Don't go anywhere for me, I'll be right back." Marlin straightened and disappeared back into the house, the screen door banging in its frame. I looked out over the peaceful and idyllic scene of the trees rustling lightly in the breeze and I relaxed, leaning back in the chair. The screen door opening up brought my attention back around, Marlin stepping out of the portal with an honest to god foot bath between his large hands.

"What are you doing?" I asked, laughing.

"You trust me?"

"You know I do."

"Then you'll see."

He set it at my feet and ran the cord to an outdoor socket, flipping back its cover to plug it in. He returned and lifted my skirt, tucking it between my knees to preserve my modesty before lifting first one foot then the other into the bath. I watched him curiously, this big, strong, man on his knees at my feet. The water was warm and when he switched on the bath, the smell of lavender and eucalyptus wafted up to me.

"Where did you even get this thing?"

"Drugstore while you were in with your doctor, now sit back, relax and let me take care of you."

"Why?"

He flashed me a roguish smile, "Because I love you, and it makes me happy."

His frankness stole my breath away, and his words made it slow to return. I watched in rapt fascination as he went back into the house, returning with a couple of bags of items, taking his time to rifle through them. He brought out nail polish remover and cotton balls first, and laid a towel over the top of one of his thighs; he brought out one of my feet and took care to strip the chipped and flaking polish off of each toe.

I blinked, and couldn't believe it. This powerful man's man, fisherman, biker, fighter... was giving me a pedicure. His hands were rough against my skin, but so gentle with how he handled me.

At one point I heard laughter, and turned to see some of Bobby's workers standing by and watching. A couple of them called out to Marlin, mocking, but he ignored them, holding me fast when I tried to pull away. He captured my gaze with his and something passed between us. He didn't care, not one bit, about them or anyone else who had an opinion. I found myself becoming strangely emotional. Something I couldn't quite define, something that had no name but didn't feel bad; quite the opposite actually.

I was suffused with a warm, tingling, golden glow. I felt loved, cared for and cherished. He was amazing in so many ways and I found my hands shaking lightly with how fiercely I wanted to pull his mouth to mine and show him just how much this grand gesture meant to me.

He took his time and extraordinary care, clipping, filing, and buffing the nails. He did everything exactly right and I found myself blurting through one of the tenderest massages I'd ever received, "Where did you learn how to do this?"

"Looked it up on YouTube yesterday while you were napping."

"YouTube?" I asked incredulously.

"That's right," he wasn't looking at me, he was paying close attention to what he was doing, rubbing small circles with his thumbs, pressing with just the right amount, into my shin to either side of the bone, fingers gliding effortlessly in the lotion and oil he applied to my skin.

I found myself going limp, submitting to the sublime relaxing sensations he wrought with his fingers along first one leg, then the other; paying special attention to either foot. I was a melting puddle of bliss in the old wooden rocking chair by the time he was using a bit of alcohol on a cotton ball to cleanse the nails of any residual oil or lotion. Apparently this was full service and he really didn't care what anyone thought. Several workers had taken up working in the nearby trees, and quite a few of them were staring unabashedly.

"Marlin…"

"Fuck them, they want to say anything I'll gladly realign their jaws for 'em. This is about me and you, nobody else's business but ours, Baby Girl." He punctuated his statement with a crisp look in my direction and by cracking open a bottle of clear basecoat, studiously and carefully starting in on painting the nail on one of my big toes while my heart swelled with love for him, and with gratitude.

I was struck by a thought that I chose to keep private for the moment, but that I promised myself I would share with him when the time was right. I thought to myself: *Everything, all of the pain, the misery, and sorrow of New Orleans, was worth it because in the end I'm able to sit here with a man like him.* I traced the metal filigree behind the key plate in the wristband and thought to myself further, *If only the boy knew how right he was.*

I watched, grossly fascinated, as Marlin painted my nails a beautiful metallic color that shifted between a blue and sea green, two or three shades darker than the actual waters around here, but no less beautiful. He blew gently on my toes and it made me giggle, but as with everything he did, the paint job was perfect. He did everything with equal care and precision I noticed. From fishing on his boat, to repairing an air conditioning unit, to painting his woman's toenails. I admired him beyond words for that.

"Sit and let that dry," he said quietly, voice heavy with an unknown emotion and I marveled at him, nodding.

I caught his hand as he stood to clean up after us and he looked down into my face, "Thank you," I murmured and he smiled, a self-satisfied smile and nodded gently.

I sat and enjoyed basking in the relaxing aura Marlin had created for me. I smiled and laughed at myself when I likened it to a bubble, my nickname among my sisters being 'Bubbles' and all. He came back after he'd put everything away and sat on the steps, reaching one hand back and caressing my calf while he had a cigarette. By the time he was through with it, I was sure to be dry, but I had no real desire to move just yet. Rather, I simply enjoyed looking at him. Letting my eyes wander over his tattoos where he had them, and the freckles caused by the sun, spattered like paint droplets across his shoulders and back.

My daydreaming and admiration of him was dispelled when he

stood and held out a hand down to me. I took it and reluctantly got to my feet.

"Come inside with me," he murmured and I nodded and followed him into the house and up to our room. He'd pulled the wingback chair that sat in the corner to beside the foot of the bed and he gestured for me to sit, so I did. He closed the bedroom door, and turned to look me up and down.

"What is it?" I asked at his grave expression. He shook his head, the energy between us crackling as he reached for the waistband of his jeans. He undid the button and zipper and let them fall to the floor. My breath caught again when it was revealed he was nude underneath and I found myself squeezing my thighs together with want. It was still kind of a foreign concept to me, desiring a man as I desired Marlin, after all was said and done, but the relaxed state I was in, the calm and peace... I wanted him and I was *okay* with wanting him.

He knelt at my feet again, this powerful man, and raised my skirt, reaching up beneath it to hook his fingers into the waistband of my panties. He kept his eyes on mine, the air between us electric. His so blue eyes checking with me and asking permission silently, every step of the way which just served to turn me on even more.

I lifted my hips, and he slid my panties out from beneath the skirt of my dress. I went to stand and he put his hands gently to my hips and settled me back into the chair, tugging me forward so I sat on the very edge of the seat.

"What are you doing?" I whispered.

"Worshipping my personal goddess."

Marlin lifted my skirt and spread my thighs, he kept eye contact with me the entire time he moved his mouth toward my sex, and I swear it was the most erotic thing I had ever had a man do. He breathed me in with a satisfied sound and my eyes closed, fingers tightening on the arms of the chair as he kissed me first, then played his tongue against my pussy.

I arched, my hips thrusting forward of their own accord to meet that velvet probing touch. I was surprised when he slipped a finger inside of me, at how wet I was, my body getting with the program a little faster than my mind. I groaned softly, and he hummed, pleased, against my flesh which sent my blood scorching through my veins. The deference he showed me nearly brought me to my own knees, but he placed an arm across my hips, effectively pinning me to the chair while he took his time, tasting me, making love to me with his mouth. He twitched his fingers inside of me and I nearly shot off like a rocket when he found that secret spot that drove me wild.

"Oh, god... Marlin," I gasped, my chest heaved with my panting as he worked me into a tizzy. He had me right on the edge, so very close and I wanted to come so badly. It felt so natural with him, so *right*, and it made my heart glad beyond words that he had been the one to initiate contact this time. It meant so very much to me.

"That's it, Baby Girl, come for me," he growled against my body and the vibration from it sent shivers down my spine. He sucked my clit and teased that place inside of me with his fingertip and it was so perfect, so right, that lightning shot through my body, fizzling down every nerve ending and lighting them up with that blue white glow, even as the blood rushed through my ears like thunder, drowning out my own cries of release.

I melted, and when I came back to myself, settled back into my own skin, it was to Marlin's bright blue eyes gazing up at me with a mixture of love and adoration, my fingers tangled in his shoulder length blond hair, where I'd gripped him to my body as I'd ridden out my orgasm against his face. I quickly, but carefully disengaged my fingers from his hair and he laughed, the grin on his face speaking volumes about his own satisfaction, but we weren't done. We couldn't be done. I needed more of him. I needed to show him back just how much I appreciated him, how much I loved him, too... even if I weren't ready to say it out loud quite yet.

CHAPTER 37
Marlin

I'd stripped and left her clothed to give her some of the power, make her more comfortable, but I couldn't stand it anymore. I needed to love her and after taking care of her downstairs, the energy had just felt right. I didn't have any condoms on me, but fuckin' test results be damned. It was my ass on the line and reckless as it was, I was all in. I don't think she remembered herself. She was so caught up in the moment, and I wasn't about to douse her in the ice cold water that was reality. If it came up later I'd deal, but for now I kept my fuckin' mouth shut.

She wasn't having any more of the dress or of me on my knees; she slipped out of the chair and hoisted her dress over her head. I helped her out of it, amused by the sudden shift in the energy between us, even as her fingers wrapped gently around my cock, stroking it.

I closed my eyes, my head turning as I moaned out, it felt so good. She stopped stroking just long enough to twine her arms around my neck and to press her mouth to mine. She kissed me deeply, pressing her body so tightly to mine, I almost thought she wanted to meld us into one being. Truthfully, I was okay with that, but I had a better way. I let her climb into my lap, legs to either side of my thighs, my dick perilously close to finding her entrance, but instead of going there, of fucking her on the floor, I got my legs under us and basically power lifted her, standing with her in my arms. She squealed and laughed, holding to me tightly as I laid her back onto the bed.

"No floors for you," I murmured, before kissing down her throat, taking one of her pert nipples into my mouth. I let my cock go on a quest of its own as I captured the tight bud between my teeth, tugging at it gently, and Faith's eyes slipped shut, her head tipping back as she made a throaty, sexy as fuck, moan escape her. A moan I turned into a gasp by sliding into her hot, wet, grasping, cunt.

God she was perfect, so tight, so wet, and when our bodies met, it was like I was meant to be there; one with this woman. I returned my mouth to hers and we kissed, passionately, as I drew back and gently surged forward. Faith's legs went around my hips and she held onto me as I moved back and forth inside her, slowly, deliberately. I wasn't going to rush this for anything. You didn't rush making love, which is exactly what I was going to do. I was going to make love to this woman, pour every ounce of feeling I had for her into our bodies meeting, and fill her up so she had no way to talk herself into believing she deserved anything less.

Her moans and cries were fucking intoxicating, and I wanted suddenly, so badly, to see her move above me again that I rolled us on the bed. She yelped with surprise and let out a peal of laughter that set every fractured bit of our world to right. I smoothed my hands over her body, ignoring the odd imperfection of scar here and there as she arched above me. She didn't lift herself and slam back down over my cock, instead, she gave this sultry roll of her hips, grinding herself against me, opening up new dimensions of pleasure I'd never experienced before.

She was something wild in that moment, free, and beautiful, and fuck I wasn't about to resist her siren's call. She had me, hook line and sinker and I just wish there was more I could do to let her know…

She looked down meeting my eyes with those amazing aquamarine globes of hers and with a shuddering gasp, gave herself to me completely by saying, "I love you."

Fuck. Yes.

I reared up, and caged her body with my arms, my hand tangling in her long blonde hair as I drew her mouth to mine. I must have hit the spot or something because she cried out, her sweet pussy convulsing around my dick making my fuckin' eyes roll into the back of my head. That didn't stop me from kissing her, though. Our mouths locked, tongues lashing out and tasting one another. She wriggled her hips and I gripped her ass with one hand to still her, just enough so I wouldn't go off. I wasn't ready yet. She'd only come twice and that was unacceptable.

I turned her, and laid her down, mouth's still locked on one another's mouths before I resumed slowly thrusting into her again. She turned my blood to quicksilver in my veins, her soft, silky, body molding to mine so perfectly, those miraculous eyes of hers shining with perfect love and perfect trust as I brought her two or three more times, until she pushed against me, thrashing to get away from the probative touch of my thumb against her clit. I took my hand away and captured one of her nipples with my teeth, gently, while I stroked a few more times to allow myself to finish. She was so fucking wet, so aroused, that slipping in and out of her was effortless.

When my balls drew tight and I shot inside her, I swear to Christ it felt like it went on forever. Like she took all of me, not just the best parts, but the parts of me that were arrogant, demanding and unfair as well. She took me as I was and I felt so grateful that she would allow me to share her body after everything… I simply couldn't hold it back. I thanked her.

Faith panted below me, her hands finding my face as she held it between them and drew me down for another one of her soul stealing kisses. I was okay with that, though. I knew she would take good care of it. She was a good woman, underneath all that hurt and the shit that'd been dumped on her. She was a good woman who deserved a man that could and would take care of her, and I was confident that man was me.

"I'd walk through fire for you, Baby Girl," I breathed against the side of her neck and she wound her arms around my shoulders and held me tight.

"I already did, to get to you… and I wouldn't change anything that's happened to me, because it meant that I got to meet you. You make me happy, Marlin, even when I don't think I entirely deserve it."

"Hmm, Baby, that's where you're wrong. You deserve the world."

"I don't want the world, I just want you."

"You've got me, Faith. I'm right here, you've got me."

We had each other and I aimed to fuckin' keep it that way.

***

We rested, but neither of us were sleepy. We simply lay, tangled in one another until Faith's stomach growled. I chuckled, and she gave that tinkling laugh that sounded to fuckin' surreal, like she were some kind of nature goddess or something.

"What was your favorite food growin' up?" I asked suddenly, and she froze.

"We ate *a lot* of mac and cheese when I was growing up because it was cheap. Hope can't stand it and I think Char is pretty much indifferent about it, but I always loved it. It reminds me of when things were good and mom was alive."

"Yeah? What kind?"

"The cheap shit, in the blue box. What other kind is there?"

"Alright, alright, no need to get uppity over mac and cheese," I teased her and earned myself another one of those infectious giggles. Who knew that joy was some kind of disease? Of course, fuck if I ever wanted to be cured of it.

Faith rested her head against my chest, and I traced idle patterns over her skin with my fingertips.

"What about you? What was your favorite thing to eat when you were a kid?" she asked.

"My mama made one of the best key lime pies in the state. I swear to Christ, I couldn't get enough of it. It just melts on your tongue, cool and refreshing, the flavor of that thing is outta this world."

Faith had gone very still and I looked down at her, doubt clouded her beautiful face, those bright and beautiful eyes of hers going distant.

"What's wrong, Baby Girl?"

"I…" she stopped and let out a breath that carried hopelessness with it.

"Talk to me, Baby Girl," I said soothingly, "Can't fix it if I don't know what it is."

"That will make for one very awkward meeting, don't you think?" she asked quietly and her tone was somber and hurt.

"What, when you meet my folks? Nah! I'll walk you right up, proud as hell to have you on my arm and say 'Mama, Daddy, this here is Faith, one of the strongest, most beautiful females I have ever had the pleasure to meet."

Faith laughed but it was slightly bitter, "Oh and what does Faith do for a living, Dear?" I snorted.

"If that was supposed to be my mama, that was pretty awful," Faith slapped playfully at my chest.

"Hard to imitate someone you've never met before!"

"Hey! Alright, alright, no need to tear a page outta your sister-mom's playbook; damn!"

Faith laughed, smothering it behind her hand into giggles. I pulled her hand away from her mouth and brought it to mine, kissing the palm.

"Don't you ever hide that sound from me, it's my favorite music."

She gasped softly and I smiled, turning back to the problem at hand, "You can tell my mama whatever you want in that regard, Faith. Hell, you can pour the whole ugly truth onto the table. My mama and daddy aren't like most folks. They're true Christians and real salt of the Earth kind of people. Dollars to pesos, you tell 'em what those fuckin' animals made you do, my mama will remind you that Jesus hung with Mary Magdalene and *she* was a whore by choice."

We lay in silence for a long time after that, Faith cuddling closer into my side, one leg over the both of mine as she smoothed the sole of one foot up and down one of my legs. She was thinking and I smiled to myself.

"Why don't you come with me out on the boat tomorrow? Meet my brother Johnny for real; see if he says I'm lyin'."

"I'd like that," she said carefully, and the longing in her voice couldn't be ignored. She finished by confirming what I'd thought I'd heard, "I miss the water."

I kissed the top of her hair and had to smile to myself, "That more than anything tells me that we really are meant to be."

She chuckled and kissed my chest, the closest bit of my hide she could reach with her lips.

"Thank you," she said softly.

"For what?"

"For asking me to try the medicine, you were right, this is the most I've felt like *me* in a long time."

"I'm glad to hear that, I really am."

"This has been a good day," she murmured.

"The best day."

"The best day," she agreed.

I knew it wasn't always going to be like this. That her moods would shift like the wind and the sea and some days would be stormier than others, but this was good. It felt like we were finally moving out of some of the treacherous waters we'd been navigating the last couple of months.

Truthfully, she was doing remarkably well, coming out of this thing like a real champ. Moving past all the ugly with some sheer iron will and determination. It was good, but it was also dicey. I just had to have a steady hand and fight the pull when she tried to go back under. It was a lot of patience and a lot of understanding on how this thing worked… trauma, PTSD and the like. I'd be a liar if I said I hadn't done my homework about all of it. Mostly while she was in the throes of that fuckin' poison. I like to be informed, liked to know what came next, and I'd been just as committed then as I was now to see this thing through to the end with her only now, it was so I could live in a fuckin' happily ever after with her. I had no intentions of turning her loose and it seemed like we were on the same page there too.

I couldn't remember a time when I was fuckin' happier.

CHAPTER 38
Faith

I loved riding on the back of Marlin's bike, and after the trip to New Orleans and back, the short twenty minute ride to Dr. Sheindland's office had felt like a sorry consolation prize. The ride to Ft. Royal, at a little over an hour, had felt much better. I was smiling when we reached the marina. Bobby had ridden with us on his own motorcycle, which had surprised me. I just hadn't imagined that he would ride, I don't know why. His bike was some kind of classic, a Harley, but from the 60's or 70's and *loud*. It was a bright, deep, sparkly blue, the paint on the tank almost like the nail polish on my toes with metal flake in it, adding a dimension to the color that made it shine like a diamond. It was a pretty machine, and it fit him somehow.

I wondered why he wasn't a part of the Kraken, but I figured it probably had to do with how busy he was with his orange grove, and the hour long commute. The Kraken didn't really seem bothered with expanding their borders outside the limits of the town. Maybe that was why. It just didn't seem like a thing I should ask, and besides, I could almost pick up on a tension in Bobby whenever the club was talked about.

I got off of Marlin's bike and waited beside Bobby while Marlin backed his bike into the little cinderblock garage that was his on the marina property. Marlin came out to stand with me while Bobby did the same. There was a tension in him, which I think had to do with us being back here without the majority of the rest of his brothers to keep an eye on me. I had the feeling that Marlin was keeping some information back from me when it came to the situation with the men who had held me for two years. I wondered how much of their ire was for me having been freed, versus how many of them had died in the process of releasing me. I remembered the blood, and I knew it would come at a steep cost eventually.

I was worried about it. Worried that cost would come in the form of Hope being sacrificed for my escape. I would worry about that until she was out of that jail full of corrupt men that had been in the hip pocket of the men that'd held me and trafficked my body for their own greed. I hugged myself and shivered in the bright white heat of the day and it had nothing at all to do with being cold.

Marlin put an arm around me and I leaned into his hard body gratefully, drawing strength. He looked down at me but I couldn't see beyond his sunglasses what he may be thinking, I think it was the same for him because he asked, "What's wrong, Baby Girl?"

"Thinking about Hope."

"Don't you worry about that; Cutter's with her, and the rest of the boys, too. Hope is going to be fine. Don't forget, she whooped *my* ass once."

I blinked and drew back looking at him, "When?" I demanded. Marlin laughed and Bobby pulled the garage door down.

"I'll tell you later," he put his lips near my ear and whispered, "He'd never let me live it down."

I laughed, I had to, I knew how my sister could be, but taking on Marlin? Or any one of the other Kraken? Why would she do that? Why would she be so… I could feel my face fall into lines of sudden understanding.

"Yep. Had to do with you," he said with a smiling nod.

"Oh, *this* I have to hear."

"Later, I promise."

"What's the matter, afraid whatever it is I'd hold it against you?" Bobby asked, cluing in to the conversation.

"Yes."

Bobby shrugged unapologetically and gave a nod, "Meh, you're right, I probably would."

I laughed again, "You two are insufferable aren't you?"

"Pretty much," they both said in unison.

I let out with a loud peal of laughter and Marlin hugged me into his side. I liked how both of them smiled at the sound and I liked that I could make it again. I wasn't all better, not by a long shot, but I felt good yesterday, and I felt good today, the medicine was working and I almost felt bad for the people around me that I'd resisted taking it for so long. It took the edge off and let me feel almost normal again and I cherished that, even as it scared the hell out of me. That voice of self-doubt whispering out of the dark, *what if you need it? What if you crave it so bad you can't give it up?*

Except it wasn't like that with the pills, I didn't feel this driving need to take more. I didn't wish with every waking moment for the little tablets to hit my palm. I didn't think about them at all, really, at least not until my insecurities whispered out of the back of my mind and tried to take hold... except every time they started in, there he was with that smile that set my heart a flutter and I forgot everything else except the man at my side, holding my hand or holding me tight. I forgot everything except how he made me feel like I was, indeed, worth the world to him. I still marveled at it every time.

We walked to Marlin's boat, my body vibrating with excitement and joy. I really *had* missed the water and the sound made me excited. I wanted to spend all day on it. If the opportunity arose, I wanted to swim in it and walk along it, this big, vast ocean that made me and all my problems seem so very small and insignificant by comparison.

I felt safe, warm and protected when Bobby flanked my other side and walked with his arm around my shoulders, even as Marlin's rode along my waist. The riding gear was hot, and I was looking forward to ditching it in favor of something lighter.

Johnny was already on Marlin's boat when we arrived, and he didn't look happy. Marlin jumped up and helped me up after him, Bobby followed me and I felt like I was a celebrity or something, realizing belatedly that their movements were exceedingly protective and sent the message to anyone watching that it would be a very bad idea to try anything.

I felt a lightness in my chest, as if a weight I hadn't even known I carried had been lifted. The shadows were lifting off my heart a little bit at a time, and it felt good. Still, there were a lot of shadows and a few good days were nice but I was well aware I was still severely limited and had a very long way to go towards healing.

"'Sup, Man?" Marlin asked his brother, but Johnny's gaze was fixed on me.

"She isn't going to go all freaking out in front of the clients again, is she?" he asked by way of greeting, and it felt like clouds scudded over my good mood, the smiles and joy of just a moment before dampening under a sense of guilt; the shadows returning.

"Nah, Man, and fuck you for saying it like that," Bobby said and shook his head.

Marlin just smiled, but it was tight with anger, "Not sure what crawled up your ass and died, Little Brother, but after the clients are gone, I'm whooping your fuckin' ass again."

Johnny looked a little less certain and I sighed inwardly, "Look, I'm sorry about how I was before… that morning, but I'm trying really hard not to be that way. I'm working on it, okay? I promise to try not to freak out." I fixed him with my gaze and tried to look as sincere as I felt. Bobby put his arm around my shoulders and I jumped slightly from the unexpected contact, it didn't deter him at all though, he smiled down to me and gave me a reassuring squeeze.

"Don't pay that douchepickle any mind, Sweet Thing, go get out of all that hot leather and get yourself settled."

I looked to Marlin, "Go on, Baby Girl, I moved all your stuff from the house into my quarters. It's part of what took me so long. Just search through until you find everything, by the time you're back up here, we'll be underway."

"Okay, just try not to hurt each other on my account, please?"

Marlin stepped over and leaned down, kissing my forehead, "I'll be down in a minute to change. I won't punch him until we're done with this trip."

I scoffed, "Insufferable," I lamented and Marlin winked at me. They let me go, and I went below deck to the stately bedroom. It felt like an age, rather than a week since I'd woken up back here after being drugged on the beach.

I went through all the myriad cupboards and storage, some of them being drawers under the raised platform the bed rested on. I found my white, two piece swim suit and settled on it, looking through the drawers until I came up with a long, light aqua, skirt wrap cover up and a thin, white cardigan that wasn't sweater material, but rather a thin, cool, stretchy cotton or polyester type blend that felt soft against my skin.

A light rapping at my back made me turn around before I started to take anything off; I startled and turned to find Marlin in the doorway.

"Just me, figured I should let you know I was here. Didn't want to sneak up on you."

I smiled, he was always so thoughtful, "Thank you, you take such good care of me."

"Do I?" he asked and I nodded, smiling. The affirmation made his chest swell in a deep breath, obvious pride in himself shone out of his true blue eyes and I loved him even more for it. It'd been scary, admitting my feelings out loud, but he hadn't pushed or made a big deal about it, which put my heart and nerves at ease.

"Everything okay?" I asked softly, and he smiled even more.

"Johnny has a problem, but it's not with you, Baby."

"Oh, anything I can do to help?"

"Naw, only person that can help Johnny is Johnny. I'm sorry he came off like that, Bobby's setting him straight." He laughed at my expression. "Just talk, I'll readjust his attitude later if it calls for it."

"I hope it doesn't come to that."

"Me either."

We were quiet for a bit, as the moment built between us. He leaned down and kissed me softly and my eyes drifted shut, sinking into the sensation of his arms around me, of his mouth on mine.

Marlin kissed along my jaw and put his lips near my ear, saying so softly in that sexy, low voice he got when he let his desire take over, "Can't wait to make love to you in our bed."

"Our bed?" I asked softly, breath tremulous.

"What's mine is yours, Baby Girl. You live here too now."

I closed my eyes, and held myself to him tightly. His words didn't frighten me, like I expected them to. They didn't fill me with doubt, or with dread. Instead, they filled me with hope that I indeed had a future with this man, and it was one of the most solid, and real, positive things I'd felt since I'd been rescued. So honest, and so real, it very nearly brought a tear to my eye.

"You okay?" he asked softly.

"Are you with me?" I asked.

"Always."

"Then yes."

CHAPTER 39

Marlin

I changed along with Faith, forgoing boots, denim, and leather for a work tee, a pair of faded, in some places torn, but seriously fuckin' comfortable cargo shorts and flip flops. I shrugged my feet into the pair of brown leather thongs I wore around the boat, and with one last lingering appreciative look, left Faith to finish getting into her sexy as hell outfit. Of course, when it went onto the woman you loved, she could wear a fuckin' garbage sack and still be sexy.

I went back up on deck where Bobby was giving my little brother a flat, unfriendly look and I arched a brow. Fuck if Johnny wasn't having a shit time with Lynn again, but that didn't warrant him taking it out on Faith and I wasn't about to fuckin' stand for it either. He had the whole trip to fuckin' apologize to my girl, or I was going to readjust his attitude problem the hard way.

Bobby gave me a chin lift and I rolled my eyes and shot a prayer skyward that I would have the patience to make it through the fuckin' day with my brother. It looked like he was going to be a full on ass bag, which made me wonder what his bitch wife had pulled now, because let's face it; Lynn was an ever loving fucking cunt. There wasn't any which way around that fact.

"Ahoy, there!" someone called from the dockside and I exchanged another look with Bobby who smirked. I turned and greeted the clients with a professional smile.

"Welcome aboard! I'm Jimmy, but folks call me Marlin and this is my boat, the Scarlett Ann." I held out a hand and helped the older guy up over the side and onto the deck, Bobby got up and did the same for the lady after him and the next dude after that. I got the last woman, and we had a damn near overfull boat. It would be okay if I could get Faith to entertain the ladies on the foredeck. I exchanged a look with Bobby and he nodded, picking up what I was putting down. He'd stay near Faith and help out with keeping my girl and the two women entertained.

"This here is my brother Johnny, and I take it you two gentlemen are here to fish."

"That's right!" One of them said, "I'm Dave and this here is my brother, John."

"Nice to meet you Dave, John." I shook their hands in turn.

"This is my wife, Janice," John said, and I shook a woman's hand with short, auburn dyed hair. An expensive dye job for sure, but the fine lines around her eyes gave it away as being one. She smiled broadly and I liked her instantly.

"And this is my wife, Arlene," Dave introduced.

"Well, Janice, Arlene, either of you two interested in putting a line in the water?" Johnny asked from over my shoulder.

"Oh, no, not us!" Janice laughed.

I couldn't resist and I was sure I was going to pay for it somehow, but I gestured over to Bobby, "Well, my cabana boy, Bobby here, would love to take care of you ladies. He'll take you up to the foredeck and the loungers up there to catch some sun with my girl Faith, won't you Bobby?"

Bobby grinned at me in that way that told me 'you are so going to get it you fucker,' but he held out his arms to the two women and said, "Absolutely, follow me."

He went off with the two ladies, just as Faith made her appearance. She drifted up to me and I leaned down. She kissed me gently on the cheek and with a warm smile, drifted off after Bobby. Both Dave and John looked after her with admiring expressions and I suppressed the urge to say something. She was on board with me, she was safe with my best friend, and the two men weren't going to do anything more than look with their wives on board. I needed to let it go, so I did.

What I didn't let go was Johnny's scowl at me when I turned around. I scowled right back and the first chance I got, hauled his ass below deck.

"Just what in the absolute fuck is your problem today? What the fuck did Lynn do now?"

Johnny looked visibly upset, not angry, but upset, which was unlike my brother. I crossed my arms and waited for him to spill it.

"Traded in her car and traded up, man… I can't afford keeping up with her. Our fuckin' kids are going without while she's riding around in a new fuckin' BMW. I left her ass. I've been stayin' here on the boat while you been gone, but Jimmy, she's holding our fuckin' kids over my head. I don't know what to do."

I put a hand on my brother's shoulder, "We'll figure it out, Man. We always do, but I can't have you takin' your shit out on Faith. She didn't do nothin', she isn't Lynn, she ain't asked for nothin' I've given her. She doesn't ask for anything, come to think of it. She's got enough to deal with without you bein' a full fuckin' ass hamster to her."

"I'll fuckin' apologize."

"Yeah, you *will*. As for Lynn, I'll be here more, we'll do more gigs, but not to pay for her shit. We'll find you a divorce lawyer and a fuckin' kick ass family lawyer."

"Mama's gonna have a fuckin' fit."

"Good, you can draw fire; Faith is scared to death to meet our parents." I gave him a pointed look and he grimaced.

"She's a pretty girl," he supplied.

"Yeah, she's worried about divulging her latest line of work, despite the fact I keep telling her that sexual slavery ain't exactly a job description."

Johnny looked even more crestfallen, "Shit, I didn't think about that."

"No, you didn't, and you keep thinking about her like she's a whore, I'm going to kick your fuckin' ass so hard your own kids won't recognize you. You get me?"

Johnny looked at me for a long minute, "You really love this chick, don't you?" he asked.

"Never felt the way I do about her with anyone else."

He nodded, "Lynn's being served the papers today. Can we get the fuck out of here *before* she gets them and makes a scene?"

"Damn, you really did it, Bro?"

"Yeah."

"Who'd you get to serve 'em?"

He looked embarrassed, "I couldn't serve 'em, and you couldn't either being family. I had to get a third party unrelated to either myself, Lynn or the kids. I called up Cutter and asked for help."

"The Captain?" I asked startled.

"Yeah, he said I'd owe a favor to the club, but he's got one of the guys that stayed behind doin' it."

"Looks like I owe the Captain a favor or two myself then."

Johnny looked spooked, "What do you think he'll have me do?"

"Never mind that now, it ain't nothing you gotta worry about. Cutter knows you're family and that you've got kids. Shit you've hung out with us long enough." I lowered my voice, "Whatever he asks might not be this side of legal, but he'll keep you well clear of it. He's got a soft spot for kids and taking you out of the equation would leave yours without a functioning parent."

Johnny teared up at that and nodded. My brother, though he could be a fuckin' idiot, and sometimes lost his brain to mouth filter… at his heart, he was a good man. He lived for his fuckin' kids and would do anything for them. I was struck, suddenly, by a crazy idea.

"Faith might be willin' to watch 'em while we work."

"I don't know about that," Johnny started in dubiously.

"Listen, she would have Hope around to help her out for the most part, as soon as Hope gets –" I stopped myself before I said 'outta jail' and went with "back into town."

"Whatever Man, I can't think about this right now, and we can't keep these guys waiting."

"No, you're right, let's cast off and do some fishin'."

We did just that, Bobby poking his head into the wheelhouse long enough to tell me, "Guess what, fucker? Your 'cabana boy' is raiding your wine selection for these old broads. They're nice, and your fuckery earned them the VIP experience."

I laughed, "Go right ahead. How's Faith doing?"

"Other than the fact that we heard your entire fuckin' convo with

Johnny, and she looks like she's completely moon struck in love and misty eyed over you? Meh, she's alright. She's navigating a minefield of questions outta Arlene and Janice though, so I ought to get back down to her."

I grimaced, hard, and got us out to sea. As soon as I could viably have Johnny take the wheel, I had him do it. I went down to the foredeck after handing out a couple of cold beers to Dave and John and found Faith softly and politely answering questions to both Arlene and Janice who wore empathetic and horrified expressions. Faith caught sight of me and I mouthed, *'I'm so sorry'* at her. She smiled, the most beautiful and forgiving smile, in my direction and mouthed back *'it's okay; I love you.'*

I wasn't sure I could fall any more deeply in love with Faith Dobbins, but I did, right then and there.

CHAPTER 40
Faith

I didn't mean to make either Janice or Arlene cry, but I suppose it was hard not to when it came to a story like mine, even as unbelievable as it might be. They made such sad and empathetic noises that I very nearly teared up a time or two, but I would not give in to self-pity; not on such a beautiful day.

It helped when Bobby showed up with a bottle of chilled white wine in a bucket. He set down a glass of ice water with a wedge of orange rather than lemon and I smiled at him. He poured two generous glasses out of the bottle for the women, and took himself into the wind and spray at the front of the boat. He was still within earshot, but respectfully pretended not to be.

The day went quickly; it was nice to move from the heavier topic of my captivity to the stories of children and new grandchildren that Janice and Arlene had to share. The women were in their sixties, they and their husbands newly retired, having turned their husband's family business over to their sons and daughters. Arlene and Janice had both worked alongside their husbands at the stonecutting business. Arlene handling the company finances while Janice handled customer relations and the sales floor.

They both agreed that they'd led charmed lives, marrying their high school sweethearts, and living the American dream. They were honestly almost as idyllic as American apple pie. A life that I now longed for. Quiet, simple, beautiful. Before I hadn't had any hopes or dreams, now I found myself dreaming of a life surrounded by family, even if I couldn't have children. Marlin and The Kraken MC he belonged to had shown me over the intervening months since my rescue that family came in all sorts of ways and didn't always have to include children. That still didn't stop me from a brief sense of loss and mourning that I would never have a child of my own.

I'd never wanted to be a mother before, but now that the choice had been stripped away, I couldn't really argue the philosophy of you always wanted most what you couldn't have. Of course, just because my uterus was scarred and wouldn't allow me to carry a child, and just because, even if I did manage to conceive, my cervix was ruined and wouldn't allow me to carry that child to term, didn't mean my biological clock stopped ticking. It was a weight and sadness I would likely forever carry, but one that, for today, was bearable.

Cheering from the back of the boat snapped me out of my reverie, and the three of us stopped chatting, exchanged a look, and began to laugh. Bobby had even perked up and was looking over the side down the boat.

"You don't *have* to stay with us!" Janice exclaimed.

Bobby looked to me, as if to make sure it was alright and I laughed lightly and nodded. It was all he needed, before he made strides along the side of the boat and was out of sight around the high structure in the middle. I didn't really know what you called it.

The rest of the day passed quickly with the good company, the sunlight, and the wind kissed freedom of being on the water. I could see why Marlin loved it so much as to live aboard his boat full time. I could also understand why he rode his Harley like he did. When you were stuck on land, riding was a pretty close second to the freedom that the open water provided.

Marlin made an appearance or two back here throughout the day to check on us himself, at one point he drew me carefully aside and apologized profusely for having been overheard, but he was already too late; I'd forgiven him. I couldn't hold this much love in my heart for this man who had saved me, seen me at my worst, had continued to put up with me at my worst and who was still here, despite my having lied to him and despite every attempt I'd made at pushing him away. He was my rock in the tempest, and though right now, things were calm, I knew that the bad days were far from over, just as surely as I knew that when they came, he would be there, providing shelter in his arms.

I was so blessed in that, I couldn't even.

When we arrived back at the Marina, it was quite a bit of work for the men. Dave and John had caught quite the fish, and apparently, it was one they could legally keep. Their wives looked on with smiles, photos were taken and the fish, a beautiful green that faded to yellow and silver, well it was almost as tall as I was.

I was relaxing on the back of the boat while Johnny, Marlin, and Bobby set about with the long task of cleanup when Johnny took a seat beside me and gave me a soulful look that reminded me of a basset hound's, all sad puppy dog eyes. I tried not to giggle but it did draw a smile out of me. I could tell that Johnny could be quite the charmer when he wanted to be.

"I owe you an apology," he said shortly and I started to shake my head. "No, really, I do, and I'm sorry for the way I acted when you got here. I wasn't around for all the bad stuff and I've been a self-absorbed assclown, and I'm not just saying this because my brother's going to beat my ass if I don't."

I laughed nervously, I didn't want to believe Marlin would, but I couldn't help but think about his scraped and bleeding cheek, or the bruised and cut knuckles he'd had weeks before. A business meeting, he'd called it, and I hadn't pressed, even after he'd assured me that it was just a tiff between him and his brother. I wondered to myself now, just how often those 'tiffs' happened.

"It's alright," I said softly, "I would much prefer no one had their ass beaten on my account."

Johnny smiled, and I took a deep breath and held out my arms for a hug. I don't know, it just seemed like the thing to do. He hugged me, quickly and let me go.

"Thanks," he uttered and got up to finish what they were doing.

The idyllic peace of the day was shattered when we disembarked the boat with loose plans to have something to eat at one of the nearby beachfront restaurants.

"You *fucking* son of a bitch!" a woman screamed. She was striding up the dock towards us in ridiculously high heeled sandals, at least for walking on the gapped wooden surface. She wore tight, so light blue of a skinny jean that they were mostly white and a loose, fluttery salmon colored top. Her breasts were obviously paid for, and expensive, and she oozed money, from her expensive blonde dye job that was remarkably close to my natural hair color, to her well-manicured and pedicured nails. She raised her Dolce and Gabbana sunglasses up onto her head and her brown eyes snapped furiously at us.

I blinked and stood, pretty much between her and the men as Marlin had just lifted me from the boat. She eyed me up and down and I didn't like it, but waited to see what she would do. Her hands went to her hips, gold bangles ringing as they slid down her wrist and she eyed me with contempt.

"What, are you his whore? Is that why he's leaving me and his two children?"

"Lynn," Johnny started in an exasperated tone, but I already knew, I *really* didn't like her, and after overhearing Marlin and Johnny earlier, and thinking back on how I would never have the opportunity to have any children of my own… well anger replaced any hurt I might have felt, even if it was a tad misplaced.

I think I may have channeled Hope for a moment there, because some of the old me, the me from before I had ever set foot in the city of New Orleans, surfaced for just a split second and the words were out of my mouth before I could stop them.

"Nice outfit; did it come with daddy issues and a pole?"

Her perfectly lipsticked mouth in a color that perfectly matched her shirt, dropped open.

"*What* did you just say?" she demanded.

"Oh, I think you heard me."

Marlin, Bobby, and Johnny all stood aside, equally as shocked as she was, mouths hanging open in surprise. The woman, Johnny's wife, scoffed and demanded, "Who the fuck are you, Skank?"

I stepped into her space and she turned to face me, I put my nose almost touching hers and gave a tight little smile, "No one," I said and put my hand in her stomach and shoved. She teetered on those stupid stripper shoes and arms flailing for balance went on her ass, precisely as I intended, over the open water. She shrieked before the filthy, oil slicked marina water closed over her head and she came up sputtering.

"I'm hungry," I said dispassionately, and walked away, leaving Lynn screaming for her husband to help fish her out. Johnny looked at me like he was seeing me with new eyes and Marlin and Bobby, laughing, caught up to me.

"What was *that?*" Bobby asked me, tears of laughter very nearly leaking out of his eyes.

I looked at Johnny, then Marlin in his and said, "He's family now, and if it's one thing I learned from my sister, Hope, no one, not anyone, is allowed to mess with family."

Marlin put his arm around me, his smile reaching from ear to ear, and Johnny looked from me to him, mystified.

"When are you bringing your girl home to meet Mama?" he asked.

"How does this Sunday, sound? After church, you should bring the kids. It's been a while since Mama's seen her grandbabies."

"Oo, think you can talk her into making one of her key lime pies?" Bobby asked and I felt myself smile.

"Bring her a flat of oranges and I bet you could talk her into just about anything."

"Fuck I'll bring her the limes, too. Got a plot of 'em at the back of the south grove."

The men talked amicably about Marlin and Johnny's mother's cooking and I felt like I belonged with them. Like whatever barrier I'd had between myself and Marlin's brother had been lifted, despite the guilt I felt for having given in to my flare of anger. I had been and always would be a firm believer that violence couldn't and wouldn't solve anything, but still, it'd felt really good to do what I had done, even though I would likely pay for it later. Technically I had just committed assault, and I expected Lynn would turn me in to the police.

"Hey, what 'cha thinkin'?" Marlin asked, shaking me gently by the shoulders.

"Well, I was thinking that I've already been to jail twice, now.

This last time I actually remember the whole thing, so at least I know what to expect."

Marlin laughed, and Bobby looked at me like I'd grown a second head, "Honey," Bobby said, "We don't know what you're talking about. We all three saw it, one of those dumbass hooker heels of hers got caught in the dock and she went right over. You have three witnesses that all saw it to her none."

"Seriously, don't worry about it," Johnny agreed.

I blinked, I hadn't considered that they would lie for me, although, I should have suspected they would. Marlin chuckled, "I may be your white knight, Baby Girl, but to the rest of the world, I'm still an outlaw."

I tucked myself against his side, "I don't care what the rest of the world thinks, I know what kind of man you are and I love you for it."

He hugged me around the shoulders and kissed the top of my head, smiling a satisfied little smile. Neither Bobby nor Johnny commented, but they were both smiling, too. Though Johnny's held an edge of sadness which made my heart break a little for him. Having lived through what I lived through, it was hard not to recognize abuse when I saw it, and Lynn? Lynn might as well have 'abuser' branded on her forehead in neon letters. I reached out without thinking and grasped Johnny's hand giving it an empathetic squeeze and he startled, before giving me a shy little smile.

"Where're we eatin'?" Bobby asked as we reached the main boulevard, Johnny let out an explosive breath as first one, then another police car pulled past us and into the marina's parking lot.

"How about Tommy's fish shack?" he suggested.

"Sounds good," Marlin said and we walked at a leisurely pace in the proper direction.

CHAPTER 41
Marlin

We had a good dinner, the boys and me walking Faith from the restaurant, strolling easily along the boulevard. When we reached the marina, on the way back to the Scarlett Ann, Johnny cast a sideways look in my direction before casually saying, "Y' know, it's getting late. Why don't you guys stay on the Scarlett Ann tonight? I'll bunk down on deck or in the living quarters.

Faith looked up at me and nodded silently, picking up as much as I was what my brother was putting down. He didn't want to be alone in case his crazy ass soon-to-be-ex-wife decided to show up and cause trouble. We looked to Bobby and he asked, "You got beer?"

"What the fuck you mean, 'have I got beer'? When do I not have beer you happy bastard?" Bobby gave me a shove and I careened into Faith who lost balance right along with me, we giggled, going foot over foot off to the side to bounce off my little brother like a human rendition of pong. Johnny laughed and gave us a gentle shove to help us get righted.

"Cool, thanks guys," Johnny said and Bobby shrugged.

"Don't mention it," my best friend said and Faith gave a soft, contented sigh beside me.

When we got back to my boat, we hung out on deck and had a round of beers, except Faith, she had water. She didn't want to drink with the new meds and I didn't blame her. I think she'd had enough of living in an altered state for her lifetime and then some.

It was late when she and I finally went to bed, and I have to admit, I'd been fighting the urge to rush her there all evening. When I shut the door to my master cabin, she stood in the dim lighting and looked like a fuckin' angel.

I went to her, stripping my tee off over my head, and pulled her to me when her breath caught with desire. Those incredible aquamarine eyes of hers wandered over my chest and arms and it was like she was drinking me in, the way she did it had me instantly fucking hard and I asked her, "It alright if I make love to you?"

"Yes," she breathed and her hands were tangling in my hair, dragging my face to hers, even as I slipped her flimsy cover up, sweater thing off her shoulders and off her arms. It dropped to the carpet, pooling behind her and before it'd settled completely, I was working at the aqua wrap that hung low on her hips, the gauzy material lighter than air. It fluttered to the floor two or three seconds later, Faith's hands finding their way to the front of my shorts, working at the button and zipper.

I groaned into her mouth when she reached inside and wrapped careful fingers around me. She grasped me, her palm soft against the head of my dick and I found my hips jerking forward all on their own to meet her firm strokes.

"God, Baby Girl, that feels so good," I moaned and tipped my head back to just enjoy it for a few seconds. Her kiss on my chest was light and reverent and I smoothed my hands up and down her arms, my fingers going up under her hair to work at the halter of her swim top. It gave way and I eased it down, following it, going to my knees so I could take first one, then the other nipple of her pert breasts into my mouth. I loved her body, every curve, every angle, every supple inch but my woman had breasts to die for.

Faith's fingernails scratched lightly against my scalp, her voice a hoarse, muted cry as she threw back her head and allowed me to pay homage to her beautiful fuckin' tits. I smoothed my hands up her ribs and around to her back where I found the catch to her swim top and got it loose, pulling it off completely, leaving her in just the bottoms. I pulled *those* aside and buried my face at the juncture of her thighs, kissing; tongue questing for that small prize, that pearl of nerve endings that would set her on fucking fire.

Her legs shuddered and she bit her bottom lip, trying to keep her voice down and I chuckled, backing off her long enough to pull the bottoms down her lithe legs. She shuddered and I stood, leaving my shorts on the floor, stepping out of them and my flip flops. I picked her up and she twined her legs around my hips. It was a few steps up and I was laying her back gently and carefully in my bed.

"Marlin," she gasped, a slight edge of panic in her voice and I realized I was looming, and tonight it was setting her on edge.

"Whatever you want, Baby Girl, just tell me," I said and held myself off of her, my arms to either side of her body. She had her lip between her teeth with apprehension and when she finished searching my face, realizing I meant every word I'd just uttered, she relaxed, slowly.

"Kiss me," she said softly and I lowered myself, placing my lips softly against hers.

She kissed me carefully, her hands holding my face, cradling them gently and I pulled back just enough to ask her again, "Is it okay if I make love to you, Faith?"

"Yes," she said, unequivocally, and so I slipped inside her.

She was wet and ready, despite the demons inside her head and I moved slowly, maintaining eye contact with her. The moment she let go was a beautiful thing, her eyes drifting shut, her body relaxing beneath mine and her breath escaping in a shuddering sigh.

"That's it, Baby," I murmured and it was the wrong thing to say. Her eyes flew open and I immediately pushed myself up. Her eyes were wide and frightened and I instantly made a mental note to *never* say that again.

I pulled out of her and she covered her breasts with her arms, tears springing to her eyes making them luminous. I made soothing noises and moved off to the side, asking her, "Can I hold you?"

Faith nodded, and I gathered her into my arms and she wept. I sighed inwardly, and didn't fault her one bit. It would be silly of me to expect that we would never have one of these kinds of setbacks. I held Faith tight and let the tears fall. As soon as I'd seen the fear in her eyes, my erection had flagged, and somehow I think that actually *helped* in this situation. She whimpered that she was sorry into my chest and I felt a fission of anger travel down my spine, though I would be damned if I would show it. I wasn't angry at her, and I didn't need her thinking I was.

"Shh, no need to apologize, Baby Girl. It's gonna happen, I understand."

I hushed her and I soothed her and I pulled the sheet and blanket up over us both, cuddling her near, and letting her cry it out, until exhausted, she fell asleep. I lay awake for a long, long time after that, absently stroking her back as she whimpered and slept fitfully in my arms.

It was probably the toughest night we'd had together to date, since the earlier days when she was still in the throes of her body's addiction. It'd been a real good day, too. I had to imagine, if there was anything that'd set her off, it wasn't me; I was thinking it had to be Lynn. Abuse is abuse and if ever there was a more abusive broad, Lynn was exactly it.

I closed my eyes and sighed, trying to think of how we would handle this come morning, whether or not we would speak on it, if I should bring it up, or if we should ignore it. I settled on asking her if she wanted to talk about it, because ignoring a problem never solved anything. With that decided, I fell into an uneasy sleep of my own.

CHAPTER 42
Faith

I woke before Marlin, and spent a good deal of time simply watching him sleep. He had deep circles under his eyes, telling me he'd likely fallen asleep long after me and I felt bad about that. I didn't want him to think he'd done anything wrong, because he hadn't. He really hadn't. It was just that *phrase*, those exact *words*. He'd said them and I hadn't heard his voice, I'd heard another and it was as if I'd gone back in time, and instead of his neat cabin on his boat I was back on that dirty mattress in one of their fucking livestock pens.

I trailed light fingertips down Marlin's arm and his eyes flew open. He looked over at me and he reached out, but didn't quite touch my face. I finished for him, turning my cheek into his fingertips and closing my eyes.

"Want to talk about it?" he asked, voice rough with sleep and I thought about it, finally I nodded and when I looked, he was listening, I mean *really listening*, and so I spoke. I told him everything and he listened, asking a question here and there, and probing gently to figure out what would and would not work so we could avoid similar trouble in the future.

By the end, tears of gratitude slipped down my face and I was back, cuddled against him, some of the deep, fractured ache of my trauma sealing itself shut under his tenderness and love.

A soft knock at the door, and he made sure we were covered before calling out, "Yeah!"

Bobby poked his head in, "Hey, Johnny's gone to get his kids, we heading to your parents?"

"The fuck? Is it Sunday?"

"Uh, *yeah*."

"Shit, I lost track of the days," Marlin stretched, and he smiled at me. I nodded and he nodded back.

"We'll be right out," he said and Bobby gave a nod and shut the door.

"You up for this?" he asked me, and I was surprised to find that, *yes*, yes I was. I felt phenomenally better after spending the time talking it out with Marlin. We got up, showered and dressed, although sadly the little shower on his boat was only good to fit one of us at a time. It was as if I felt a little more fragile today, and as a result, I craved his nearness, his strength.

When I got out of the shower and dressed, I found him in the little kitchen, a glass of water in one hand, a slightly worried look on his face, as if he wondered if I were about to be offended or not. I smiled, and held out my hand for the pills and relief crashed across his face, as fast as lightning into the sea. I took the two pills, one tablet, and one tiny anti-anxiety med and washed them down with copious amounts of water. The little one liked to melt before I could get it down and it tasted awful.

Marlin took the glass from me, and before I could protest the after taste of the medicine might get him, he kissed me, and I have to say, his taste was far better than that of the much needed drugs.

He pulled back and said, "Thank you," like I'd done him an honor and I shook my head faintly.

"I'm so sorry," I started but he placed a finger against my lips.

"Just a bad night, Baby Girl. One bad night. They're gonna happen, this won't be our last. We don't have any control over when they crash the party, the control we *do* have is in how we choose to deal with them."

"We don't let them slow us down," I said softly, with sudden insight.

"No, we don't," he murmured, "One bad night, no bad days."

"One bad night, no bad days," I repeated and he smiled.

"You guys ready or what!?" Bobby yelled down.

"We're ready!" I called, feeling lighter inside, and I knew it had nothing to do with the medicine, it didn't work *that* fast.

"Alright then let's go! Church lets out in a few minutes and I wanna get there when they get home!"

"Why is Bobby so excited to see *your* parents?" I asked quizzically.

"Because his folks passed a while back, his dad from cancer and his mama from complications from her diabetes, although a lot of folks argue it was from a broken heart. She gave up after Ken passed."

"Oh, that's so sad," I felt my brow furrow in empathy for poor Bobby. Marlin smiled a little sadly and stroked my forehead with a gentle touch, smoothing the frown away.

"No bad days, Baby Girl, especially not today."

I smiled and agreed, "Okay."

* * *

The ride out to Marlin's parents was a bright one, even with my sunglasses on. The wind did it's best to cool us, but the hot Florida sun seeped into our black leathers and I felt a trickle of sweat glide down my spine beneath my 'property of Marlin' vest and the leather jacket beneath it. I was glad Marlin had insisted on us packing cooler clothing to change into once we got there.

I didn't know what to expect when it came to his parent's house. Honestly, I hadn't put any real thought to it. I was surprised to find a quaint little home with a perfectly manicured front lawn and equally perfect flowerbeds. The ride hadn't been a long one, maybe twenty or thirty minutes or so, and when we pulled up, it was behind a late model Honda, a boy and a girl bouncing out of the back seat to either side, and Johnny climbing out of the driver's seat.

He looked drawn, but his children were all over it when it came to Marlin, screeching "Uncle Jimmy!" jumping and bouncing, waiting for him to stop and shut off the bike. Johnny was calling to the kids to calm down and wait for Uncle Jimmy to get off his bike when Marlin tapped my knee, reminding me I needed to get down first.

I got off the back of the motorcycle in my form fitting leathers and felt vaguely self-conscious standing in front of the two kids, a boy and a girl, who were looking up at me as I took off my helmet.

"Who are you?" the boy asked.

"My name is Faith," I said smiling.

"My name is Violet, that's my stupid brother, Holden."

The girl gave me a gap toothed grin and Holden shoved her, exclaiming "*You're* stupid!"

"Hey!" Marlin barked, "The both of you knock it off, and gimme a hug."

The kids, who couldn't be more than five and six, the girl the older of the two, shouted and laughed, shrieking in delight as Marlin picked them up and tickled them, hugging them and playing like any good uncle would. I smiled faintly and felt a wistful pang, wondering if he would someday realize that he wanted this, wanted children of his own... children I couldn't provide.

"Why so sad?" Bobby asked me, he and Johnny were standing with me, watching Marlin in the beautifully kept front yard and I sighed softly.

"I can't give him that," I said honestly and both of them looked at me. I closed my eyes and sniffed, breathing deep and counting in my head to keep more tears at bay. I was honestly tired of crying so much, no matter that I came by it so honestly.

"What do you mean?" Johnny asked, and he looked perplexed.

"I got pregnant, while they had me. They did a back alley abortion. Took my baby and scarred me up so bad on the inside that even if I did manage to conceive, I'd never be able to carry to term." I swallowed hard. I didn't have to tell them any of that, but Dr. Sheindland had encouraged me to speak my truth whenever possible. That confronting the painful events, over and over again, being brave and taking them head on, would encourage the healing process along. She told me to look at it a certain way, that no matter if it made people uncomfortable or not, that I had been the one to actually live with it. That the discomfort I had endured to this point was nothing on the fleeting moments they would bear and that too often, victims remained silent because they didn't want to hurt or displease those closest to them.

That by being open, and honest, about some of the things I'd gone through would allow the ones that loved me, the chance to help me grieve my losses and would foster a better understanding. Of course, she meant this more about my family than acquaintances, but Marlin's family was supposed to be my family and last night, Bobby and Johnny had told me to consider them all in.

Both of them were looking at me with a mixture of sympathy and pain and it hurt to see, but it also helped lessen my burden, too. I was grateful for that, and it was Johnny who put an arm around my shoulder and gave me a squeeze.

"I didn't know, I'm sorry," he said, tone laced with guilt.

"You *didn't* know, and it's okay, really."

The ruckus that Marlin and Johnny's children were causing eventually caused the front door of the quaint little house to open, a woman much older than I expected, coming outside. I'd honestly anticipated Marlin's mother to be in her sixties, but the woman standing stooped and frail on the front step looked like she was already in her mid to late seventies. The man appearing behind her looked much the same. Both of them held the air of happily married retirees and the glad cries that emanated from them caused me yet another pang, this time one of nostalgia mixed with wishful thinking.

My mother was gone and my father we had no contact with, and no idea where he was mixed with no desire to see him. I firmly believed my older sister and what he'd done, and I harbored a deep sense of shame over it. Charity had been too young, and had been hard on Hope. I didn't know if things had changed but she had always been a daddy's girl growing up whereas I had been mommy's little girl up until mom had died.

Marlin put down his nephew and came over to me, tucking me under his arm. I banished the rainclouds from my mood and took a deep, cleansing breath.

"C'mon Baby Girl, I want you to meet our parents."

We walked up to the front steps and Marlin and Johnny's mother held out her arms to her two sons. She hugged first one, then the other, though Marlin was stiff around both her and his father.

"And who might you be?" she asked, beaming and friendly.

"Mama, I'd like you to meet my girl, Faith."

"Oh, look at you! You're so very pretty, come here, around here we give hugs. Jimmy I didn't know you had a girlfriend!"

Hugs were exchanged, a whirlwind of activity ensued and before I knew it, both Marlin and I were changed and seated at the dinner table, talking and plates being loaded with food; although my plate was seemingly loaded for me, Marlin's mother, Eileen, kept eying me and I knew I was still thin, a couple of months had done wonders for that, but apparently I still wasn't up to standard around here. By the time she finished I had enough for almost four meals on my plate.

I was sitting between Bobby and Marlin and Bobby leaned over and muttered in my ear, "Save room for the pie, it's to die for."

He looked up suddenly and asked, "Mama, you get the limes I had sent over yesterday?"

"Of course I did and I made six, I figured each of you boys would want to take one home."

"Shit, we came on the bikes," Marlin muttered and Eileen gasped, a scandalized sound.

"Jimmy! Language at the table, and in front of your niece and nephew no less!" she turned to me, "I'm so sorry dear, I raised him better than that, I surely did."

I laughed lightly, "You think that was bad, you should meet my sister Hope."

Of course, that turned the topic of conversation to me, and of my family, which invariably led to sympathetic coos from Eileen over my mother, and admiration for my older sister for raising Char and I the rest of the way like she did.

"I'm pretty lucky," I agreed.

Then came the dreaded question from Marlin's father, "So what do you do for a living, Faith?"

I smoothed my lips together and thought on how to best answer the question, Marlin squeezed my knee under the table and I said the only thing that came to mind, "I was a full time college student two years ago."

Craig, Marlin's father, frowned, and sat back in his chair. Johnny stood up, his children by far done eating and more playing with their food than anything, waiting for the adults to finish their meals.

"Okay, kids! How's about we go outside and play?" Bobby asked and Johnny shot him a grateful look.

The two men took the kids out the back door and I sighed, Marlin helping me out, "What happened to Faith, isn't really something that the kids need to hear," he said quietly.

Eileen and Craig both looked worried, so I took a deep breath and spilled my truth, believing in Marlin that they wouldn't judge me.

"Two years ago, I took a trip to New Orleans with my college roommate…"

I spared the excruciating details, keeping it simple, that I'd been sold by Tonya into sexual slavery, that the men that'd held me had used heroin as a method to keep me both in line and close and that it'd taken two years for my sister to find me. That when she did, it had been her and their son, Marlin to come and get me and that Marlin had been instrumental in my recovery, both from addiction and working my way through the mire of psychological after effects my time in captivity had caused.

Marlin's fingers had found the spaces between mine beneath the table, and I clung to his hand as if it were a lifeline. Eileen was in tears by the end of my story, and even Craig's eyes shone as he looked at his son like he'd never seen him before. Craig stood up and came around the table, Marlin and I stood up too, in reflex.

Craig captured his son in a bear hug and said to him, "Boy, I have never been prouder of you than I am now." He looked at me over Marlin's shoulder and sniffed, saying, "I'm right sorry for what happened to you, Faith, but I'm glad my son has been there for you. That he gives you some peace." I smiled faintly and nodded.

Marlin pulled back and looked his father in the eye, "The thing is, Pops, Faith gives me peace, too."

Eileen came around the other side of the table and swept me up into a tight hug of her own which startled me, "Sounds like I should welcome you to the family, my girl," and *that* is what started the tears in *my* eyes. Tears of absolute relief.

The pie really was as phenomenal as all the men had said.

CHAPTER 43
Marlin

"What 'cha thinkin'?" I asked her, and she stirred against my shoulder. We were laying in the hammock out back of my parent's place while Johnny and the kids chased lightning bugs, and Bobby talked with my parents, laughing, around the fire pit.

"No bad days," she whispered and I chuckled, kissing her temple.

"Not today, anyways."

"I love you," she said spontaneously after a long silence.

"I love you, too, Firefly," I murmured, using the Captain's nickname for her.

She smiled and gave a little laugh, she was staring drowsily out at the kids and my brother chasing the little bugs in the deep twilight. "I've never seen them before. I grew up in California, remember? We don't have them there."

"Kind of a sight to see, ain't they?"

"Mmhm," she agreed.

We were quiet, swaying gently back and forth when she just as suddenly asked, "What happens now?"

"Now? Well, we head back to Bobby's and wait, for one. When the Captain and your sister get back," I lifted a shoulder in a shrug, "We go back to the Scarlett Ann and go from there."

"I want to find something to do. I want to be useful."

"Might need you to watch Johnny's kids while we're out on the water, think you could be up for that?"

She was silent for a long time, mulling it over, "Are you sure he would want me to? I mean I am still… I have… Maybe I'm not the best person."

"Snakes bother you?" I asked.

"Snakes?" she asked confused, "Like poisonous ones?"

"Naw, constrictors."

"I hadn't thought much about it, but not overly much, I suppose, why?"

"We could put you and the kids with Hossler and her kids, so you could help each other. Would that make you feel better?"

"Maybe. That's an idea… but why would I need to not be afraid of snakes?"

Marlin chuckled, "She breeds 'em."

"Oh. So not like really big snakes then."

"No, not really big, no."

"I think I could handle being around that."

I smiled and hugged her a little tighter, "That's my girl."

We got up slowly, neither one of us really *wanting* to move for being so full of my ma's good food and being so relaxed. Still, we needed to get changed to ride and a move on back to Bobby's house and it was time. I led her back to where our gear was stashed in my folks' spare room and she slipped inside.

I went back out and waited so I could take my turn, my mama coming up to me, "She seems like a lovely girl, despite all her problems."

"Yeah, that's what I'm finding, too."

"I worry about you, Son. I'm proud of you, but are you su–" I stopped her gently with a look.

"I appreciate it, Ma, but I'm a grown ass man and I'm sure."

She slapped my shoulder and made an exasperated noise, "Language!"

I laughed and she laughed too, the back slider opened up and we turned to watch Faith slip out. I couldn't help it, the sight of her in my rag, and all the rest of her form fitting riding gear gave me one hell of a chub.

Bobby wandered over and sighed, "We about ready to hit it?" he asked and I nodded.

"Yeah, stay with my girl, I'll be right back." I bent down and kissed my mom on the cheek and went back to change myself, double timing it into my riding gear and back out.

Faith was saying goodbye to Johnny, my folks, and the kids and I joined in. Bobby was a reckless fucker and was riding in his shorts and tee shirt, without the benefit of any protective gear. I liked my hide intact and road rash free, so no thank you.

We slipped around the side of the house to the front and left Johnny to break the news of his impending divorce to my deeply religious and commitment oriented parents. He didn't want us around for it, and I didn't want Faith to see it get ugly. I was actually surprised my ma had kept it as low key as she had, then again, my parents weren't *stupid* people. They saw the difference between Faith's addiction and Danny's as clear as I did.

I was buckling Faith's helmet on when she placed her hands on mine and made me stop. I looked into her so serious face and cocked my head to the side, inviting her to say her piece.

"Do you think we could try again tonight?" she asked quietly and I smiled.

"Absolutely, Baby Girl."

She smiled and it was a brave little quirk of her lips. I got on the front of my bike and she got on up after me. We rode back to Bobby's, her face pensive over my shoulder in the side view mirror, and I couldn't help but wonder what was weighing so heavy on her mind now.

We got back to the grove and Bobby's house and I brought the bike to a stop, switching off the engine which stuttered to silence. The frogs and nightlife provided a soothing backdrop as I dropped the kickstand and leaned my machine onto it. Faith got down and took off her helmet, handing it to me and I hung it off one of the handlebars.

Bobby had split off and pulled into a bar on the way back, so it was just me and her. I had a key though, so it was all good. Faith was looking out into the rows of trees, flanking one side of the house, a troubled and lost expression on her face when I turned back to her. I stood, waiting her out patiently, to collect her thoughts and to speak on it.

"You know I can't give you what Johnny has, right?" she said so faintly, I almost didn't hear her.

"What, Vi and Holden?"

"Children, yes."

I pulled her by the wrist gently, until she turned and looked at me, but I kept pulling until her arms were settled around my waist and my arms were around her.

"Don't get me wrong, I love my niece and nephew to death, but Baby Girl, I'm the vice president of what is technically an outlaw motorcycle club. That doesn't exactly make father of the year material."

"I know what you are, Marlin, I'm not talking about that though, I'm talking about *me*. Asking you if you're *sure*, because I don't know if I could live with it if one day you woke up and decided you wanted something I couldn't give you and you pitched me –"

I put a finger to her lips and smiled down at her and I knew it was a little sad. Shit, what she was sayin' kind of hurt. That she would think of me that way… but I knew where this was coming from, and I knew it didn't have so much to do with me as it did her and her insecurities.

"Faith, if ever there comes a time you want a child, or that I want one for some god forsaken reason, we'll talk about it. Just like we're talkin' now. I've never been much interested in bein' a daddy, but if the urge suddenly decides to come on strong, there are a hell of a lot more ways to go about bein' one than knocking my woman up."

Faith stared at me in silence, and I sighed out softly, "Shit, I meant adoption and that didn't come out right. I'm sorry."

"No, it's okay, I understand… I don't think it came from me right either."

I rested my forehead against hers and we just existed for long minutes, in each other's space, each drawing comfort from the other.

"It's been a long day," I murmured.

"An unexpectedly busy one, too," she agreed.

"Can I please just take my woman upstairs and make love to her?"

"I think I would like that," she said softly.

"Okay then."

Hand in hand I let us into the house and led her up the stairs.

When we reached the bedroom, I shut the door behind us softly. When I turned, it was to the blue light of the moon illuminating one half of my girl's face. Man, Faith was one of the most beautiful and ethereal lookin' women I had ever seen. Like she'd been swimmin' in the sea, tail and all and had done that miraculous change, walkin' up onto shore.

"You're so fuckin' beautiful to me it hurts sometimes," I told her, and it was true.

Her expression, her *body language*, softened. Tension easing from her shoulders and the tightness around her eyes and anxiety in her face melting away some. I went to her and kissed her gently, tracing light fingertips along the side of her neck.

The clothes came off slowly, hands exploring and that was fine by me. I was in no rush and neither one of us had any place to be. I moved us over to the bed and laid her down, opting to kiss every inch of her supple skin while she fisted the sheets and arched to meet my touch, jerking back and giggling when I found a ticklish spot. I liked it when she did that, her smile and laugh infectious.

I started with oral on her, having had sex a few times, this is what seemed to put her in a relaxed state enough to keep the memories at bay, holding her in the now. I wanted that for her. I wanted to keep her here, with me, until a time I could send her shooting into the stratosphere.

My efforts paid off in that department, with a lingering swipe of my tongue, Faith's spine arched, bowing impossibly, until not even the crown of her golden hair made contact with the mattress or pillows. She was drawn tight, like the skin of a drum, and let out the most beautiful, satisfying sound as her pussy milked my fingers in an even pulsating rhythm.

I felt a savage victory over that, I'm not even going to lie.

CHAPTER 44
Faith

I collapsed back to the bed, panting, fingers clutching the bottom sheet, tight. Marlin was laying butterfly kisses along my hip, up my flank before pausing to take one of my nipples into his mouth. I cried out again and writhed beneath him and felt him smile against my breast. He finished with his attentions there and laid his hands on my chest between them, resting his chin on them.

"You good, Baby Girl?" he asked and I nodded, unsure of my ability to speak. "You want I should keep going?" he asked softly and I could see in his eyes that he really didn't want to stop. That he would, when I know he was so obviously aroused, likely to the point of pain, touched me. I didn't want him to stop, though, I wanted him to climb my body the rest of the way, I wanted him to kiss me and I wanted him inside me.

I untangled my hands from the sheets and gestured for him to finish coming up here. He smiled at me, and placing his arms to either side of my body, complied, holding himself carefully off of me so as not to overwhelm me.

Every little care he took towards my wellbeing like this, I noted it. Every time he gave me a nuanced look, checking on me, checking to see if this or that was alright, every time he kissed me with such reverent care, every time he stopped at the first sign of my distress, every time he'd squeezed my knee in reassurance, or kissed the hurt away, or touched me with the reverence he was showing me now… I fell more deeply in love with him.

He lowered his lips to mine and gently slipped inside me, eliciting a deep, impassioned moan from me. I pushed at him and he smiled against my lips, turning with me, holding me close so that he lay on his back and I rose above him, his cock still seated deeply inside of me as I looked down at him from my perch along his body. I wanted to love him as thoroughly as he loved me, and I loved that he let me do it.

I rose and fell gently along his length and loved it when his eyes drifted shut and he moaned, giving himself over to the sensations of our bodies meeting. I made love to him for a long time this way, until time melted and distorted in the haze of euphoria we shared and we either had to finish or Marlin had to take over, my legs trembled so badly from fatigue from the sustained, unfamiliar position I had them in.

It ended up being the latter, Marlin sitting up and curving his strong arms behind my back. He lifted me and turned me without slipping free of my body, but still managed to not lean on one of my legs in the transition to where it felt like the bone very nearly bent. I loved that about him, so thoughtful and he thought of *everything*.

He took over, and I closed my eyes, drowning willingly in the feeling of him moving above me and inside me. Relishing how the pleasurable glow of our lovemaking coalesced into sparks of energy, flowing through me and alighting on my skin. Glowing off and on like the random little fireflies in his parent's back yard.

When I came, it was with him, and it was, in fact, as if the earth moved. Like my axis reversed polarities and settled, just a little bit more, into who I had been before my trauma, only more like it settled into who I would be and it only had one word to apply to it: *stronger*.

Marlin gathered me to him in the dark of the room, and we lay, pressed together, breathing heavy, safe in a world of our own making.

"I love you, Faith," he whispered when he'd caught his breath enough.

"I love you, too."

It was nice, because in that moment of post lovemaking bliss, I felt it as sure as the sun would rise tomorrow… I was going to be okay. We were going to be okay.

Here was a new beginning. One full of potential… one without end. Marlin hugged me tighter and placed a kiss against the top of my hair. I sighed out, and laid even more of my burden down.

***

Three weeks later…

"Are you looking up my skirt?" I asked laughing. Marlin caressed my calf, running his fingers lightly up behind my knee, taking the liberty of continuing all the way to my lower inner thigh. I shivered, and stilled on the ladder and he chuckled.

"Maybe, but can you blame me?"

"No, I suppose…" I trailed off, standing straighter at the roar of pipes growing closer. I started leaning this way and that, trying to see through the trees and Marlin laughed outright, Bobby with him.

"Easy, Baby Girl; I don't want you to fall, come down here."

I took a step or two down and Marlin gave a pull, with a surprised squeal, I fell into his arms. He laughed and kissed me, before setting me on my feet.

"There you go!"

We rushed back to the house and around front where Cutter, my sister, and the rest of The Kraken who had stayed in New Orleans were getting off their bikes.

"Hope!"

I ran to my sister and hugged her tightly. She looked surprised, bewildered even and hugged me back tightly.

"Are you okay? I mean what happened?"

"Calm down, Firefly! We'll get to it." Cutter wrapped an arm around my sister's waist and hugged her into his side.

"You *are* okay, right?" I asked her anxiously.

She gave my hand a squeeze, "I will be after I get some real food," she said and she was as closed off and shut down as I'd ever seen her, which meant that no, she wasn't alright. I had only spent a night in that place and Hope had been with me… I can't imagine what a month with no one familiar had been like.

"Are you done?" I asked, and I was apprehensive, I mean, what if she had to go back?

"Yep! All charges were dropped and the cops that picked you up are under some hardcore review," Radar crowed.

"So, what happened?" I asked.

Cutter laughed, "I said we'd get to it! Relax Firefly, damn, although it's good to see you bein' you." He winked at me and I blushed.

"Can we call Charity? I mean, can she come home?" I asked. I'd talked to my younger sister more and more over the intervening weeks; the stronger I'd begun to feel, the more outgoing I'd begun to feel too. Hope had the shine of tears in her eyes and pulled me into a tight hug.

"Yeah Bubbles, It's time I had both my girls home," she said. I couldn't disagree with Hope. This was home, or Ft. Royal was anyways and she was right, I wanted all of us together again. It was past time.

"So we can call her? Do you think she'll be able to leave?"

"Bubbles, this is Blossom we're talking about here, you think anything is going to stop her? She'll just outsmart them."

I nodded and hugged Hope again, and it felt like I was me, like we were a family again. Marlin smiled at me, pleased, from behind my sister's back as he clasped hands with Cutter and pulled him in for a hug. Something passed between the two men in that enigmatic way that was between two brothers of the MC. As soon as he and Cutter had their bromantic moment, Marlin moved to greet the rest of the men... the rest of my extended new family.

I smiled and couldn't think of a time that I had ever truly felt like I was a part of something before, but it was true... This is where I belonged. Safe, happy, and loved.

EPILOGUE
Charity

"Ack! God fucking damn it!" I went diving over the edge of my bed in my dorm room and snatched my buzzing phone off the nightstand.

"Hello?"

"Blossom!" My two sisters crowed into the phone and I held the phone away from my ear to keep from going deaf in it.

"What?" I asked, laughing back. *Faith is laughing…* It'd been so long since I had heard that laugh. I missed my sister, *both* my sisters, with a fierce ache in the center of my chest.

"When are you coming home?" Faith demanded, like she hadn't been the one keeping me away. I rolled my eyes exasperated. *Some things never change.*

I looked around my dorm room. I had six weeks of class left, but I *really* wanted to go. I did some quick math and sighed out.

"I can be there in three, maybe four weeks?" I hazarded.

"Will you be graduated?" Hope asked suspiciously.

"Close enough, I'll have all my classes done, all my credits in, and will just be waiting on my diploma in the mail."

"Charity…"

"Oh, whatever Corporal Badass! I don't need to walk down some stupid aisle and across some fucking stage, in front of a bunch of gawking people I don't know, to feel like I accomplished what I did."

I heard a male voice that could have been Cutter or Marlin say "Damn!" on the other end of the line and Hope and Faith dissolved into peals of laughter, which made me laugh too.

"By my estimation you have six weeks of classes left," Hope said and I rolled my eyes.

"Yeah, so what? I can do them in the time frame I gave you."

"Charity –"

"I do what I want!" I said in a mock tough-guy tone; more laughter ensued. I'd never been one to take my oldest sister too seriously, Faith did and then some, covering us both on that front.

"Fine, you do what you want and get your ass down here, *with* your diploma or I'm kickin' your ass!" Hope said.

"Aye, aye, Captain tight wad!" I crowed and I heard Cutter in the background say, "Hey! Watch it now."

It took a few minutes for the laughter to subside and for the three of us to get a grip and say goodbye. I smiled after I ended the call and breathed in deep and let it out.

It was time for the three of us girls to inhabit the same space again… I couldn't wait.

From the Author of
SHATTERED & SCARRED
THE SACRED HEARTS MC

AJ DOWNEY

CHARITY FOR NOTHING

The Virtues

Other books by A.J. Downey

THE SACRED HEARTS MC

1. Shattered & Scarred
2. Broken & Burned
3. Cracked & Crushed
3.5. Masked & Miserable (a novella)
4. Tattered & Torn
5. Fractured & Formidable
6. Damaged & Dangerous

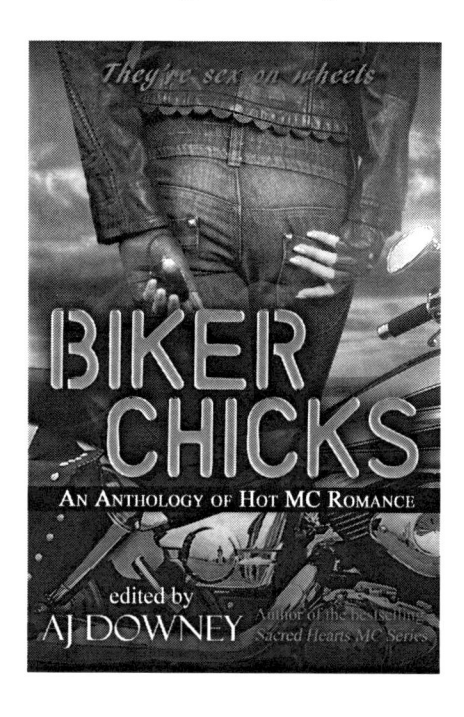

Paranormal Romance
I Am The Alpha (with Ryan Kells)
Omega's Run (with Ryan Kells)

About the Author

A.J. Downey is the internationally bestselling author of The Sacred Hearts Motorcycle Club romance series. She is a born and raised Seattle, WA Native. She finds inspiration from her surroundings, through the people she meets, and likely as a byproduct of way too much caffeine.

She has lived many places and done many things, though mostly through her own imagination… An avid reader all of her life, it's now her turn to try and give back a little, entertaining as she has been entertained. She lives in a small house in a small neighborhood with a larger than life fiancé and one cat.

She blogs regularly at *www.ajdowney.com*. If you want the easy button digest, as well as a bunch of exclusive content you can't get anywhere else, sign up for her mailing list right here:

http://eepurl.com/blLsyb

CPSIA information can be obtained
at www.ICGtesting.com
Printed in the USA
LVOW10s2359020118
561473LV00036B/541/P

9 781530 627929